Assignment for a Mercenary

Books by Howard R. Simpson

Assignment for a Mercenary

To a Silent Valley

Assignment
for a Mercenary

Howard R. Simpson

Harper & Row, Publishers

NEW YORK, EVANSTON,
AND LONDON

To M. A.

Assignment for a Mercenary

Chapter 1

:

The S.S. *Owerri* swung in toward shore and ran parallel to the short sand beach. The vibration of her engines slowed as she moved through the motionless water. She was painted black from the top of her short funnel to the water line. A heavy, tarry black that drank in the African sun and held it for days.

The strip of sand beach fell behind and was replaced by gray mud flats and mangrove swamps. Behind the swamps the first stand of tall palms spread desiccated branches toward the leaden sky. The heat pressed down as a solid weight, soggy and stifling. The land threw off the sweet odor of vegetable decay.

The buildings of Port Akodu came into sight as bright sun reflections from corrugated tin roofs. Then huts, shaky wharfs and canoes appeared. The freighter turned her bow toward the small harbor. The hoarse whistle of the S.S. *Owerri* blew twice; strident, insulting to the calm ashore. An agitated flight of white birds rocketed up out of the mud and circled over the town.

The captain made his appearance on the bridge, grumbling and rubbing his eyes. He stood behind the mate, breathing heavily, filling the already thick air with the acid redolence of cheap Dutch gin. The mate steadied the wheel and rang HALF ASTERN. The ship slowed, gliding silently toward the sagging pilings of the Port Akodu dock. The captain moved out onto the bridge wing. He watched the Africans come out of the shade and prepare to receive his mooring lines.

There was more jangling of the engine room signal. The ship shook like a stricken whale, a muddy froth churned up under her stern and her plates made contact with the dock, grinding and squeaking against a tattered buffer of automobile tires. Lines were tossed ashore and the dockers made them fast with the same deliberate slowness that never failed to infuriate the captain. He cursed silently, scratching his huge stomach through his soiled undershirt. A steward appeared, his serving jacket open over a bare chest. He pushed a mug of brown tea toward the captain, who took it without a word. The mate left the wheelhouse to shout instructions to the deck crew and a wide gangplank was run out to the dock. The captain sipped his tea and watched one of the Africans swing aboard to secure the gangplank. He frowned and his small eyes were almost lost in the folds of his pudgy face.

Two weeks down, he thought to himself. Two weeks down and at least three back. And a bloody fine trip it's been so far what with engine trouble and busted water pipes and the stupid bloody cook forgetting to put aboard the bloody Brussels sprouts and letting the ants get into the treacle. He took another sip of tea and walked back into the wheelhouse. He glanced at the clock and returned to the bridge wing.

The passengers were coming out on deck. Several African

§ 2

porters had come aboard and the captain could hear them arguing over a pile of luggage near the gangplank. The Lebanese was the first passenger to debark. The captain frowned as he watched him walk carefully over the gangplank to the dock. Greasy little bastard. Look at those shoes, color of cow cream, and wearing a hat like a West Indian spiv. And here comes his Royal Highness, the District Officer. Too good to eat with the others and always complaining about the food. Let 'im travel on the bloody *Queen Mary* if this isn't to his liking.

The captain turned and started to walk back into the wheelhouse as the third and last passenger was leaving the ship. The captain paused, still holding his half-finished mug of tea, and watched the American go ashore. Now there's a strange one. Don't quite know what his game is. Not a tourist, that's for sure. Seems to know a little bit too much for his own good but claims he's never seen Africa before. Wanted ice with his drinks. The captain laughed and entered the wheelhouse. He put down his tea mug on the chart table. The steward was talking to the second mate.

"Smyth," the captain called, interrupting them.

"Yessir," the steward replied, gathering up the tea mugs in one hand.

"How did the ice hold up, what with the Yank asking for it every day?"

"Oh, it's all right, about three big cakes left. But it's just as well he's getting off here. Chief Oluwo's beginning to smell a bit."

The captain laughed and clapped the steward on the shoulder. "Well, the old bastard smelled worse when he was alive, I can tell you. We'll have 'im off-loaded tomorrow so the fam-

§ **3**

ily can bury 'im in a hurry." He reached over among the charts and pulled out a weathered pipe. As he filled it he laughed again. "We can bloody well say we gave that particular Yank his first taste of Africa!"

The police post at Port Akodu had been built in the late 1800s. To rank after rank of British police officers it had been a last assignment. Long before DDT, Atabrine and swamp control, the mosquito had been king. Seething off the gray mud and fallen mangroves in humming clouds, the deadly insects had been the first all-African, anti-European defense force. One after the other the pink-cheeked young British officers had taken to their cots, shrunken and yellowed. Many had died.

Now the mosquitoes were simple pests but they still flew at will in and out of the wide windows of the Akodu police post. The building was of whitewashed mud with black hardwood door and window frames. A well-swept path edged by two fan palms led to the front door. A bulletin board was fixed to the front of the building. A covering of chicken wire kept the larger lizards off the official notices. A flagpole surrounded by a ring of whitewashed stones held a limp Union Jack over the post's corrugated tin roof.

Constable Okwatola walked briskly up the main road from the port. It was still morning and the thick leaves of the plantains threw a lukewarm shade on the yellow dust. The constable was in a hurry and bright beads of perspiration covered his broad black forehead. He swung off the road and walked up the path to the police post. He entered the office, slammed down his heels and swung his hand up, palm out, in a rigid salute.

Officer Pluckett watched him over the rim of his tea cup.

§ 4

He put down the cup and returned the salute. "Stand easy, Constable," Pluckett said sighing. "Well, is it our bird?" he asked.

Constable Okwatola grinned. "Yes, sahr, he is the man. I look at the passport as he come through the customs shed. He is a Yankee for sure. Here is the form."

Pluckett pushed his chair back and read the form Okwatola handed him. Pluckett was young. He was red-haired and birdshot with freckles. He had the look of a Midland farm lad who had somehow taken the wrong turn and suddenly found himself in a different world, doing the wrong type of work.

"Michael Craig—that's him all right," Pluckett said, putting the form down on the shaky, plain wood table that served as his desk. He got up and walked to a window. He wore a short-sleeved khaki shirt and military shorts slightly frayed from the hammering of streamside washing, but starched and pressed into sharp creases. The wide muscles of his lower legs were covered with regulation knee socks. His exposed knees were scarlet from the sun.

"Where's the Yank staying?" he asked, yawning and stretching by the window.

"At the Bristol Arms, sahr."

Pluckett slapped his hands together. "Well, Constable, we better get cracking."

He walked to his desk and picked up the phone. "Hello, hello, operator? What? No, damn it, I'm calling, not answering. What? Yes, that's it, old boy. Officer Pluckett here, Akodu police post. What? Hello, hello!" Pluckett put his hand over the mouthpiece and raised his eyes to the ceiling. "Goddamn it to bloody hell!" he murmured through clenched teeth.

Constable Okwatola shifted uneasily. A large lizard entered

§ **5**

the open door very slowly. He lifted each leg in slow motion and pivoted his orange head like a papier-mâché movie monster.

"Look, you bloody idiot, this is Officer Pluckett speaking! Yes, damn it, I'm Pluckett. Good, fine. Now listen carefully. I want to call the capital. Got that? Good. Seven, six, five, three. Got it? No, no, seven, six, *five*, three. Right. I want to speak with Commissioner Innes at the police officers' club. Innes! I . . . N . . . N . . . E . . . S! That's it, perfect, very good. Ring me when you get him, eh? Good, fine, you're a fine fellow."

Pluckett slumped against his desk. He sighed and replaced the telephone in its cradle. He pulled a handkerchief out of his pocket and mopped his brow. Suddenly he stopped, glaring past the folds of his handkerchief. "Constable, there he is again," he said quietly, pointing to the lizard that had now reached the center of the hard-pounded mud floor. The constable reached down and grasped the lizard firmly behind the head. He carried it to the door, its bent, stumpy legs gyrating slowly and its tail flicking from side to side. He swung the lizard in a circle and sent it flying out over the road.

Pluckett shook his head despairingly. "He'll be back," he murmured to himself, "in about two hours."

Commissioner Innes had finished his fourth bottle of Alesopp's Ale when they called him to the telephone. The bar of the police officers' club was crowded and noisy and he had a hard time pushing his way through the beery crush of red-faced officers, their wives and girl friends. But the ale had mellowed the commissioner and his difficult progress was more of a pleasant game than an irritant.

§ **6**

He picked up the phone and shut the door of the hot little booth with a smile. "Hello, hello, Innes here," he shouted over the noise from outside that penetrated the thin walls of the phone booth. He heard an empty humming and he slumped back against the wall patiently.

Malcolm Innes was tall and thin. He was a Scot and he had worked his way up in Her Majesty's colonial police, leaving far behind the sergeant's stripes and the burr of his Highland accent. He had seen a lot in his time and he knew Africa well enough to realize he would see a lot more before he was finished.

He glanced out of the booth at the crowd milling around the bar. Empty glass mugs were being passed to the bar over the heads of the crowd and taken away full. It was about noon and most of his lads were well stoked. He found himself staring at the ample bottom of a young brunette from the Government House office force. He quickly shifted his gaze to the hunting trophies over the bar.

"Hello?" A very weak voice vibrated from the telephone. "Officer Pluckett here, sir, calling from Port Akodu."

"Oh, yes, Pluckett, what's up?"

"The American chap has arrived, sir. Came in this morning on the S.S. *Owerri.*"

The commissioner frowned, forcing his mind back to his desk and the case file and away from the noise and gaiety of the club.

"Oh, yes, Pluckett, ahh, good work, er, what's he up to?"

He didn't really listen to Pluckett's reply but he shut his eyes and tried to recall the details. A telegram from London received last week. One Craig, a Yank, expected to land at Port Akodu and head inland for Ikiri near the border, supposedly on an education grant to study the regional tribes. Intelligence had other ideas.

Pluckett was still talking. ". . . he's staying at the Bristol Arms here. I've put my constable on to him and we'll know when and where he wants to go next."

"Very good, Pluckett, glad you called. I may call you later tonight but if not I'll definitely call tomorrow. Let me know the minute he leaves Port Akodu and keep a sharp eye on him. I want to know who he talks to and what he does down there."

"Right, sir, I'll keep you informed."

"Jolly good, how are things?"

"Oh, not bad, sir, I—"

"That's it, keep your pecker up and have a pint on me. I'm ringing off now."

"Thank you, sir, goodby."

Commissioner Innes hung up and pushed open the phone booth door. His jacket clung to his back, damp and soggy with perspiration. He straightened his belt and walked back to the bar. "One Alesopp's," he shouted to the African constable serving as barman. Two officers made room for him at the counter. He put his bony hands on their shoulders. "How goes it, lads?" he asked, reaching between them for the cold bottle and empty glass mug that the barman held out to him.

"Very fine, sir. It's a good day for beer."

"Looking at the pot you're putting on, Finchley, I'd say a bit of tennis would be good for you." He poured his ale and took two deep swallows.

"Ah, that does it, fine," he murmured, smiling. "Say, Finchley, be a good chap and go find Major Bedwell for me. Tell him I'd like to see him for a moment."

§ **8**

"Yes, sir, right away."

Finchley disappeared into the crowd and the commissioner poured some more ale into his mug. He spoke to the other officer. "Well, how goes the Riot Detachment?"

"All right, sir. We received the new tear gas the other day and I gave it a try. Quite effective. Blew the wrong way though and mucked up our mess a bit that night, but they're much better than the old grenades."

"Yes, I heard they were good. MacClain used them up in the north for the first time last week and got good results. Some hassle over a cow or a wife or some foolish thing and two villages were all ready for what-for. MacClain tried to reason with them and they tossed a few rocks his way and started to wave their hunting spears about so old Mac let fly. Cleared them off in nothing flat, he reports. Good stuff, for a change."

Major Bedwell suddenly appeared, a serious Kriss Kringle, with curly gray hair, a waxed gray mustache, the collar of his tunic black with perspiration. The major was Commissioner Innes' intelligence officer. He was dead serious about his work. One of his military ribbons had come loose and it hung by its metal clasp.

"Hey, Robbie," the commissioner said, poking at the major's chest, "you're about to lose your M.C."

"Oh, my God! Thank you, Malcolm." He fumbled one handed with the clasp, perspiration coursing over his face. The other hand held a full mug of Guinness. "What's up?" he asked, twitching his mustache.

"Well, Robbie, your Yank has arrived."

The major frowned and glanced around uneasily. He lowered his voice and moved closer to the commissioner. "This is

§ 9

a touchy case, Malcolm. I'd prefer to discuss it in the office."

"Oh, come off it, Robbie, no damn Yank has ever been that dangerous, or even interesting."

The major buried his chin in his Guinness. He came up licking the creamy foam from his lips and mustache.

"This one is, Malcolm," he said quietly, "and it's no laughing matter."

Chapter 2

.
.

Commissioner Innes climbed out of his station wagon and strode up the path to the wide glass doors of the American consulate. He enjoyed his visits to the consulate because of the air conditioning. He luxuriated in the coolness and the quiet after the wet heat and din that entered through the open shutters of his own office window.

Consul Hargrove was expecting him. The receptionist led the commissioner directly to his office. The commissioner followed along behind the young African girl, his swagger stick and his black, leather-billed police cap in hand.

The commissioner liked Hargrove. He was a nice chap and they always enjoyed each other's company at social affairs. Unfortunately, most of their business contacts were of an unpleasant nature, usually having to do with American seamen picked up for drunken brawling or Africans accused of stealing by those shepherds of their souls, the American missionaries. The Craig case was the first really serious matter he had had to take up with Consul Hargrove.

§ 11

Hargrove was waiting for him and they shook hands as he entered the outer office. "Good morning, Malcolm," Hargrove said. "Glad to see you. Come on into my office." They entered the cool semidark room and another man rose to greet them. "Commissioner, I'd like you to meet Harvey Klein. Mr. Klein has come down from Paris to fill me in on our friend . . ." Hargrove reached over and closed the door. ". . . our friend Craig."

"How do you do," the commissioner said in an official tone.

"Glad to meet you, Commissioner," Klein said removing a cigarette from his mouth.

"Sit down, gentlemen," Hargrove suggested. "I thought we might as well meet as soon as possible on this case." He cleared his throat and opened a file that lay on his desk.

Tom Hargrove was a middle-aged Foreign Service career officer who hadn't quite made the grade. His present assignment was a symptom of his unfortunate career. He'd been in many small posts in South America and Asia. He had seen his counterparts rise slowly up the ladder from small to medium posts and finally to special assignments with the Department in Washington or to influential posts in European capitals. He had continued the milk run from one hardship post to the next. Suddenly he had found he was no longer a young officer with the world at his feet but a middle-aged consul conveniently buried in Africa far from the important and influential friends now riding high on the ship of state. His old friends rarely looked behind them to see if one of their comrades might be bobbing along in their wake.

"Well," Hargrove said, "I think it would be best for all of us to take a good look at the subject of our conversation." He picked up two small photos and handed them to Commissioner Innes. They were informal shots, obviously lifted out of a larger photo taken at a reception or cocktail party. In each Michael Craig was smiling. Commissioner Innes examined the photos in his usual neutral, meticulous manner. Not a bad-looking chap, he said to himself. About medium size with short-cropped hair, graying hair according to the written reports, and blue eyes. Fairly muscular; must be a sportsman or have done some heavy physical work in his time. But, Innes reflected, the only standout in these photos is the smile and the eyes. The eyes were hard. They canceled out the smile.

"Looks like a nice enough chap," Innes ventured.

The consul grimaced and the commissioner handed the photos to Mr. Klein. Klein punched his cigarette out in a silver ash tray and pushed his black-rimmed glasses up onto his forehead before examining the photos.

If this chap is C.I.A., the commissioner said to himself, I have lost some faith in the Yanks. Looks more like an Irgun type I once helped hang. He caught himself. Mustn't be unfair, he reasoned, might be a good man for all that.

"Yes," Klein said, "that's him." He handed the photos back to the consul.

"Suppose you tell the commissioner what you found out in Paris," the consul suggested.

"Yes," Commissioner Innes agreed, "I would be most interested."

"Well," Klein began, resettling his glasses. "He's a rare one. An American who foreigners will actually pay to handle a tough job of political intrigue. To go back a bit; he came from a normal American middle-class family, went to American public schools and graduated from college just before World War II. I think the war was the disorienting factor

§ 13

here. He was a good skier so he went into a mountain infantry outfit. From there they sent him to a special demolition school and from there it was O.S.S. and some highly dangerous special missions in Europe.

"After the war he entered the Foreign Service and spent most of his time in Asia. He worked as a political officer and, I think Consul Hargrove will agree, he was doing a fine job and his future looked assured."

"Then," the consul interrupted, "the man went haywire!"

Harvey Klein smiled. "Well, Mr. Hargrove, there are two sides to that story."

Hargrove gave a derogatory snort of disagreement.

Klein continued. "I think to understand Craig we have to be objective," he said, taking his glasses off and twirling them in his hand. "We've also got to remember that the man lost his wife at about this time. She died of a miscarriage in some understaffed local clinic. She'd refused to fly to Hong Kong and he was off on a field trip. He turned down the offer of a reassignment following his wife's death and continued his work. Some people thought he showed a lack of feeling. I've talked to some of his friends since and they tell me that the loss of his wife cut much deeper than he let on."

"And since," the commissioner asked, "have there been other women?"

"Well, he hasn't lived the life of a monk. He lived with a young American girl for about two years in Paris but it was what we might call a sensible arrangement—no tears, no recriminations. Incidentally, she turned out to be a tough nut when I tried to pump her on Craig. Made like a clam—not one word. To summarize—he takes his women where and when he needs them and we'd be wasting our time if we thought women were his weakness. The same goes for alcohol."

"Well, to get back to his career: Craig is a freewheeler. He doesn't pay much attention to the rules."

Consul Hargrove interrupted again. "He certainly doesn't. Why, he almost compromised the American Mission."

"Not so fast, not so fast," Klein replied, a slight edge in his voice. "I'm not defending Craig. I just want the commissioner to know the facts."

Commissioner Innes fiddled with his swagger stick, hiding a smile. This was quite a little show as far as he was concerned. American officials arguing, with him the innocent spectator.

"Well," Klein continued pointedly, "regardless of what the State Department thinks, Craig did one hell of a job for a short time. He helped organize a local counterguerrilla force that later, under his 'indirect' direction, helped fight the communists to a standstill and put off their takeover of a certain Asian country—at least temporarily."

"Hardly the job cut out for an American Foreign Service officer," Consul Hargrove added.

The commissioner watched Klein. He could tell he was making a special effort to remain calm. The younger man rubbed his hands together slowly.

"Mr. Hargrove," Klein said, barely hiding his exasperation, "I think we Americans tend to put more faith and trust in titles than we should. Craig is no sudden monster. The fact that he was a Foreign Service officer only means that he brings a certain specialized experience to his present work. It's nothing extraordinary. There are Americans, scattered around the world, who get themselves into the same sort of trouble. In the past our unemployed pilots took a job barnstorming—

today they fly paid missions over Indonesia. The Foreign Legion is 'out'—it's for clods—and the high-paid lone wolf operator, the mercenary, is 'in'!"

"Men like Craig are dangerous," Consul Hargrove said, seriously.

"You're so right. Men like Craig are dangerous. They do things. They're the type we look for during a war. We beg, borrow and steal to find them. I . . ." Klein paused. He resumed speaking in a much calmer tone. "My point is this: if we keep shaking our heads over Craig as a straying Foreign Service officer we'll waste our time and complicate things needlessly. Now, to get back to our all-American boy. He resigned from the Foreign Service and lived in France on his savings after his Asian experience. Unfortunately, he seems to have developed a taste for dabbling in the affairs of other countries. I've been working on this case in Paris. I'm afraid he's tied up in something very unsavory.

"From what we can put together, Craig has been hired by an organization of European business interests and Right Wing extremists who do not want the Trust Territory of Bomasha to become independent. He has been paid a sizable amount of money for this. How much we don't know. But a certain amount has been deposited in a Swiss bank. If this organization can cause enough trouble in Bomasha in the next few months the French government and the U.N. may have to reconsider the date now set for independence."

Consul Hargrove shifted nervously in his chair. He reached across his desk and offered cigarettes to Klein and the commissioner.

"Isn't there some way we can act now?" the consul asked. The commissioner shook his head. "I'm afraid not. His

§ **16**

papers are all in order. Even his research grant seems legitimate."

Klein lit his cigarette and slumped back into his chair.

"We also know that this organization has hired a very distinguished European lawyer to keep watch over him. They're ready to hit us with every legal weapon available if we attempt to get in his way."

"Another case of catching someone with the goods," the commissioner remarked. "It's not going to be easy."

"Oh, nothing's easy any more," Consul Hargrove said bitterly. "Nothing. The whole world has become too complicated."

"My men are already watching him," the commissioner stated. "I talked to one of my officers in Port Akodu yesterday. He said Craig planned to head for Ikiri soon."

"Ikiri is on the Bomasha border, isn't it?" Klein asked.

"It's about two miles from the actual border. It's one of our big problems. Full of smugglers and renegade political refugees from Bomasha."

There was silence for a moment. The three men seemed lost in their own thoughts. The air conditioning hummed and the street sounds and shouts of the mammy traders working the nearby market were muffled and seemed far away.

The commissioner sighed and slapped his swagger stick against the starched khaki of his shorts. "Well, I must get on. One thing, however, that I wanted to check," he said seriously. "Tom, have you spoken to the French consul about this business?"

"Not yet," Hargrove replied, coming around from behind his desk. "But I plan to see him soon. I think we ought to keep them informed."

§ 17

"Could we let it ride for a bit?" the commissioner asked, glancing at the new green rug under his regulation boots.

"Well, I suppose I could wait a few days."

"Good. I'd appreciate that. Well, glad to have met you, Mr. Klein."

They shook hands and the commissioner left, his swagger stick tucked under his arm.

Klein got up and walked over to the consul's desk. "Quite pukka, your friend, the commissioner," he said smiling.

Hargrove frowned and adjusted his necktie. "The French are going to be upset if we don't keep them informed. I can't see what difference it would make if I told them now."

"I think we better go along with Commissioner Innes," Klein replied. "He seems to know what he's doing."

The commissioner did know his business. He'd learned it the hard way. A lot of things had changed since he came ashore on the Gold Coast with two suitcases, an unburned skin and new sergeant's stripes. His first case had been a juju murder that turned his stomach inside out and taught him a great deal about Africa.

The murderers had made a great mistake. They had unwittingly killed a chief's son. Of course it really wasn't their fault. They had come upon three young boys swimming and splashing in a muddy water hole. It had been an easy hunt, a simple massacre. If they hadn't killed the chief's son the police might not have heard about it.

They had been after heads. The fat, aging chieftains to the north were constantly in search of an elixir to improve or reactivate their virility. A gelatinous salve made from the brains of young boys was the best juju available. Each head

§ **18**

brought a good price from the juju men and the murderers were good at their trade.

Smeared with ashes and monkey urine to protect them from the eyes and spears of irate parents, the hunters had fallen upon the children with their machetes and left three small, headless bodies by the side of the water hole.

From the moment the mourning chief and his retinue had come into the courtyard of the bush police post to the moment the murderers dangled lifeless on a scaffold in the capital, Innes' daily routine had been a long chain of shocks and surprises.

One of his constables had been struck by a juju curse and had become paralyzed from the waist down. The chief's warriors had brought in the heads of two men from another tribe who they had claimed were the murderers. They were not. Innes' houseboy and cook had collaborated in mixing a stew of unmentionable ingredients for his supper in the hope its absorption would allow their master to see through the dark, the mountains and the jungle, to where the murderers were hiding. Two attractive young girls had appeared unheralded before his bungalow, sent as a bribe by the parents of the murderers.

Finally, a strong juju had been put on him. With every fiber of his Scots logic protesting, he had felt himself become weaker each day, nauseated at the thought of food and sunk in a deep depression. It was nothing he could have explained at the time. A bottle of whisky had helped him break the spell. The hang-over that had followed was much more understandable and less disconcerting. He still couldn't explain juju, but he didn't laugh at it.

The memory of the murderers' filthy hut and the young

§ **19**

heads rolled together like fly-covered coconuts in the blood-stained sacks had never left Innes, but the immediate shock had been dulled by time and other horrors.

When the commissioner returned from the American consulate to his own office he cursed the heavy heat and the street noise. He picked up some of the papers on his desk and began to read through them. They were reports and orders for his signature and a long dissertation on proposed customs regulations to be applied when dealing with an independent Bomasha. A one-day-old report caught his eye. He sat upright and read it with sudden interest.

A young boy had been struck down in the market place of an outlying village. The boy had been urinating by the side of the road and the killer had struck in broad daylight, swinging his razor-sharp machete in full view of the terrorized mammy traders. He had then calmly gathered up the child's head and disappeared into the bush.

The commissioner sat silently for a moment, rereading the report. He took his pen and scratched a brief note on its margin. "Put a young officer on this," the note said, "and keep me informed." He signed his initials and put the report aside. He sighed and turned his chair toward the window. The color changes in an African sky never failed to fascinate him.

The tiny green lizard remained motionless upside down on the ceiling. The morning light from the closed shutter threw a ladder of gold over the walls and ceiling of the room. It was difficult to spot the flies. Suddenly the lizard shot forward. He snatched a fly and his head moved in slow convulsions as he worked his jaws further and further along the fly's body. The

§ **20**

frantic buzzing died as the fly disappeared from sight. Michael Craig put his pipe on the bedside table. It was too hot to smoke. He flopped back down on the lumpy bed. Each movement brought down a slow-falling cascade of dust from the dirty mosquito net folded over his head. He had stripped to his shorts and he lay full-length on his back, his hands behind his head. He didn't feel well. The iron fist of dysentery was hovering over his belly. If he hadn't been so tired he would have opened one of his suitcases and taken a few Vioform pills. He didn't like pill-taking and it was all he could do to remember his biweekly malaria preventive.

He had one of the best rooms in the Bristol Arms. The floor smelled of disinfectant, a good sign. But the mattress threw off the sharp, cloying odor of perspiration. The perspiration of many men, long before him. The ceiling fan was broken. Some exposed wires hung from it like forgotten party decorations. He had tried the rusty wash basin but only a trickle of warm brown water and a very surprised cockroach had come out of the tap. He could see the antennae of the cockroach over the rim of the basin, the two hair-thin wands combing the air slowly, suspiciously.

Craig climbed out of his bed. He lifted one of his suitcases off the floor and swung it up on the bed. He opened it and rummaged through the shirts, handkerchiefs and shorts. He reached deep under the clothing and pulled out a small cloth-wrapped package. He undid the wrapping and put it aside, hefting the 38-caliber Colt on the palm of his hand. He yawned and glanced across the room at the washbasin. The cockroach had ventured up on the basin's rim. Craig leveled the .38 at the cockroach. "Bang," he said unenthusiastically, a half smile on his face. "You've had it, pal."

§ **21**

Later he stood by the window of his hotel room watching the harbor of Port Akodu. The dugout canoes seemed to be suspended several inches above the yellow-green water. He walked to the bedside table and brought his half-finished quart bottle of German beer back to the window. He sat on the edge of the bed, put his feet on the low window sill and lit his pipe. He watched the living ebony figurines of the fishermen as they swung their nets from the bows of the dugouts. The nets spread in frail mothlike patterns before settling quietly and without a ripple into the tepid water. The dull throbbing of a drum and the eerie sound of someone making music with empty bottles hung in the air.

A sharply double-ended Japanese freighter was loading palm oil near one of the dock sheds. Puffs of white smoke rose one after the other into the sky long before the chugging sound of the loading crane crossed the water to the hotel. Craig took a sip of beer. He was enjoying his introduction to Africa. He had touched Africa before, during the war. He'd been traveling in an army air force transport, coming back to Europe via the southern route and they had put down at Kano for fueling and minor engine repairs. He remembered only the heat and the laconic Hausa traders.

For a moment the dangerous coil of memory unwound and he remembered his wife. He felt the same jagged blade of pain and loss enter his chest. In temporary weakness he let her image linger. He again heard her laughter, felt her touch. At the same time he experienced a sense of guilt at how blurred the image of her face had become. With considerable effort he wrenched his mind away and pushed it forward in time to a more recent image. He had said goodby to Anne in the cold grayness of the Paris winter.

He lay back on the bed and shut his eyes, replaying the

§ 22

scene like a scratchy film clip. He had told Anne the vague outline of his new job. Her reaction had been violent.

"For God's sake, you must be mad! Surely you're not serious?"

He had stood by the window watching the rain slanting down on the Jardin du Luxembourg and the Sunday afternoon drivers passing slowly, hesitantly, as if in search of diversion.

"Yes, I am. Very serious."

He had sensed a hollowness in his stomach and he'd wished he'd kept his mouth shut. She could if he couldn't. He had had to reassure himself. She had walked to another window, a few feet away and when she spoke he had known that she was on the verge of tears.

"Hold them back, hold them back," he had whispered silently to himself as if his wish would have some effect on her tear ducts.

"You goddamn fool," Anne's voice had been low with anger and sadness. He had felt sorry for her. She had tagged along with him for two years. She was young, intelligent and coldly beautiful. The money he had saved during his government service had evaporated and she had been helping him find a job. As an assistant editor of a fashion magazine she had contacts. She was willing to do anything for him.

She had cried then, as if the emotion was something she could shake off by holding herself erect and finding something of interest outside on the shining, damp streets. Her black hair had been pulled back in a stark chignon and the silk shirt and capri pants had accentuated the fine, thin lines of her figure.

He had put down his brandy glass on the piano and he remembered her toneless warning, "It'll leave a ring."

"The hell with it," he had replied, watching a tear slide

down her cheek, carrying with it a slight residue of mascara.

"God," she had said, sighing, "you're a bastard."

"Look, Anne, I told you because I wanted you to understand."

She had turned on him, her eyes flashing. "You want me to understand? How can I understand? What you're doing is completely crazy. Don't you see what you're getting into?"

His face had hardened at that. He didn't love Anne. He respected her and he had lived with her. They had shared their lives for a certain period of time. He had felt an obligation to tell her something of his plans. He quickly realized he had made a mistake but once launched it was hard to find a verbal brake.

She had collapsed on the couch, her head in her hands. "I spoke to Carl Owens the other day about that slot for an editor at Radio Free Europe. He was interested in you. I'm sure you could have it if you tried. But this . . . Do you realize what it can mean?"

"Perfectly. I'm going to be paid well to do a job and I've accepted the terms."

Clasping her thin hands between her knees, she had spoken without looking up at him, as if her words embarrassed her.

"Look, Michael, I don't want to sound like your conscience. I know I couldn't if I tried. But let me get this out. I've known you for about two years. I might be in love with you. I thought I knew you pretty well but I guess I don't. Wait a minute—" She had held up her hand, searching for words. "I'm floundering but I'll get to the point. Please don't hold what I'm about to say against me." Then she had taken a deep breath and spoken rapidly.

"Let's put aside all the personal risks and dangers mixed in

§ **24**

with what you plan to do. That's your business. It's your life. But have you thought of the other side? Look, we're both Americans. I'm not a flagwaver and since I've been living in Europe I haven't been much of a citizen of the republic, but for God's sake—there are certain things we don't do! You're not a criminal." She had sniffed and gone on. "I'm no do-gooder and I'm not going to exhume Washington, Jefferson and the Four Freedoms or talk about the wonderful gift of independence for people that are still eating their grand-mothers, but stop and think, Michael. Think what you're getting into!"

She had jumped up and walked back to the window. He had spoken to her jerking shoulders.

"I've taken this job because I wanted to. Who has a clear conscience today? Most of us are morally dead but we don't know it. Look, I've seen a lot. I've seen the good being bad and the bad being good. I've seen mutilated children piled up like cordwood because they were unfortunate enough to live within certain coordinates on a military map. I've seen fascists die like heroes and my friends die like frightened dogs. I've made decisions that meant death for men, women and chil-dren I'd never seen before."

"Then stay away from it," she had groaned, "stay away from it."

"No!" he had replied, suddenly angry. "I won't. I'm not going to stay in this phony city, dying a slow death on vari-ous bar stools. I'm fed up with it all!"

He had softened his voice then. "Try to understand. I'm different than the others. Don't hit me with the moral routine. Hell, just look around you. Read the goddamn papers. Our enemies are our allies. The wheel of history grinds slowly but

§ **25**

it makes a God-awful hash. Hiroshima, Dachau, Dresden, Vietnam, Algeria, Budapest—throw them all into the grinder and what comes out? A purée of death and broken bodies and an enormous fund of forgetfulness and new political arrangements."

He had walked to the window and pulled her back against him, trying to force some humor into his voice. "Look, if it will make you feel any better, call me an irresponsible adventurer. Who knows? Uncle Sam may decorate me some day for a job well done."

"Get out," she had said softly.

"You mean that?"

"Yes."

He had walked to the parlor and put on his coat. She had remained standing by the window. Once outside he had felt a great relief. He had walked through the sifting mist to the Brasserie Lipp, taken a table on the enclosed terrace and ordered a grog. Sipping the hot drink he had suddenly realized that Anne had been his last link with the past. With the link broken he finally felt free. It had taken a long time.

A lazy fly flew under the rolled mosquito net and buzzed around his nose. He waved it away, still lost in the past.

In 1943 he had parachuted onto a flat, windswept plateau in southern France loaded physically with the tools of a demolition expert and mentally with all the stirring catch phrases and motivations of a young American crusader with a Galahad role.

His crusade had been short-lived. A husky communist Resistance leader had greeted him with a solid blow from a rifle butt, stripped him of his equipment and locked him in a

§ 26

manure-filled pigsty. Two days later he had been released from his fetid prison and told that the bridge that had been the objective of his mission was not to be blown. He had been fed and given wine and ignored.

In the weeks that followed, his bruised eye opened on a whole new world of political realism. He had learned of the Right and the Left and the in-betweens. He had seen with numb shock that his gallant Resistance companions were thinking ahead—to the end of the war and beyond. Although they had fought and killed Germans it had been obvious that they considered the Boche a temporary problem—not quite as serious as the rightist Resistance group led by a retired army colonel that operated in the adjacent territory.

He had learned the ageless continuity of European politics in a school taught by tough realists in blue overalls who were ready to die for an ideal but preferred to pick the time and place.

He had profited from his first lesson. Back in England, while other O.S.S. agents had studied maps, practiced with new weapons and listened to periodic headquarters pep-talks, Craig had marked his area of operation, read as much as he could of recent political events and combed London for contacts that knew or had known the local politicians and Resistance leaders.

He had met and spoken with socialists, radicals, communists and royalists. He had questioned them, tactfully agreed with their political vehemences. He had weighed and judged, adding valuable information to the sketchy and often inaccurate official picture.

The next time he had jumped he knew the strengths and weaknesses of the local Resistance groups. He had known

§ 27

with whom to work. He had become one of the most effective American agents operating in France and one of the most unpopular among his less effective colleagues.

The by-product of Craig's practical education in applied political science was a deep and abiding distaste for official incompetence and the words of glory so often used to disguise it.

Both his moment of glory in the Far East and his ignominious resignation had been direct results of this attitude. The ambassador had been furious when he had learned of the extent of Craig's activities. Even then, there would have been a chance had it not been for Craig's reaction.

He had been called in from his para-military project, from the tough little bronze partisans who had thought of him as their chief, and tongue-lashed by the ambassador. To point out to the ambassador the incompetence of his immediate advisers had been bad enough. Adding to this the direct implication that the ambassador himself didn't quite understand the political situation in his country of assignment had been too much. The Department had requested his resignation. After that even the C.I.A. wouldn't touch him.

Paris had been fine in the beginning. He had had his government back pay, insurance and refunded retirement money. He had made it last. He'd picked up some money from an occasional translation job, a film-dubbing assignment or a travel article. Anne had been more than generous. He had accepted more from her than he liked to admit. Then everything had begun to close in.

Paris, the City of Light, had a sinister undercurrent. The food was too good, the women too easy, the liquor too abundant. Anne's world had to a large extent become his and he had felt its luxurious velvet tentacles closing around him. When the opportunity to escape had come he had not hesitated.

He had been contacted in Paris by a French journalist he did not particularly like. The journalist worked for a Right Wing weekly and tried his best to look like an aristocrat but it didn't quite come off. He was so used to taking bribes that he had almost slipped the luncheon bill into his pocket without looking at it when the waiter had handed it to him.

The journalist had put him in touch with a gray-haired gentleman with the red *tomate* of the Legion of Honor on the lapel of his expensive wool suit. Craig remembered the well-manicured fingers shaking under his nose.

"The communists will take over one week after independence," the elderly gentleman had said gravely. "We are proposing to pay you for something your own government should be doing. Every new flag thrown up a pole in Africa is another blow to Western civilization."

Fifty thousand dollars. He rolled the sound of it on the end of his tongue. Twenty-five thousand already deposited for him in a numbered Swiss account. The remainder would be his at the completion of his assignment.

It wasn't just the money. Anne would never understand. She couldn't. He was too far from her world. He was going to work again. His kind of work, with no ambassadors to get in the way. No empty moral judgments to complicate things.

He opened his eyes and stared at the ceiling, interrogating himself. Finally a slow cynical smile spread over his face. Yes, it is true, he said to himself calmly but with a slight trace of bitterness. I just don't give a damn any more. I don't care.

A blast of high-life music forced his attention to the small

§ **29**

open stall across the street from the hotel. It served as both a sweet shop and a bar. There were several rickety wooden tables, a few dilapidated chairs and a fat mammy trader sitting stolidly behind the counter crunching a chewing stick between her white teeth and occasionally chasing the flies away from a plate of sticky fried plantains.

The police constable was still there. Craig felt sorry for him. He was trying to be unobtrusive with his nose buried in a local newspaper but he wasn't accustomed to this type of work. He was visibly ill at ease. Once, when the mammy trader had talked to him about the white stranger and emphasized her conversation with gestures in the direction of the hotel, the poor constable had steadfastly looked away from the hotel, rolling the whites of his eyes as if he were faced with a wild animal that might go away if one didn't look at it.

Craig finished the beer and walked to the wash basin. He stood looking at the stained enamel for a moment. He shook his head in disgust and toweled himself dry of perspiration. He took a clean shirt out of one of his suitcases and slipped it on. His flight to Ikiri was in one hour's time. It would take the hotel's battered Land Rover a good half hour to reach the Port Akodu air strip. It was time to get moving. He decided not to wear a necktie. Before closing his suitcase he took out two thick volumes bound in stained leather. He examined them carefully, fingering the thick binding. *Tribes of the Border Territories* by James Stone-Parkinson was undoubtedly one of the most boring and obsolete anthropological works in print but there were ten one-hundred-dollar bills sealed between the layers of leather in each book. His contingency fund or "bug out" money was comparatively well hidden. He shook his head, smiling as he thought of the sixty-odd volumes of various anthropological studies he had ordered from London. Wait till they arrived in Ikiri! Every dried-out bore of an anthropologist in West Africa would probably make a point of dropping in on him when the word got around. He packed the books, tucked his coat under his arm and went downstairs to pay his bill.

The Greek wife of the proprietor raised her dull eyes from a cheap illustrated magazine and gathered up the pounds and shillings with the languor of a gorged boa. An African boy came out of the kitchen and went slowly up the stairs to fetch Craig's baggage. Craig finished paying and grudgingly left a tip on the counter. The boy struggled back downstairs, a heavy suitcase in each hand, his white shorts sliding dangerously low on his thin hips. Craig said goodby to the Greek woman. She smiled at him briefly, arching her heavy eyebrows, and went abruptly back to her penny dreadful.

A tall, skeletal African in the remmants of a military uniform stood by the hotel's Land Rover. He saluted Craig gravely, his splay fingers almost knocking off the dented red fez set at an angle on his clean-shaven skull. Craig nodded in return and waited for the boy to load his luggage. When the boy had finished he came over to Craig smiling.

The boy had trachoma. His right eye was coated with the milky white gelatin of the infection. "Dash, Mastah," the boy said. It was both a demand and a question. Craig dug into his pocket for some change. He took the boy by the shoulder and turned him to put his good eye in line with the sweet shop and bar shack opposite the hotel. "Do you see that policeman?" Craig asked.

"The black constable?"

"Yes. You take him these shillings and tell him to buy a beer for himself."

The boy grinned and held out his hand for the money. "I

§ **31**

go tell 'im, he go drink beer pretty nice from one English fellah."

Craig corrected him. "No, from one American fellah," he told the boy.

"Good, Mastah, I go tell 'im."

"That's it," Craig said, climbing into the Land Rover, "Here's something for you."

"Ahh," the boy said, his fixed grin broadening. "Ah, you one fine mastah."

The lanky driver clamped his bare foot over the clutch pedal, wrestled with the long-suffering gears and they pulled slowly away from the hotel in a cloud of black exhaust.

Craig looked back over his piled baggage. The boy was carefully counting the money he had given him. He saw the boy glance cautiously in the direction of the constable, then slide all the money into his drooping shorts and walk nonchalantly back into the hotel.

Chapter 3

.
.

Big Boy Eniki was drunk. He had started with beer and shifted to palm wine. Now, as he danced slowly in a shuffling circle outside the hut, his eyes were glazed and his mouth hung open. He held a half-finished bottle of palm wine in one hand and when he spun in rhythm to his own monotonous chanting he splashed dollops of the wine over the dusty ground.

A young Fulani girl crouched by the door of the hut, watching Big Boy's dance in silence. Big Boy had purchased her from her cattle-driving father for two nights. The second night had passed and she was waiting for Big Boy to fall asleep so she could run away.

"Oh, Big Boy, he some fellah," Big Boy chanted, almost falling down in the middle of a senseless pirouette. "Man, look that black fellah, B-i-i-i-g Boy!" He stopped, swaying, the powerful muscles of his legs visible through the thin material of his trousers. He raised the bottle to his lips and drank, leaking the palm wine down over his chin and onto his dirty shirt front.

He threw the bottle at the top of the hut and roared with laughter as it rolled down the dry thatch and bounced off the ground. Big Boy Eniki stretched his six-foot frame and flexed his muscles. "Goddamn Jesus," he shouted, "how you make a man so strong and good as this man?" Then he burst into high-pitched laughter, the tears rolling down his cheeks as he ran around in a tight circle kicking at the ground with his bare feet.

The Fulani girl pulled the blanket closer over her face. This slight movement caught Big Boy's attention. "Hah!" he shouted, leveling a long black finger at the girl. "You not worth one sick cow. You no good at loving me. Bugger off, you!" he shouted, launching a kick in the girl's direction. She dodged it with a sudden agility, dropping the blanket from her shoulders. The sight of her dusky nude body and young, firm breasts kindled a spark in Big Boy's wine-dulled eyes. "Hello," he said softly, with renewed interest. The girl remained crouching, breathing heavily and licking her lips. Dark bruises were scattered over her body from previous encounters with Big Boy.

Big Boy moved closer, his broad, scarred face lit with a crafty smile. The girl started to back away along the wall of the hut. Big Boy shouted, "Yaaah," and made a lunge for her. She jumped lightly aside, spit at the curly head that flashed by her and ran off past the huts, her muscular buttocks jiggling frantically and her feet kicking up small puffs of dust as she disappeared from sight.

Big Boy had fallen to the ground. He watched her go with his back braced against the wall of the hut. He belched and looked around for the bottle but he couldn't find it. A small black bird swung in low over the dusty ground and settled into one of the nearby mango trees. Big Boy watched the bird as it flitted soundlessly among the green leaves. He reached into one of his trouser pockets and pulled out a kola nut. He wiped it off and popped it into his mouth.

Big Boy was bored. He had been in Ikiri for two days waiting for the American and he was restless. The cool bite of the kola on his tongue revived him. He pushed himself upright and yawned. He felt hungry now and he decided to walk back into town.

He walked away from the hut, weaving slightly, toward the narrow dirt road that led into Ikiri. Two small boys came around from behind a hut, their round bellies jutting out over their skinny legs. They stood in silent wonder watching Big Boy's departure.

From a distance the town of Ikiri looked as if it were about to be swallowed by the surrounding jungle. The thick bush rolled over the hills and to the edge of town like cool, green lava. There were a few trees left in the town, sprouting up among the roofs or isolated along the edges of the main street. The poison of lorry exhausts had condemned them to a leafless, living death.

The district officer's home and the government Rest House stood well above the town. Both buildings were buried in the hill scrub under the gray-trunked trees that rose straight and tall, trailing yellow bands of vine and moss until they exploded toward the sky in umbrellas of thick green leaves.

The district officer's home was a low five-room bungalow built by the government public works department. It had been inadequate in 1930. It was doubly so now. One had the immediate impression that someone had made a great mistake, that the guard house and its occupant in his red, tasseled fez and gold buttons would soon be loaded into a truck and moved to a home more fitting for the representative of Her Majesty's government.

The Ikiri Rest House held an unblemished record for serving the worst meals in the border territory. A family of deadly black mambas lived under its shaky front veranda.

The one main street in Ikiri was identifiable by the three-story cement building of the Ikiri Hotel. The hotel dominated the northern end of the dirt street with its heavy ugliness. The government police post marked the other end of Ikiri's main street.

The town's other commercial buildings were of thick red mud. Their walls were cracked by the heat and the rains and shored up with logs or mud bricks. Their roofs were of battered corrugated tin. Grouped around the central business district were the one- and two-story homes of the Lebanese, Pakistani, Indian and African merchants. They were ugly constructions of concrete with sagging walls and flaking pastel paint.

Huts of mud and thatch made up the rest of the town. There was no street pattern, only a series of evil-smelling alleys full of flies, garbage, shouting naked children and goats. There were black goats and white goats and goats of blended browns. Their underslung bellies dragged over the refuse heaps, their short tufted tails flicked like frantic metronomes.

Big Boy Eniki weaved his way up the main street of Ikiri. He paused occasionally to spit a jet of kola-nut juice onto the dusty road. He passed the stands of several Yoruba mammy traders. One of the women adjusted the folds of blue material over her ample bosom and laughed as Big Boy staggered slightly and recovered himself. He stopped, frowning. "What for you laugh, you woman?" he said, taking a threatening step toward her.

Like buffalo grouping to face a marauding lion, two of the other mammy traders got up from their stalls and waddled silently over to their friend, who continued to eye Big Boy with a broad grin on her face. Each woman was huge. The folds of blue cloth and their butterfly-like turbans made them look even larger. One of them had a deep scar running across her chin. They chattered together in Yoruba and Big Boy didn't understand them.

"Go, big man," his antagonist said in English. "Yahh, yah," she said as if she were chasing a chicken away from some corn. The other mammy traders laughed, throwing back their heads, holding their bellies.

Big Boy retreated a few steps. He spit on the ground and made an obscene gesture.

"Ahhh," the woman with the scar on her chin shook her finger at him. "You want that?" she asked, swinging her broad hips in gross invitation. "C'mon man, I give you plenty."

The other two roared with laughter, their white teeth shining. Big Boy shrugged his shoulders and walked away. He was no longer drunk but he mumbled to himself, glancing back over his shoulder at the mammy traders who were now re-enacting the whole encounter for the benefit of some truck drivers.

"Let them laugh, ha ha," he mumbled, frowning. "They don't know nothing! I fix pretty good those damn fools when the time come. I am a captain, a secret captain and a

§ **37**

damn good fightin' man. Yaah, pretty Jesus, I'll show them."

Big Boy reached the front steps of the hotel. He pushed past the Hausa traders sleeping on the veranda and walked into the bar and dining room. He wrinkled his nose and looked around the room. Several mulatto children were playing around one of the oilcloth-covered tables. An infant was screaming in a corner, a dirty, full diaper hanging low between its bowed legs. The Armenian owner of the hotel lounged behind the bar reading a battered copy of the *Daily Express* and chewing a silver-banded cigarette holder.

"Man," Big Boy said in a loud voice, "this place smells!"

The Armenian glanced up at Big Boy. He put down his paper on the stained plastic of the bar top and rubbed his watery eyes.

"Hello, chappie," he said in a painful imitation of an English gentleman's delivery. "Like some good gin to make the day happy?"

"No," Big Boy said, slumping down at one of the empty tables. "Want some good chop. I want two fried chicken eggs and some gari and one big cup of tea."

"Aha," the Armenian said, smiling and climbing down from his perch behind the bar. "You are hungry."

Big Boy waved some of the drowsy blue flies off the oilcloth in front of him. "Mistah Magabian," he called plaintively, "can't you put that pickin' outside?" Magabian paused by the infant, glancing down as if he had just noticed the child for the first time. The child stopped screaming and turned his curly head up toward his father, his eyes glistening with tears.

Magabian picked the child up. Holding him under the arms

§ **38**

and at a distance he carried him outside. The screaming doubled in volume.

Magabian came back inside. He paused at the bar, picked up a stained dishtowel and wiped his hands on it. Then he walked across to Big Boy's table and gave the table top several swipes with the same towel.

"Say," Magabian said, as he straightened up. "There was a telephone call from the Rest House for you. A European calling. Didn't sound like an Englishman. Asked for you, 'Mr. Rodney Eniki,' he said." Magabian laughed. "I didn't know your name was Rodney, Big Boy."

Big Boy made an irritated gesture of dismissal with his hand. "You have them eggs fried by Crismas?" he asked.

Magabian left the dining room whistling and rubbing the perspiration off his neck and forehead with the dishtowel.

Alone, Big Boy grinned with satisfaction. "Man," he said to himself, "now we goin' to roll." This American was supposed to be a big mastah and Americans were tough. He had seen them in movies. They shoot first and ask questions later. That's how Big Boy liked to operate.

Craig finished his dinner and walked out onto the sagging veranda of the Rest House. He filled his pipe hurriedly, anxious to blot out the unpleasant taste of charred Brussels sprouts that lingered on his palate.

It actually felt cool now that the sun had slipped behind the mountains. He walked down the stairs puffing clouds of smoke over his shoulder as his pipe took hold. He tossed away the curled, black match. He decided to take a leisurely walk up the road that led to the edge of the jungle at the base of one of the larger mountains.

§ 39

He walked through the red laterite dust of the road and glanced back over his shoulder at Ikiri. The lights were beginning to come on. Electric lights blinked hesitantly in front of the police post, at the hotel and in a few of the larger homes. Kerosene lanterns and carbide lamps were sputtering to life throughout the rest of the town.

He reached the end of the road, which stopped at the edge of the jungle. It was strange. There was an abrupt transition that he could see and hear. The jungle began ten feet before him. It was as if he had come to the entrance of a dark cave. Scrub bush and thorny vines skirted the road's edge. Next came a stand of tall grass and scattered bushes with wide shining leaves. Then the eye could not differentiate. The foliage pushed together and blended under a roof of tall trees, vines and darkness. He stood listening to the evening symphony of the jungle. Wave after wave of insect sounds were counterpointed by the low croaking of toads and the occasional angry squeal of a monkey somewhere high in the interlaced branches before him. He looked up at the sky. There was still a bit of light. But it had been night for some time in the jungle. He picked up a small stone and tossed it into the bush. A sudden, artificial silence fell like the blade of a cleaver. In the small radius covered by the sound, insects and small animals paused, silent, and alert. He waited, listening. Then the first notes of the interrupted chorus began again. Cautiously the chirps, trills and croakings swelled in volume with the reassurance of mutual support.

He turned and headed back to the Rest House. He had only gone a few steps when he heard the trumpeting of an elephant. He had heard the sound before at the circus or in films. This was different. It was a weird, lost sound that came

§ **40**

faintly from somewhere very high on the mountain. It wasn't a sound of challenge or defiance. It was a sound of defeat and despair. He paused, listening, but there was nothing now but the mad jangle of the insects. Reluctantly he walked back to the Rest House, pausing occasionally to look back at the black pyramid of the mountain outlined against the night sky.

Chapter 4

.
.

Big Boy watched Michael Craig fill his glass with beer and kept talking. "Once we cross the border we go south along the river to Ache. Ache is good country. All around nobody bother us. We got twenty man ready down there with new Belgian submachine guns."

Craig made an abrupt motion with his hand. Big Boy stopped talking, a puzzled look on his face. Craig flipped off the ceiling light and moved quickly to the open window. He paused, listening, looking into the darkness. Before he came back to the table he swung the shutters closed. He switched on the light and turned toward Big Boy with a look of anger and utter amazement.

"Let's just talk about our trip, Mr. Eniki," he said in a loud voice, still looking hard at Big Boy. "I am particularly interested in the river tribes."

Big Boy was stunned by the sudden change in atmosphere. To cover his puzzlement he gulped several swallows of beer.

Craig busied himself over the maps. My God, he thought,

this man is a menace! He had been told that Eniki was one of the better men he had to work with. A veteran of World War II, supposedly tough and skilled in small arms. He couldn't afford snap judgments, but one thing was certain, Eniki talked too much and too loud. The sooner they got out of Ikiri and away from civilization the better.

Big Boy got up and stood beside him looking down at the maps. "Do you think we can leave in two days?" Craig asked.

"Ah, we go leave tomorrow if you like," Big Boy replied. He bent low over the map and grimaced. "No damn good," he said, puffing his lips in derision. "These maps don't show nothin' right. River filled in that corner one time, long ago."

"We'll start day after tomorrow," Craig said. "I have a paper to do on the burial rites of the river tribes and I want to get some facts together first."

Big Boy turned his huge head slowly and looked at Craig for a moment, blinking. Then he understood, and a conspiratorial smile spread over his face.

"Yes," he said, enjoying the new game. "Them river fellas not much for Christian teaching. They just toss 'em into the water, splash! and ol' crocodile chop 'em."

"Well," Craig said, folding the maps and tossing them onto his bed, "I think I better get some sleep. We'll get together tomorrow. I've a lot of questions to ask you, Mr. Eniki."

"Yes, sahr, I will show you Ikiri," Big Boy said, eyeing the half-finished beer bottle. "I have been glad to meet an American man," he said solemnly as he walked to the door.

"Good night," Craig said, feeling Big Boy's muscular hand close over his.

"Good night, Mastah," Big Boy said. He hesitated for a moment in the doorway. Maybe Mr. Craig would like one

§ **43**

nice woman for the night. He frowned for a moment as Craig waited impatiently. Big Boy decided not to say anything. This man acted strange, like a damn fool missionary. Big Boy took his leave shrugging his shoulders and murmuring to himself.

Craig shut the door and collapsed into the uncomfortable chair by the window. He glanced up at the bare bulb hanging from the ceiling. He shut his eyes to lessen the glare and listened to the throb of his headache. He reached for the beer bottle but it was warm to the touch. He wanted to stay awake a bit longer. He wanted to think things out. Eniki was to be his military assistant, his strong right arm. Craig smiled and shook his head. Someone had been sold a bill of goods. It was too late to change things now, but he would have to watch Eniki. Once they got to Ache he would make contact with Colonel Durand. Maybe then he would be able to make some sense out of the situation.

He finally found enough energy to get up and turn off the light. The thin whining of a mosquito reminded him of his net. As he adjusted it, pushing the ends under his mattress, he re-examined the plans for his meeting with the colonel, seeking gaps in the logic or loopholes in the reasoning. It seemed to hold together. It had been Colonel Durand's idea. Craig grudgingly gave him credit. It rather surprised him that this colonel, particularly a French colonel, could be concise and uncomplicated.

Craig stripped to his shorts and climbed in under the mosquito net. He yawned. He wanted to sleep but his mind idled on. He wasn't young any more. Forty-two years still had an aura of youth about it when you rode to work and lived in the luxury of a modern city. You could still fool yourself by skiing in the winter or sailing in the summer or

§ 44

by ogling the young secretaries and performing in bed. Here it was different. He thought of the jungle at the end of the road. He knew he would soon leave to enter the jungle as a resident, that the vine-choked trails would be his commuter run and that even the shabby mosquito net now enveloping him would be a fondly remembered luxury. He was going to earn his money the hard way.

Commissioner Innes was waiting for Harvey Klein at the bar of the Queen's Gardens. They shook hands and sat down at the bar. Innes ordered two bottles of iced stout.

"I hope you don't mind," he said, "but the whisky here is vile and I have my reasons for ordering stout."

"Reasons?" Klein asked puzzled.

"I've got a surprise for you later on."

"Oh," Klein said smiling, "well, here's mud in your eye!"

"Cheers!"

They sipped their stout in silence. Klein examined the Queen's Gardens. It was an open beer hall with a green cement floor, palm-frond roofing and tables pushed up against the high concrete walls that closed out the fetid slums of the capital.

"Quite a place," Klein ventured, looking at the colored bulbs that lit the bar and straggled up and over the palm-frond roof.

"It's not too bad," the commissioner said, "I'd advise you not to try the W. C., however. At least not before you eat. On the other hand the food here is not bad at all. An old French chap runs the Gardens from his sickbed. Couldn't care less about the look of the place but his bed is in the room next to the kitchen and the old duffer checks every plate. A bit touching, you know. Just a skeleton of a man and yet he can

§ 45

tell what's happening in the kitchen by the sound and the food odors. Raises an awful rumpus with his help when things don't go right."

A small, bent African with gray hair shuffled through the swinging doors behind the bar. "Mastah come," he said peremptorily to the commissioner.

"That means us," Commissioner Innes said, smiling. "We'll take our stout to the table with us."

They followed the waiter to a table against the wall. It was lit by a lonely green light bulb and it took some time for their eyes to become accustomed to the semidarkness. When they were seated the waiter shuffled off again toward the kitchen.

"Frankly," Commissioner Innes said, "this is one of the few places in town I can really talk. My bungalow is full of small African boys with big ears. Even my office is more of a public place than a private enclosure. Here we have a good high wall of twelve-inch concrete between us and a noisy slum and a good view of everyone coming in. Ah, here we go."

The waiter reappeared carrying two large trays. Now he was smiling and he echoed the exclamation of surprise and pleasure from the two white men when he set the platters down on the table.

"Oysters!" Klein said, stupefied, "on the half shell!"

"Flown in by Air France this morning," the commissioner replied, reaching for a lemon, "packed in seaweed and fresh as the Atlantic spray. Now you can see why I prefer the Queen's Gardens to the boiled beef and potatoes of the better hotels in town."

The waiter put a plate of brown bread and butter on the table. "Bring us two more bottles of stout," the commissioner ordered as he dug into his first oyster.

The waiter returned with the iced stout and the commissioner waited for him to disappear through the swinging doors before he spoke. He pushed three empty oyster shells aside on the metal table top and selected a full one from its bed of seaweed.

"You can probably imagine why I wanted to speak to you alone. Hargrove is a good chap, one of the best, but I'm afraid he tends to be overly officious. Stop me if I'm being unfair . . ."

Klein smiled, looked up from his plate and shook his head.

"Well, I imagine you people are on to Colonel Durand?"

Klein nodded affirmatively, his mouth full of oyster and brown bread.

"Durand is the reason I did not want Hargrove to speak to the French consul, at least not yet. The French consul's all right. A bit ga-ga over the ladies, maybe, but a fairly stable type—for a Frenchman. I'm more worried about his staff. I'm sure he'd waste no time in consulting his vice-consuls about the Craig business and I think we'd stand a good chance of having everything we told him delivered to Colonel Durand on a silver platter, probably accompanied by an engraved calling card.

"Is Durand being paid for his part in this?" Klein asked.

"No. At least not as far as we know. I think he believes in what he's doing. That's what makes it so bloody difficult. I've never met the man but from all I can gather he certainly is the type one would admire and like under different circumstances. He's one of those rare beings that are so hard to come by today—a leader of men.

"Do you think he and Craig are going to get along?"

"That I don't know. Durand certainly doesn't like Americans. He makes no bones about it. Seems to feel you chaps are to blame for most of the ills of the world. Pretty bitter

§ **47**

about your support of these newly independent nations at the expense of France. He's a very intense type. A very dangerous man to have against you."

"Well, Commissioner, I'll be frank. My time down here is limited. My assignment applies strictly to Craig. I came down to confirm what we suspected and my authority at this time doesn't extend beyond gathering information. I'll return to Paris soon to make a full report." Klein put aside an empty oyster shell and frowned, thinking. "But," he continued, "there is always the human element in something like this. I'd like to talk to Craig myself."

"American to American and all that?"

"It sounds dated but there's that one chance in a thousand that it might work. I'll probably catch hell for it but it might be worth the effort. It could be very rough if anyone knew about our meeting. I wouldn't want any links with Craig and his project. Too many people would be only too happy to say my organization was mixed up in it."

"Well," the commissioner said, "I don't suppose you'd be able to nip into Ikiri and out again without people knowing about it. It's one of those spots where the arrival of every new white man is an event and a subject of local speculation. Besides, I don't believe you'd be able to catch him before he leaves for his first field trip. We understand he's planning to do some research on the river tribes shortly after his arrival at Ikiri."

Klein shook his head. "I guess you're right. I'd better forget my trip to Ikiri." He sighed, "My Boy Scout days are over."

The commissioner smiled. He lifted his glass. "I'm glad you made that decision yourself. I was about to advise you against it, informally, of course." He paused, looking at Klein. "I have some other news for you—and it's not good."

§ 48

"More trouble?"

"Yes, I'm afraid so." We know that an African named Rodney Eniki has contacted Craig at Ikiri. Eniki is an unsavory character with a strange background. He fought with an African battalion in Burma and distinguished himself against the Japanese. Picked up some very respectable medals in the process. At one point, things being somewhat quiet and no Japanese about, he and a few friends stole some medical alcohol and proceeded to drink themselves blind. Eniki then led them on a rampage. According to reports they came upon some wounded from a Gurkha unit and proceeded to chop them up with machetes. Eniki later claimed he thought they were Japanese. The incident was hushed up for fear of clashes between the Gurkhas and the Africans and Eniki got off easy. He finished the war in a work camp.

"Since then he's been in prison several times, once for killing a man in a beer shack brawl, twice for rape, and the last time for smuggling on the Bomasha border. He has given himself the rank of captain. In reality he did make sergeant at one point. He's supposed to be a wizard with small arms."

The waiter came and removed the plates piled high with empty oyster shells. He turned his wrinkled face toward the commissioner.

"Good?" he asked frowning.

"Top, number one," the commissioner replied. "Tell Mr. Lancome we are ready for our steaks."

The waiter left and Klein offered the commissioner a cigarette. "I wonder," Klein said seriously, "if Craig knows about Eniki's background?"

"I don't know," the commissioner replied. "But, that isn't all."

"You mean it gets worse?"

§ 49

"Exactly. Eniki won't be the only advocate of Mars working with Craig and Durand. Someone has seen to it that more professional talents are available. I have definite information that two Europeans—a South African and a Frenchman—will soon be added to the team."

"Professional mercenaries?"

"Yes, I'm not sure about the South African but I know that the Frenchman was one of Durand's comrades-in-arms."

Klein finished the last of his stout. "Jesus," he sighed, "what a mess."

"Quite," the commissioner agreed. "But that's enough business for now. I hate being a Cassandra. Life's too short. I've ordered a good wine and although the local beef isn't choice I'm sure the sauce they whip up here will disguise the flavor."

They finished dinner, said goodby and Klein went back to his hotel. He finished packing and relaxed in the shower, letting the water pour over his head and down through the thick mat of black hair on his chest. The stout had given him a slight headache but it faded with the first touch of cool water. It helped to take his glasses off for a while. Without them the world took on a slight haze, a pleasant blur, not at all uncomfortable. It helped him relax.

This was the strangest assignment he'd ever had. Harvey Klein, Phi Beta Kappa; M.A. in literature; tempered liberal; C.I.A. desk commando; expert at Research and Intelligence evaluation—what the hell, he asked himself, are you doing in Africa?

He smiled as he stepped from the shower. He had always wanted an active assignment. He had felt he was stagnating at his Washington desk, evaluating reports, balancing percentages, becoming a so-called expert on Western Europe. Well, his assignment to Paris had been all he'd dreamed of. But he hadn't thought it would bring him to Africa. Assignments no longer seemed to be clear-cut and static. Jets had pulled countries together till they overlapped politically, economically and militarily like badly poured pancakes. He pulled on his pajamas and flopped down on the bed.

This Craig case seemed to be snowballing. Now that he had his teeth into it he hated to let go. There was something that bothered him about the case. He knew the dossiers of the men who had hired Craig. It was inconceivable that they would hire an American for anything from cleaning out their offices to assassinating de Gaulle. And yet they had. That fact alone overrode his incredulity. Well, he told himself, there's bound to be a follow-up. He turned out the light, punched the hard hotel pillow and went to sleep thinking of his wife and children waiting for him in Paris.

Chapter 5

:

The Trust Territory of Bomasha was shaped like an exclamation point, its broad top resting on the southern edge of the Sahara and its thin bottom squeezing out into the Atlantic and the Gulf of Guinea. For many years the peoples of Bomasha remained untouched and undisturbed by the cautious European prodding and exploring along the west coast. The Portuguese and the British had run their slave ships in against the coastal mud shallows but the impenetrable mangrove swamps and the unimpressive physical attributes of the coastal tribes had discouraged the flesh traders and they had upped anchor and sailed north to dicker with their Arab counterparts along the sand beaches of the Slave Coast.

The coastal tribesmen were short, ugly, unfriendly people who spent three quarters of their time immersed in the brackish waters of coastal inlets fishing for the suckerfish that made up the bulk of their diet. There were no tribal wars as their primitive society had never evolved into tribal divisions.

There had never been cannibalism as all Gokas shared a monumental loathing for meat of any kind.

To these people the shark was the God Father. Occasionally, when the rains sent the rivers crashing through their shaky stilted settlements and drove the fish out to sea, their priests would choose several infants at random, tie them together at the ankles and throw them as an offering into a sheltered inlet where the gray coastal sharks nestled into the soft mud to ride out the storms.

The more adventurous of the coastal people had ventured hesitantly north along the rivers until they came into contact with the Yoruba cattle drovers of the central savannah and the fierce Bomasha of the northern region.

Their emigration then stopped and recoiled back to the thick jungle and steamy mud of the river banks. These pioneers of the coastal people were labeled the "river tribes" by the early French and British explorers, and lumped together with their brethren on the seacoast under the tribal heading of "Goka," an indecipherable word stemming from the repetitive guttural shout of the fishermen as they drove the sluggish suckerfish into their primitive fish traps.

The French pushed down into Bomasha from the southern Sahara in the late 1800s and staked their claim. The young major of spahis who led the small expedition had not been too impressed but his superiors were overjoyed to slap another bit of possessive color on their maps of Africa. An Africa that the European nations were then slicing and dividing like a rich, succulent pie.

Bomasha's first export had been fighting men. The northerners seemed to take to the military life and France had been able to put them to good use. As the years passed other exports developed. Hides, palm oil, groundnuts, bananas and timber were shipped out of northern Bomasha by rail. But the coastal shallows and mangrove swamps had discouraged any major port construction in the south.

In 1936 the first tin mine began operation in Bomasha and suddenly the possibilities of mineral wealth prompted a new interest in the dormant colony. Dusty records were reopened and files for columbite and coal were added.

Two battalions from Bomasha went off to help crush Hitler and the colony moved sluggishly through the war, divided by European political intrigue but basically bored by the faraway clash of arms.

When Bomasha was made a Trust Territory following the war, the Vichy sympathizers packed their bags and moved on to more fertile ground in North Africa or the Far East.

During the postwar readjustment, as other African nations flamed with nationalism, observers in Bomasha could report only a weak flickering of independent feeling. Strangely enough, this seed of independence first appeared among some members of the coastal and river tribes who had been exposed to the Protestant missionaries from the nearby British colony. The French authorities had long ago decided that anyone who wished to work with the Goka were more than welcome to the task. Later, they noted with surprise some of the products of the mission schools. The sons of the semi-aboriginal fishermen had shown an unexpected flair for learning. Not being amateurs in the colonial business, the French had quickly picked several of the brightest graduates of the mission schools and sent them off to Paris, at government expense. Thus, while their northern brothers were still prostrating themselves before emirs or straining their unexercised

§ 54

brains over the sighting distances on French army machine guns, the sons of the fisheaters were applying their strange gift of awakened native intelligence at the Sorbonne and listening to radical political theories in the student cafés along the Boul' Mich.

Faced with the necessity of hurriedly forming a native governmental cadre in compliance with the U.N. regulations for a Trust Territory and in preparation for eventual independence, the French authorities reluctantly turned to their educated black sheep from the south.

There was little doubt that Jean Jaurès Tibaki would be the first prime minister of Bomasha. Following his Paris studies he had worked in the native government as a civil servant. He had been promoted to the highest post held by an African —Assistant Director of Public Works—and had recently been the first African elected to the local assembly. A move suggested quietly the previous month by the French high commissioner.

He was a small coal-black man with a forehead marked by deep muscular furrows. His black curly hair was clipped close to the skull. He wore round gold-rimmed spectacles that he was continually removing and wiping with the white handkerchief he wore tucked up the sleeve of his black double-breasted suit.

He was quiet and retiring. He dressed like a Calvinist minister and carried a black umbrella to ward off the sun. His smile was warm and disarming. His colonial mentors were pleased that the word yes came so easily to his lips. An unofficial joke among French officials had it that the only time Monsieur Tibaki ever said no in earshot of the French high commissioner was in reply to the offer of a drink.

§ **55**

Sitting through the official dinners nibbling at the fish course that didn't taste to him like fish and tactfully avoiding the sickening meat plates, he nodded continually through the dull, condescending conversations that had been constructed for him with great care by his polite but overbearing hosts.

His softly ennunciated *"oui"* was reassuring to the influential Europeans who saw the insignificant little black man as an unhappy necessity, a dark fetish that the new Africa demanded and which they were only too glad to provide in order that they could get on with their business.

The soft, kind eyes behind the thin lenses of the gold-rimmed spectacles watched the boisterous officials and colonists with great interest. Once, at the high commissioner's, when his smile had been broadest, a visiting official from the Quai d'Orsay had been prompted to describe him as "a silly looking little monkey." Monsieur Tibaki had actually been thinking how pleasant it would be to tie several of the more portly guests together at the ankles and have them tossed into the shark-filled lagoon near his own village as an offering to the Shark God of his poor, ignorant and exploited people.

Jean Jaurès Tibaki had been raised in a sagging village on the banks of the Bomasha River where mud, water and fish were the three symbols of life. He had known his mother but he had never been sure of his father. The Goka lived and mated as a community and families existed only insomuch as breast feeding kept the child close to its mother.

A missionary woman had taken young Jean Jaurès away from his village along with several other male and female children. She was a well-meaning, fire-eating English Protestant who saw the Goka river tribes as the greatest challenge

§ 56

of her career. To the day she died she felt the mud-smeared savages had been a heaven-sent test of her faith and ability as a missionary. Her poor, dried-out corpse would have revolved painfully in its grave had she known that the scheming French would choose several of "her boys" and send them off to Paris, the capital of sin, to undermine their good Christian education with Papist theory and Continental affectations.

She had given the serious young man the family name of Tibaki. She had picked it out of a census sheet as she had done for all the Goka children in her flock. To this was added the good Anglo-Saxon sound of Harold. After a year of study and café conversation in Paris, Monsieur Tibaki became Monsieur Jean Jaurès Tibaki, a dark specter in a turtleneck sweater and dirty corduroy pants. His friends were young, radical and of all sizes and colors. His poor, glutted head, ready to burst from his studies, was filled with a charge of new ideas and theories. He was courted as an African and chastised for his political ignorance. Rightist students invited him to smoky meetings in well-furnished rooms, where he drank aged cognac to the accompaniment of American jazz and was lectured on the perils of international political life. He winced at tales of the diabolic Leftists, heard for the first time of the international communist conspiracy, detected what he thought were hidden threats that "Africans like you must wake up before it's too late." He drank more aged cognac, listened to more jazz and inevitably found himself in bed with some drunken young blonde student searching for a unique thrill.

On other nights he would flow with a tide of Leftist students to a sixth floor walk-up near the Boulevard Saint-Michel to drink raw red wine to the accompaniment of American jazz. There he was told of the Fascist threat, of International Combines and of the history of European Colonialism. His hosts attempted to shame him for his lack of progressive spirit and willingness to assist in the liberation of his country. He would sit quietly, his brow developing its deep muscular furrows, and sip the abominable knife-edged wine knowing, without being told, that the close of the evening would find him in bed with some tousle-haired, young bohemian who would chatter political theory between bouts of love-making.

It was a tiring ordeal for a student with a heavy study schedule. It was particularly trying for a young African who had need of quiet and adequate time to sort things out in his besieged brain.

At the climax of his studies Jean Jaurès Tibaki was still somewhat confused. He had, however, made up his mind on three points: European women bored him, he would never again drink alcoholic beverages, and American jazz was "formidable." The meager luggage he brought back with him to Bomasha held a dozen recordings by top American Negro jazz musicians.

Jean Jaurès Tibaki was listening to one of these records, now worn and scratched, when a male secretary announced that Colonel Durand was waiting to see him. The dreamy smile faded from his face. He reluctantly switched off the expensive combination record player and radio that stood beside his desk.

He was afraid of Colonel Durand. When he said yes to the colonel he usually meant it. The colonel had arrived in Bomasha like a whirlwind. His predecessor had been a supply service officer whose sole passion in life was orchid culture.

How he had ever been assigned as commander of the local defense forces remained an unsolved mystery.

Colonel Durand had swept down upon the unsuspecting defense forces like a sharpened cavalry saber. Time and time again he had come rushing to Monsieur Tibaki for support, dragging him out at all hours to approve new orders and projects. The colonel had not hesitated to make it clear that a newly independent country without an adequate army was a tragic joke and that the premier of such a country would not long remain in power.

This was fine in theory but Jean Jaurès Tibaki did not trust his own defense forces. The soldiers were all northerners of the Bomasha tribe who had hunted, slaughtered and made slaves of his people for centuries. He still felt uneasy when he had to review the troops during official ceremonies. As he walked along the ranks beside the high commissioner, he saw only the high cheekbones and expressionless eyes of the Bomasha glaring at him. They knew he was a Goka and he knew that underneath the khaki uniforms were the lithe, warrior bodies of the Bomasha. It was often all he could do to keep his knees steady.

At his quiet insistence the colonel had finally agreed to form an experimental company of Goka troops. It had been a great mistake. After a week of futile instruction the French noncommissioned officer in command had left the unit for one day to drown his sorrows in pastis. Upon his return he had found the charred remains of the makeshift barracks and the body of his Bomasha corporal minus certain organs that had been taken along by the deserting Gokas as an offering to their gods.

"Ask the colonel in, if you will," he told his secretary. As

§ 59

the secretary left he searched frantically through the "Out" box on the corner of his hardwood desk for some official-looking papers. He found a handful and dumped most of them into his "In" box. He kept one on the desk before him.

When the colonel was ushered in, he was studiously retracing the long dry ink scrawls of his signature on a government order for gravel. The colonel strode into the office straight as a ramrod, tanned and tough. He stopped before the desk, saluted formally and waited patiently for Monsieur Tibaki to finish his signature, a thin smile on his lips.

"Ah, Colonel!" Monsieur Tibaki put his pen aside and got up, stretching his short arm across the desk. They shook hands and the colonel fell into one of the rattan chairs without waiting for an invitation. He balanced his kepi on one knee and fished in the pocket of his short-sleeved military tunic for a cigarette. Three rows of military ribbons and the shining silver of the colonel's parachute insignia lightened the drab khaki.

"My dear Tibaki," the colonel said, smiling, his even, white teeth chopping off the words with precision, "we're all ready. I plan to leave this evening. To make it worth while I've ordered the transport company to send ten trucks north to Ache. I want to see how long it takes them at this time of year when it's dry and the roads are in fairly good condition."

Monsieur Tibaki nodded in approval. "An excellent exercise, Colonel."

"We shall see," the colonel said. "I don't know how the trucks will support the trip and I'm not too enthusiastic about the drivers. But they've got to learn sometime. Technically, the trucks are hauling ammunition but I've had them load the equivalent weight with rock ballast."

§ **60**

Monsieur Tibaki continued nodding with what he thought was an air of approval and of professional understanding. He wondered sadly how much the exercise would cost in petrol and repairs.

"I'll be visiting the 6th company at Ache. I'm not too happy about their last training report and I want to see things for myself."

"Ah, Ache!" Monsieur Tibaki was reminded of the American anthropologist. "You will then meet the American at Ache?"

"Yes, I plan to see him," the colonel said without enthusiasm, "if he happens to be there."

"But it is arranged, I think?" Monsieur Tibaki asked. "It is on my schedule."

"Very good, Colonel. I am most anxious that the American receive all the help he needs. His studies will be important to us. The Goka peoples may not have been warriors like the Bomasha but I am sure if one goes far back into their history something interesting will emerge."

Monsieur Tibaki became animated as he talked of his people. The verbosity of his student days returned and his hands fluttered back and forth over his desk like fat black butterflies.

The colonel stifled a yawn and listened. Colonel Durand would have been handsome had it not been for his nose. It was enormous and had been broken twice. Whenever he was ill at ease or bored he had the habit of running his fingers gingerly over its crenelated ridges as if he were in search of its original form.

He was clean-shaven and his hair was clipped close to his tanned skull. An abundant growth of pepper-gray and black hair curled at the open throat of his tunic and covered his muscular forearms. A strange, pitted blotch of blue and white scar tissue ran up the right side of his throat to his cheek. A young Algerian rebel had come screaming out of a rocky cave in the Aurès Mountains one cold dawn, his flesh burning and stinking from phosphorous grenades. He had discharged one barrel of his ancient shotgun at the surprised colonel before an automatic rifle slammed him to the ground, ending his suffering.

". . . the shark is more than a symbol, I believe, it is a reminder that my people recognize the strength of nature and respect it. Please do not forget to show this American some of the village idols carved from hardwood. There are carvings of strange sharks that man has never seen, the product of a mystical symbolism joined with the natural inventiveness of my people . . ."

As Monsieur Tibaki spoke on, the colonel was thinking . . . and this is the type of man that will run this country. This stupid, ineffectual black, raving about the culture of his people, this fool who will soon be expected to meet the communists and the paid agents of Nasser as an equal, who will be escorted up the stairs of the Opéra in Paris by the President of the Republic and be invited to Washington by the President of the United States. What a comedy. What a mad, unreasonable comedy!

". . . so, I shall depend on you, Colonel. I know you understand Bomasha more than most Europeans. I think it is a very good opportunity. I like Americans, don't you?"

"What?"

"I said, I like Americans. They are progressive. They get things done. Don't you agree?"

§ **62**

"Yes," the colonel said slowly, fingering his nose, "they get things done."

Colonel Durand's world had begun to crumble after World War II. He had always been a professional but he had never been overly impressed by the glory of his calling. He had been content to leave that to the cavalry officers with their tanks named after Napoleonic victories, their gloves and bamboo swagger sticks.

Jean Pierre Durand asked nothing more in life than to lead well-trained fighting men into battle. During most of his career he had done just that. He had seen the French army regain its self-confidence in Italy and later in France and Germany. He had seen the same self-confidence undermined slowly in Indo-China and Algeria, where disillusionment gave way to corruption and inefficiency.

Durand had acted. He had made his parachutists something special. They thrived on hardship and difficult operations. They had become a modern reflection of an earlier age, a band of shaven-headed fighting men resembling an order of combatant monks; they lacked only faith, or a goal, or an ideal. Their faith had been in their weapons, in their colonel, in each other. Beyond that they had nothing but a heavy void of nonfaith in everything outside their own small sphere. This nonfaith was disapproved of, then feared. On the eve of the army revolts in Algeria, Colonel Durand had been ordered to Paris for consultation.

He had taken leave of his men in the field. The sullen-faced band of hardened soldiers in camouflaged fatigues had sat in the shelter of a rocky Algerian hill and heard their colonel say goodby. He had done it abruptly, without sentiment. The

§ **63**

sick hand of politics had forced its way into their world of wind, rock, sun, blood and sacrifice.

Colonel Durand had not been implicated in the plotting. But it had been an excellent opportunity for the government to remove a question mark. In a period of revolting colonels the French government could not afford to leave the disquieting and unorthodox Durand in command of such an elite and important group of men.

He had been thrown a sop. His superiors thought they had done him a favor by assigning him to the French staff at N.A.T.O. Paris and its pleasures, the innumerable social events, the occasional voyages to N.A.T.O. member nations: all of these were considered a form of reward—in the eyes of the general staff.

Durand had disappointed them. He had been sullen and morose. He had snapped at his subordinates, insulted a British brigadier and told a Quai d'Orsay political adviser that his ideas were worthless. How could he explain it to his superiors? They were soldiers. Or were they? He had toyed with this thought as the general had reprimanded him for his behavior during the first two weeks of his new assignment.

He had found himself examining the general, eyeing his decorations, his double chin, the bulbous, vein-shot nose. Are they still soldiers, he asked himself. When did they last have the feel of it? The hot dust of a road and the sun on your face and somewhere behind the thump of howitzers. The pock and snap of small arms fire and your men going by on the double, jingling, clanking with equipment and the platoon commanders shouting orders. And ahead one of your companies swinging out and opening, crossing a field, firing as they go—an attack working the way it should . . .

The general had suggested he resign. He had been very

§ **64**

blunt about it. He was noted for his bluntness. And as Durand sat there with his whole life disintegrating into white-hot resentment, the general had stuffed a makeshift bandage into his wounded pride.

The African territory of Bomasha would soon become independent. A good man was needed to form, train and command the fledgling defense force. The general was ready to suggest Durand if he would agree.

Durand had agreed. But from that moment on, something had been broken in the machinery of his spirit. He was too strong to give way to despair. His outlet had been bitterness. He was ripe for revolt when the gray-haired gentleman with the Legion of Honor had spoken to him.

The gray-haired gentleman and his faceless colleagues had been overjoyed at the recruitment of Colonel Durand. To have a representative in such an important and exalted position in the polyglot hierarchy of Bomasha was a momentous stroke of good fortune.

It had all been carefully planned. He and the American were to work together. Once Craig reached Bomasha the colonel would arrange an inspection trip through the northern territory. He would offer assistance to the American anthropologist who was making a painstaking study of the people and history of Bomasha. A study that would be of incalculable value to the new nation in establishing its national roots and internal pride. Durand's trip would give him an opportunity to coordinate his tactics with Craig under a perfect cover.

The hot air was yellow with dust when the colonel's jeep entered the defense force compound. The transport company was preparing its lorries for the drive north. The compound

§ **65**

resounded with revving engines, gnashing gears and the excited shouts of the African drivers.

Durand jumped from his jeep and strode through the din to his office. A tall Bomasha sergeant with a chin beard saluted him on the stairs. He returned the salute and shut his office door. He threw his kepi into a chair and stood for a moment with his hands on his hips staring at the yellow and blue wall map of Bomasha behind his desk.

He turned from the map and sat on the edge of his desk. He sighed and folded his arms. Each visit to Tibaki had the same effect. He couldn't stand the man. He had more respect for the Bomasha sergeant he had just saluted.

His eye rested for a moment on the bright brass of a shell casing that served as an ash tray. It brought back his painful daydream, the field; his men going into an attack; the roar of air support overhead. Those were gone. He was shocked by his own candor. He lit a cigarette. I might not be able to lead any more attacks or win any more battles, he thought, brooding on Tibaki, but I can keep these scum from winning theirs. "Independence," he murmured to himself softly, savoring the word for its irony. He shook his head. "Idiots," he said sharply. He walked behind his desk, fell into his chair and began to read the pile of official papers waiting for his signature.

Chapter 6

.

The rattle and shuffling of goats in the rubbish pile behind the Rest House brought Michael Craig out of a deep sleep. Someone banged on the door and he mumbled a resentful "Come in!" One of the Rest House boys pushed into the room with a tray. "Morning, sahr," he said as he placed a mug of strong, hot tea on the chair next to the bed. "Thanks," Craig replied, pushing himself into a sitting position.

Craig sat quietly, staring at the steam rising from the tea for some time after the boy slammed the door shut and the sound of his bare feet had faded down the hall. Then with a groan he opened his mosquito net and swung his feet to the floor. The mug was marked with greasy fingerprints, but the scalding tea served as an excellent eye opener. As he pushed open the window shutters of his room he felt surprisingly fresh and alert.

From his window he could see down into the valley of Ikiri. The town and the valley were wrapped in a gray morning haze. He glanced at his wrist watch. It was only 7:00 A.M.

§ 67

He cursed to himself. He had thought it was closer to 8:30. Already the sun had pushed itself to the rim of the mountains. The air was fresh but the coming heat was fast dissipating the dawn coolness. He could see the Union Jack going slowly up the pole of the district officer's bungalow. Down in the town, somewhere in the morning mist, a racing of lorry engines, honking horns and occasional shouts heralded the opening of the market. He could pinpoint the market's location by the slow circling of several black vultures. He shaved before the pitted mirror of his room.

Later, over a breakfast of cold-storage eggs and questionable herring, he again pondered the significance of Rodney Eniki's services and speculated on his future relationship with Colonel Durand. The Ibo waiter in his soiled white jacket and red sash brought him a cup of weak coffee and removed the half-finished herring. Craig could feel the mounting heat. A rivulet of perspiration coursed down his back. Overhead the ceiling fans were silent.

"Could you turn on the fan?" Craig asked the waiter.

"Mastah?" the boy paused, his mouth slightly open.

"The fan," he said, pointing to the silent blades overhead.

"No, Mastah."

"Why not?" Craig said with irritation.

"The fan go on when bar be open at noontime. No fan in coolness like now, Mastah."

"You call this cool?" Craig demanded, feeling his temper rise at the boy's dull reasoning.

"Always cool in the morning," the waiter said with finality. He turned his back and took his load of dirty dishes to the kitchen.

Grimly determined, Craig rose and walked to the fan control on the nearest wall. He turned the knob, pushing the control arrow to "full" and went back to his table. The fan began to gyrate slowly, picking up speed. He was enjoying the first cool currents of air when a spiral of fly paper, dislodged by the strong draft, thumped down on his table. Craig sat staring for a moment at the curled, greasy paper, heavy with the black corpses of dead insects. The speed of the fan seemed to be increasing. Craig heard the ominous sound of grating metal. The pipe holding the fan to its ceiling attachment had taken on a perceptible sway. He jumped up from his chair, strode to the control panel and flicked the arrow back to "off." To his horror the fan continued its wild spinning. He clicked the arrow to other speeds, cursing aloud to himself, feeling ridiculous. He heard a footstep behind him.

"Here, let me." It was an Englishman in a khaki bush jacket and white slacks. He walked up to the control panel and swung the arrow around slowly. "See, you must go all around once again if you put it on 'full.' You can never go from 'full' to 'stop.'" He turned to Craig smiling as the fan slowed and the strange sounds stopped. "All part of learning about Africa, I suppose," the man said, extending his hand. "Thompson's the name. Robert Thompson. I'm the D. O. here. I presume you're Michael Craig. Welcome to Ikiri."

"Thank you," Craig said. "I just arrived yesterday." He was quickly sizing up the district officer. One thing jibed already with what he had heard. Thompson was on the bottle. He could smell the brandy as they shook hands.

"I understand you're going to do some research on the river tribes?"

"That's right. I plan to leave tomorrow for Ache."

§ **69**

"Well, I certainly don't envy you," Thompson said shaking his head. "Ikiri is no paradise but Ache is truly the end of the earth."

Thompson was short and fat. The belt of his bush jacket was pulled tight. His stomach bulged above and below it like an overloaded grain sack. He had thick hair that sprouted out over his forehead, heavy dark eyebrows and a mottled face from years of sunburn and heavy drinking.

"I received some papers for you the other day," Thompson went on. "Something about a shipment of books."

"Oh, yes. I've got some books coming up here."

"Part of your work, I suppose. Couldn't hope for some good juicy novels full of sex and all that."

Thompson leaned forward when he said this and Craig noticed the alcoholic dullness of his eyes and the water-blue limning around the pupils.

"Understand you've hired Big Boy as an assistant."

"Big Boy?"

"Yes, you know, the Eniki chap."

"Oh, Rodney."

"Rather think he prefers Big Boy. I suggest you keep your eye on him."

"He seems helpful and he knows the country."

"I daresay! Police have chased him over half of it already. I can't understand the Bomasha authorities allowing him to re-enter the territory." Thompson shrugged his shoulders. "Well, regardless, you must come over for chop tonight."

"Oh, well, I don't—"

"Don't be shy. We want you to come." Thompson grinned. "It's as much for our benefit as yours, you know. Civilized people don't come through here often and my wife and I would die if we missed someone we could talk to. You will come?"

"Yes, certainly."

"Good." The district officer glanced at the fan, sucking at his teeth. "Well, I must be off. Some damn fool chief is having a son christened today so I can look forward to standing in goat manure for several hours and drinking palm wine under a hot sun. I shall expect you . . . eightish?"

"Fine."

"Jolly good, by-by."

"Goodby."

Craig spent most of the morning packing and getting ready for the trip. Technically his Rest House room would be his base. He planned to pay for it by the month. He had already placed David Stone Parkinson's *Tribes of the Border Territories* on the small bookrack by the bed. When the rest of the books came he would have more shelves made and little by little it might become livable. Most of his work would be in Bomasha but having a base in Ikiri seemed a good idea. His long absences would be explained by the nature of his research work. He hoped his room in Ikiri would serve as a constant reminder to anyone interested that his research work was being carried out on both sides of the border and not solely in Bomasha. In the event of real trouble in Bomasha he could always put the border between him and his enemies and hope that the British police patrols on the Ikiri side were exceedingly efficient.

He decided to leave one suitcase in the room. He packed the two smallest sparingly and filled a canvas haversack with two bottles of gin, tins of corned beef, beans, pipe tobacco,

§ **71**

matches, toilet paper, hard chocolate, a compass and a pair of German binoculars. Pushing the clutter aside he placed the cloth-wrapped revolver in the bottom of the haversack and the two cartons of cartridges beside it.

During the special training for his O.S.S. missions a Scottish commando officer had lectured him. "One must begin with the premise that killing a man is one of the easiest jobs that might be ahead of you." How right he had been. Craig shook the haversack and the tins and other supplies covered the revolver and the cartridges.

He finished packing and ate lunch in the Rest House dining room. The fan was on now and there were about ten or twelve guests scattered among the tables. A group of British engineers dominated the dining room with their laughter and shouting. They had primed themselves with gin and bitters and their obvious distaste for the Rest House cuisine was audible over the steady clink of their knives and forks as they wolfed down huge mouthfuls of curried guinea hen and cold rice.

The service was painfully slow. Craig ordered two bottles of Danish beer and nodded an unenthusiastic assent when the waiter suggested the curried guinea hen. The only other item on the luncheon menu had the unlikely title of "Liver— French stile."

He ate his curried guinea hen when it came, dousing it with chopped peanuts and chutney. The cold rice was gritty with sand. The heat in the dining room was oppressive. The fan worked valiantly but had no effect. Craig mopped his brow continually with a handkerchief. He noticed that the serving boys were doing the same with the wide sleeves of their jackets. He drank his second beer rapidly for he could feel the outside of the bottle warming.

§ 72

He finished eating and pushed his plate aside. His neck and back had begun to itch. He ran his hand underneath his shirt collar and felt the tiny pimples of prickly heat burn at the touch. Thinking that there was some chance of finding a cool breeze outside, he left the dining room and walked out onto the driveway of the Rest House. Several drowsy Hausa traders looked up at him with vague interest. Their woven mats were spread with carved ebony and buffalo horn. A young Yoruba merchant had spread several rows of English pocketbooks under the entrance portico of the Rest House.

"Hello, Mastah," he said, approaching Craig.

"No, thanks," Craig replied shortly, feeling the full discomfort of his newly acquired prickly heat. He pushed past the insistent vendor and walked out onto the road, seeking the shade of some pepper trees.

He could see a Land Rover approaching, churning up a trail of dust. He moved to one side of the road to give it plenty of room. The vehicle seemed to mark him as a target. For an uneasy moment he thought it was coming directly at him.

"Hello, sahr!"

It was Big Boy Eniki, grinning with pride. He was wearing a short-sleeved shirt. The solid muscle and sinew of his arms made the steering wheel of the Land Rover appear as an undersized control of a child's pedal car. The spreading palm tree of the Queen's West African Rifles was tattooed high on Big Boy's right arm, cuttlefish purple against his black skin.

Craig couldn't help but return a shadow of Eniki's radiant smile. "Hello, there," Craig replied. "Where did you get this?" he asked, examining the Land Rover with care.

"I think last night that the border mammy wagon be not much good for you, sahr." Big Boy grimaced, enjoying an

§ **73**

opportunity to act out his thought. "I say—what for that mastah want to crimp up in the smelly wagon with all them dirty pickin's and have his teeth jiggled out? So, I talk last night to my friend, Mr. Magabian, one Armenian fellah, and he say, 'Take my Land Rover, my friend!' " Big Boy gunned the engine to dramatize his story.

Craig hesitated, feeling as if he were about to puncture the newly purchased balloon of a happy child. "Yes, well, that's very nice of your friend," he said slowly, taking in the dented fenders and the splintered windshield. "How much does Mr. Magabian ask for a rental fee?"

Big Boy shook his head slowly. "Oh no, no, sahr!" he said vehemently, frowning. "Oh no, my friend Magabian is a true friend. Besides," Big Boy leaned out of the seat to whisper confidentially, "I told Magabian we need very badly this car and if he don't give it to us . . . " Big Boy brought his fist down hard, adding a new dent to the battered hood, "I break his head open, one time!" He roared with laughter.

The booming laughter was infectious and Craig found himself chuckling.

"Come, Mastah," Big Boy said, catching his breath, "I take you for a ride through town."

Craig climbed in beside him and they drove down the hill toward Ikiri.

The evening came quickly. It seemed as if the cool mists had been hiding all day in the jungle waiting for the sun to depart. They came with the first long evening shadows, sifting slowly out of the heavy foliage, hanging in silken threads over the mango trees and bisecting the tall palms on the hills close to the town.

§ 74

Michael Craig was ready early and restless. He decided to walk to the district officer's home. He took his time, pausing by the side of the road to watch a large male lizard stalk an orange-crested female in majestic slow motion and to look out over the jungle toward the east where the border ran along the banks of the slow-flowing, foliage-glutted Bomasha River.

Three women from the Ikiri tribe hurried past him with baked mud waterpots balanced on their heads. They walked with a rapid, flat-footed shuffle to keep the pots in balance. The two eldest women picked up a free end of their brightly colored, wrap-around cotton skirts and held it over their faces as they passed. The third, a girl of twelve or thirteen with uncovered, wide-nippled breasts, shut her eyes in passing as she speeded her gait to catch up with the others.

He passed the guardhouse with a minimum of formalities and walked toward the bungalow. As he mounted the short wooden stairway to the veranda he could hear a record playing low, melancholy and modern. Through the narrow front door he caught a strange but not unpleasant blend of odors. There was the unmistakable aroma of broiling meat, blended with an undercurrent of brandy; old brandy, spilled brandy, newly poured brandy. But dominating all was the heavy scent of perfume. He paused for a moment on the veranda noting the contrast in the warm vegetable and earth smell of the African night and the pungent odors emanating from the house. He knocked and waited.

A young African boy in spotless white shirt and shorts came to the door. "Enter, sahr," he said, standing aside with a half bow. "Madam will come shortly. Will you please sit?" he asked, indicating a low-backed wooden chair decorated with red cushions.

§ **75**

"Thank you."

The boy left the room through a swinging door to the rear. Someone had made a desperate effort to decorate the house. But it seemed that two decorators with extremely divergent tastes had done the job. A semimodern bookcase of local wood was set into the rear wall. It held several rows of books and two African carvings. Above them were several prints of English hunting scenes under glass; long lean hunters going over the stone fences with red-jacketed, rosy-cheeked gentlemen gesturing to each other in humorous camaraderie. A Dufy print hung above the expensive record player. Next to it, competing for space, was a cheap print of a Thames River scene in appalling colors.

Craig filled his pipe and waited. The teak table before him was set up as a bar with two glasses, a half bottle of brandy, a full, unopened bottle of Scotch and several bottles of soda. He noted, unhappily, the lack of an ice bucket.

The record player ceased its syrupy melody and the clicking and buzz of the insects rushed into the sudden sound vacuum. Another record fell into place. This one a little faster, with a clever piano and some muted trumpets. The sounds of Africa were again pushed out of the district officer's house and back into the bush.

"Terribly sorry to keep you waiting, Mr. Craig."

She closed the door to the other room behind her and came toward him with her hand held out, smiling, and he rose to meet her, putting his pipe down on the table. The heavy perfume engulfed him. "I'm Alice Thompson," she said as they shook hands. "Do sit down and we'll have a drink in a jiffy."

Craig was surprised and a little ill at ease. He had been

expecting a more fitting mate for Robert Thompson. A district officer's wife; fat, authoritative and very British, offering a façade of protocol, carefully gauged friendliness and damp-eyed devotion at the mention of the Royal Family.

Alice Thompson sat on the couch opposite him and smiled. "What will it be? Brandy or Scotch?"

"I'll take Scotch."

"And soda?"

"Yes, please."

She was a large woman with brown hair and brown eyes. He looked at her as she poured his drink. She wasn't beautiful but she had a good figure. Her green dress was cut danger-ously low in front and the deep tan stopped abruptly at the base of the V. She was wearing circular gold earrings and a heavy-linked gold bracelet. Her hair was parted in the middle and combed carelessly down onto her shoulders, setting her brown eyes, broad cheekbones and wide mouth in a brown frame.

She handed him his glass and raised hers. "Cheers," she said, still smiling, and he noted the wrinkles around her eyes. She wasn't as young as he had thought.

She was heavily made up and when she drank she left traces of blood-red lipstick on her glass. She put her glass down on the table and reached for a cigarette. Craig struck a match and held it for her. She bent across the table, the bodice of her dress bloused as she did and in a flash of tan and white con-trast he realized she wasn't wearing a bra.

Alice Thompson sat back, blew some smoke through her nose, and regarded Craig with a look of amusement. "I'm sorry Robert isn't with us tonight. I'm afraid he's had a touch of the sun today—and a bit too much palm wine."

"He told me he had to attend a christening," Craig said, trying to sound as relaxed and matter-of-fact as his hostess. He drank the warm whisky and tried to find some rung, some shelf on which he could place Alice Thompson.

She swung her sandaled feet up under her and tapped her glass with a long fingernail. "I understand you're here to do research on the river tribes?"

"That's right," Craig replied, picking up his pipe and re-lighting it.

"Well, Mr. Craig, I wish you luck. I'm sure my husband will be glad to help if you have any problems." He didn't like the way she emphasized problems.

"I don't think I'll have any problems."

"Oh, you seem sure of yourself." She smiled. "You Americans are all so sure of yourselves."

Craig frowned. He was in no mood for exchanging insults.

"Oh, my God!" Alice Thompson put her hand to her forehead and laughed. "You're not only sure of yourselves, you're all so serious!" She stopped laughing and put her hand on his arm. He could feel her nails through the thin material of his jacket. "Relax," she said looking him straight in the eye. "Relax, Mr. Craig, while I make you another drink."

He sat with his pipe between his teeth and watched her pour out the whisky. She handed him his glass, smiling. They drank in silence for a moment until the boy padded out of the kitchen to announce dinner. They finished their drinks and went to the table.

The heavy scent of perfume hit him again as he helped her with her chair. He found it difficult to concentrate on the thick, mulligatawny soup before him. He knew he was glancing at Alice Thompson in a direct way but he made no effort to stop. She was leaning slightly forward, spooning up soup, a bemused smile playing at the corners of her mouth. His eyes traveled over her tanned, solid arms to her throat and lingered at the thin white line of untanned flesh above the swell of her breasts.

She spoke without looking up from her soup. "Are you married, Mr. Craig?"

The question threw him off balance. "No," he said shortly, knowing she had been quite aware of his inspection, aware of his interest.

"I suppose it's hard to find a woman willing to follow you around the world and set up housekeeping in jungles and deserts. Your work must be fascinating."

"It is fascinating," he replied, furious at himself for having been so obvious, "but it's hard work and it doesn't leave much time for anything else."

"Yes, I know," she said, putting down her soup spoon. "They're a strange lot. They talk and act differently than most people. In fact, Mr. Craig," she said knowingly, still smiling, "I can spot one easily, without being told his profession. My father was an anthropologist."

His mouth being full of soup he could only raise his eyebrows and nod his head in polite interest. At the same time he wished he had never accepted Thompson's dinner invitation.

Tobo Holman sat at the head of the table and told them about London. He had just come back from a year of study and he planned to continue his studies until he became a barrister. Big Boy listened to Tobo with his mouth open. The two clerks and the lorry driver broke in from time to time with a question but Big Boy listened without interrupting.

§ **79**

Magabian worked behind the bar refilling bottles but he too was listening to Tobo.

"... so I said to this chap, 'Look here, if you don't give me a room I shall report it to the Government . . .' " He paused while his audience nodded in silent approval. "Then you know what this cock told me?"

The clerks shook their heads.

"He said, 'Get out, you black scum!' "

"Ahhhh!" his audience replied in disbelief and outrage.

Big Boy leaned across the table toward Tobo. "You tell me that for the truth?"

"On my honor as an African."

"He not be Englishman," the lorry driver said, shaking his head and sipping at his beer.

"This chap was born pink and bred English," Tobo replied, frowning, "and many worse things have happened, I know."

They sat for a moment in silence. Their table was full of empty and half-full beer bottles. Flies had fallen into some, where they spun in desperate humming circles.

One of the clerks adjusted his frayed white collar. "Intolerance and man's injustice," he said gravely, "shall be defeated by good works."

Big Boy swung toward him and shook his finger under the small man's nose. "You listen too much that mission teaching. Your head go be soft like ripe mango you listen those white mission men!"

The lorry driver clapped his hands together.

"Ha, Eniki you be true too much," he said, laughing.

Tobo Holman listened to their conversation with a condescending smile. He wore a black wool suit with a broad-shouldered jacket and tight trousers. He took a tin of British cigarettes from his pocket, selected one and closed the tin without offering it to his friends. He produced a Zippo lighter, lit his cigarette and spoke with it hanging from the corner of his mouth.

"Of course," he said, with a schoolteacher's inflection, "not all English people are like that. There are many I have met who respect us as Africans."

Big Boy looked puzzled. "Why?" he asked flatly.

"Because they are intelligent enough to see into the future," Tobo replied. "They see our strength and potential." He chuckled, "Some are a wee bit frightened by an independent Africa."

Big Boy didn't understand but he hesitated to show it. "Why they go be frightened?" the lorry driver asked.

"Because they know we are rich in many things and we are strong people."

Big Boy fished a dead fly out of his glass and tried to understand. This Holman always did talk big but Big Boy had never before heard that the English were frightened. And what did he mean, Africans were rich? Big Boy glanced around the table. None of them was rich. Even Holman got his money from his grandmother who owned many cows and chickens. Big Boy became angry. This Holman goes to England one time and now is full of schoolmaster palaver. While Big Boy brooded the clerks were talking about independence.

". . . a great need for trained civil servants. You will have a very good go, I should imagine, at a post as magistrate."

Tobo Holman beamed and nodded in agreement. "Yes, I suppose I shall," he said, pleased at the open appreciation of his talents. "Mr. Magabian," he called across the room, "five more beer, if you please."

Big Boy was jealous. He was used to being the center of attention. He thought of his present work. It was a great effort for him to remain silent. He thought of Craig. Magabian brought them their beer and cleared away the empties.

Big Boy licked his lips. "You meet any Americans?" he asked, frowning.

Tobo raised his eyebrows and nodded but he didn't reply until his beer glass was full. "I met some, by Jove!" Tobo said solemnly. "They are hypocrites and cynics." He glanced up. He could see that his words meant nothing to Big Boy and the lorry driver. "They hate Negroes," he explained. "In America they hang Negroes from trees and call them 'black fruit.' "

Big Boy grunted in disbelief and wrinkled his nose.

Tobo was offended by Big Boy's doubt. "You been to America, Eniki?" Tobo asked with open sarcasm.

"I see many films," Big Boy replied.

"Ever see any black cowboys?" Tobo taunted. "Any black heroes kissing black girls? Not by half you haven't! All you've seen is black men serving dinner or drinks and working like slaves!"

Big Boy clenched his fists under the table. He thought of hitting Tobo with a beer bottle but decided against it.

"The white men in America are afraid their women will sleep with an African and never be satisfied with a white man again," Tobo stated, shaking his head gravely.

"How can it be so?" Big Boy said, "with no Africans being in America?"

"They aren't Africans, they are American Negroes!" Tobo shouted.

Big Boy frowned at Tobo and shook his head. "Man," he said, "you talking in circles."

§ 82

Tobo sighed with frustration and shrugged his shoulders, looking at the clerks for support. They both smiled. He was buying the beer.

"Did you finally find a lodging in London?" one of the clerks asked, trying to forestall further argument.

"Well," Tobo replied, "it took me some time. The government education office kept trying to put me up with West Indians but I would not comply. I told them I would rather live with a Chinese."

"They are unpleasant?"

"They are scum."

"They are black men," Big Boy stated.

"They are not Negroes! They are neither white nor black. They are the lowest of the low." Tobo pulled back the French cuff of his shirt and looked at his gold wrist watch. "My, it is late. I must go. My grandmother is going to the capital tomorrow and I promised to accompany her." He got up and went to the bar to pay Magabian.

Big Boy gave a derogatory snort. "Been to," he mumbled resentfully under his breath, referring to the capital.

"He's fit to buy you beer," one of the clerks whispered. Big Boy scowled and the clerk pulled in his neck like a frightened turtle.

Tobo returned to the table to say goodby. He carried a brown leather brief case. Brief cases had replaced the rolled umbrella in West Africa as a symbol of importance.

"Cheerio, gentlemen," he said, brushing aside their thanks as he shook hands.

The clerks finished their beer and left. The lorry driver settled into his chair, pushed his oil-stained, felt skullcap over his face and went to sleep. Big Boy was left alone with a glass

§ **83**

of lukewarm beer and his thoughts. He had been troubled lately. Things had become confusing. This independence was everywhere and he wasn't sure what it meant. He had a feeling it was bad. The Bomasha border guards had suddenly raised their bribe price. When Big Boy had protested they had talked of independence and freedom. Their words had left him far behind.

Eniki had had little education but he was clever. Through the slight beer haze a thought took shape. Independence was a new tool. Something to be used like a juju. He scratched his head and shifted his eyes to Magabian still busy behind the bar.

"Say," he called to the hotel owner, "what you think of this independence?"

Magabian looked surprised, then he shrugged his shoulders. "What independence?"

"For the African."

Magabian suddenly looked disturbed. He picked up a glass and held it to the light. "It depends, old boy," he said cautiously. "One has to be ready for independence."

Big Boy grunted. There it was again. Another unanswered question. "Goddamn, Magabian," he growled, hitting his fist on the table, "you afraid like the English. You see our strength and po . . . po." Big Boy paused, frustrated. He couldn't remember Tobo's phrase. "You just scared shitless, Magabian!" he shouted.

"Here, no, dear me!" Magabian replied surprised. "I'm your friend. No need to shout. Come, drink a beer with me."

Big Boy grudgingly moved to the bar and watched Magabian open the beer. Magabian handed Big Boy his glass. "You will be careful of my Land Rover, now, won't you?" he said, smiling.

§ **84**

"Not to worry," Big Boy mumbled through the beer foam. The beer was cooler than the beer at the table. "Ahh," he exclaimed, "that is beer, Magabian."

"It's my best! Only the best for my friends!"

Chapter 7

:

Craig had hoped to start the morning fresh and alert. Instead he felt washed out. Alice Thompson's conversation about anthropologists and anthropology had upset him and put him on his guard. It was a natural conversation for the daughter of an anthropologist but there had been a certain irony in her tone and her smile that made him uneasy.

He would have to be careful. Fifty thousand dollars was riding on his success. That wasn't much considering the risk. They'd had him at bargain rates but he needed the money.

Money bought freedom and Craig had a phobia about freedom. He had a deep, almost physical need of freedom from others. He didn't want to speak to people. He didn't want to listen to them and he didn't want to work with them. He knew fifty thousand wouldn't take him far but it would give him a few years of peace in the Balearics or Sardinia or the Caribbean.

He had never really tried to analyze this craving for solitude. He knew it was unfair to blame it on the death of his wife. That was too easy. But it was what people wanted to believe and it had saved him from a number of cocktail party analysts. There were other reasons for taking this job and he knew it.

He was packed and ready when Big Boy pulled up in front of the Rest House. He took a last gulp of lukewarm tea, swung his haversack over one shoulder and picked up the two small suitcases. He could hear Big Boy gunning the engine of the Land Rover as he walked through the empty dining room toward the driveway. It irritated him.

Big Boy's radiant smile and eager friendliness made things worse. Craig mumbled a greeting and answered Big Boy's questions and comments abruptly, hoping to forestall further conversation. But Big Boy could not be discouraged. He was a sudden fund of unsolicited information. He loaded Craig's gear with care, wedging the suitcases in between the jerry cans of petrol, laughing and talking.

"There, they no bump around, I fix it fine. We must go before the heat. That bastard sun, he come mighty fast now. Yes, sahr, Big Boy don't forget nothing. Here is one bucket full of ice and four bottles of beer. We go feel fine later. All is ready."

Big Boy was wearing a white shirt covered with a design of small red flowers. Perspiration and many washings had run the red of the flowers into oval blotches of faint color under the arms and down the back. He had on a pair of patched khaki trousers held up by a wide canvas military belt. His canvas-topped bush boots were without laces and he kicked them off before driving. Craig busied himself with his pipe and settled back as comfortably as he could in the stiff seat.

They drove away from the Rest House, up over the ridge

§ 87

of the Ikiri Valley. It was still cool. The green of the jungle on each side of the narrow road was restful to the eyes. The laterite dust was fine and deep. When they reached the crest of a hill and started down, Big Boy had to let up on the accelerator and fight the wheel to keep the vehicle from swaying. A thick red wake rose behind them, churned up by their rear wheels. The motor whined like an angry wasp as they rose and fell over the small hills.

Craig wedged his pipe under the windshield. He folded his arms and shut his eyes. Soon he had dropped off to sleep. Big Boy glanced at him and shrugged his shoulders. With one hand on the wheel he lit himself a cigarette. He blew the smoke out of his wide nostrils and smiled. He drove on, humming to himself. They passed down out of the hills onto flat land. Stand after stand of gray-trunked trees closed out the sky and shafts of light filtered down through the leaves, mottling the road in strange patterns. A mammy wagon suddenly appeared speeding toward them, hogging the middle of the road. The bright-colored robes of its passengers flapped from its open sides like lancers' pennants. Big Boy cursed and clamped his fist down on the Land Rover's weak horn. The mammy wagon swerved sideways, regained its side of the road and flashed past with a sudden clap of noise and shouting, spraying a plume of dust over them both.

Craig sat up rubbing his eyes. "What was that?" he asked, trying to see through the settling red haze.

"Damn fool driver," Big Boy replied grimly, again picking up his normal speed. The dust covered Big Boy's curly black hair and his thick eyelashes were coated with the red grains.

Now, as they shot through scattered patches of light, they could feel the strength of the sun. They ground around a series of hairpin turns and left the tall trees behind. A small flat area of scrub bush and rock lay ahead of them. "Look there!" Big Boy shouted, pointing off to the left. "There," he shouted gleefully, letting the Land Rover come dangerously close to the ditch running beside the road.

A group of baboons was crossing the road ahead of them, bounding in long leaps through the laterite. The last baboon was a mother with a wizened-faced baby hanging under her belly. She reached the far side of the road with a long leap, her thin rat tail held high and curved into a question mark. As they pulled opposite she swung around to face them. Her lips were drawn back over long yellow fangs. She backed away from them slowly, blinking her small eyes.

Big Boy cursed and braked to a sudden stop. Before Craig could ask what he was doing he had jumped out of the Land Rover. He dug around in the baggage and returned with a heavy Smith & Wesson revolver. "Yah," he yelled angrily at the retreating baboon. Craig heard the click of the hammer being cocked.

"Eniki!" Craig shouted, "What the hell are you doing?"

Big Boy was raising the revolver when Craig jumped out of the Land Rover and grabbed his arm, pushing it high, toward the sky. "Goddamn it," Craig said, furious, "put that gun away!"

They stood there together for a moment, a ridiculous frieze of arrested motion. The baboon and its clinging young one disappeared from sight. Slowly the raised arms lowered. Big Boy glanced at Craig. The mask of hate slowly dissipated and a mechanical grin spread over his face. Craig released his arm.

"I hate them damn fool monkeys," Big Boy said slowly, not meeting Craig's eyes. "Ruin crops," he said unconvincingly.

§ 89

He walked away from Craig and replaced the revolver in the baggage. Craig found that he was covered with perspiration and his throat was dry.

"Here, sahr," Big Boy came around from behind the Land Rover smiling, an open quart bottle of iced beer in his hand. "The beer won't stay cold. We better drink it up."

Craig drank from the bottle and passed it to Big Boy. The bottle was sticky from glue where the label had come off. Craig wiped his hands on his trousers and climbed back into the Land Rover. When he reached for his pipe he glanced at Big Boy. Big Boy was frowning at him. Then the grin returned as if it had never left.

"Ah," Big Boy said, climbing back behind the wheel, "beer is good when the heat come down."

Alice Thompson sat on the front veranda, thumbing through a five-year-old fashion magazine. She had slept late and she felt relaxed. She could hear Ignatius preparing lunch in the kitchen, humming softly as he made egg batter for the frozen shrimp she had found at the Cold Store the day before.

Her husband had gone off on some vague official errand while she was still asleep but she had noted the drop in the level of the cognac bottle and imagined that he would soon be home to sleep through the afternoon.

She had moved her canvas deck chair into the sun. She pulled the skirt of her cotton dress up over her knees to profit from the concentrated heat. The hair shone golden on her brown legs and she felt a reassuring pleasure as she rubbed some tanning oil over her thighs. Not bad for an old girl, she told herself, capping the oil bottle and settling back into the canvas.

§ 90

She shut her eyes and thought of last night. She thought of Craig, speculating on how and when she could see him again. Then, close to sleep, with the sun playing a kaleidoscopic design on the inside of her eyelids she half-thought, half-dreamed of the past and future.

Shortly after she had married Robert, a governor general's wife who had smelled like a sherry barrel had accosted her at a cocktail party in London and given her some advice. "There are a few things to remember, my dear," she had said, mechanically flashing her false teeth. "You must love your husband very much in this business. If you don't, you must choose between liquor or sex. And the former is not good for your health."

It had been a great joke. A joke used many times before on new wives. After the first shock Alice Thompson had laughed with the rest of them. A shadow of a frown passed over Alice Thompson's brow as she remembered the incident. A joke. The joke was on all of them. Lady Sherry Barrel, her pompous, pitiful husband and the rest of them bellowing in glee over her embarrassment. In their lives truth had been turned into a joke. It was thus easier to ignore. The truth didn't hurt—it amused.

You must love your husband very much. Had she ever loved Robert? She wasn't sure. Surely she must have at the start, but even those days had fallen far behind, been obscured in the dust of a hundred African roads, new posts and solid, permanent indifference.

At their second post she had seen the bright prints of her cotton dresses fade from the sun and the handwashing and, suddenly, she had known that she too was fading, fading like an untended plant. And Robert went his way whistling,

§ **91**

working hard for his tiny promotions, getting tiddly on weekends and kissing her on the forehead before retiring.

On one of their holidays she had seen a psychoanalyst in London. Sitting on the edge of a red leather chair in his modern, brightly lit office, she had poured out her story. Hesitantly at first, then in great rushes of bitterness and confusion. At the close of the second visit the psychoanalyst, an Austrian in early middle age, one of the best according to her friends, shook his head slowly and smiled. He had raised his hand to ask for silence. "Do not be angry, madame," he had told her, "but I . . ." He had swung his pivotal chair toward her with determination. "We are adults. Madame, you must be loved."

Her puzzled expression had made him angry. "You don't understand? Must I make drawings? You must have a man. Preferably your husband, of course." The obvious incredulity on her face had infuriated him. The English were often impossible to work with. "You don't need a psychoanalyst," he had said quietly with great restraint. "You need a man to make love to you."

She shifted on the deck chair and turned on her side. She smiled, thinking of the psychoanalyst. It seemed so long ago. It had been long ago.

There had been other men then. Quite a few. She remembered the young banker in Accra, the captain of Welsh Fusiliers during a leave in Cornwall and the Italian musician that had somehow joined their party during a pub crawl in Soho two years ago. What had they all given her? There had been quick passion and a certain relief but each affair had taken something out of her. It was as if each lover had gone off with a piece of her soul. In return they had left a certain hardness.

§ **92**

An outer crust that she could feel—and see when she looked in the mirror. Somewhere, at a certain specific time her eyes had lost their softness. She wasn't sure when or how but she knew it was true.

Craig's eyes were hard. She wondered when the change had come for him. We seem to have something in common, she thought, we are both alone.

She fell into a sound sleep in the sun, moving steadily through golden fields of silk where candle flames threw leaping prisms of colored light. A feeling of great contentment relaxed her and brought a soothing hum to her ears.

She was smiling softly when Ignatius woke her. "Madam," he repeated, "madam." She opened her eyes wide and sat up slowly, pushing her dress down over her knees. The buzz of insects engulfed the veranda. There were drops of perspiration on her forehead. Her dress was soaked through under her arms and against her back. "Madam," Ignatius said patiently, "time for chop."

By the time they reached the Bomasha River ferry crossing the sun was high and merciless. Big Boy drove off the road into a patch of shade and they waited for the ferry to return from the opposite shore.

The muddy bank leading down to the slow-moving, brown water was alive with movement. A temporary open-air butcher shop had been set up and the air was full of the chopping and hacking of blood-smeared butchers. White-robed Hausa buyers moved among the makeshift stalls examining the still-warm, ragged cuts of beef. Clusters of living cattle shifted uneasily, bumping into each other in their attempt to avoid the long poles and educated pokes of the cattle

§ 93

dealers as they moved among the herds making their purchases. Occasionally one of the long-horned cows, its dewlaps swinging loosely, would make a jogging break for freedom. Before it could get far a yelling cluster of bare-bottomed Yoruba children would sprint after it, cut it off, and drive it back to the market place with their long thin sticks.

Craig watched the scene, fascinated. There was the rich brown of the river, the yellow mud, the white robes of the merchants, the black skins, the shifting, bawling mass of doomed cattle, the flash of slaughtering knives, the bright red blood and the dull whacking of the hatchets and machetes used by the butchers. The warm, newly-stripped hides lay in a great, fly-blackened pile, collapsed and wrinkled like abandoned circus costumes. Slow-moving shadows passed over the river bank. Looking up Craig saw the gliding vultures. Once on the ground the ugly birds moved awkwardly, like drunken penguins, hopping toward the steaming piles of offal, fighting over the slimy ribbons of intestine and rushing expectantly toward the sudden gurgling of a new slaughter.

The ferry came back toward them slowly, pushed along by an ancient launch that chuffed black gouts of smoke from its wood-fed engine. The smoke hung motionless over the river, untouched by the slightest breeze.

The ferry swung into shore, fighting the current. It was a wooden barge, braced and banded by metal strips and bolts. The blunt, splintered prow nudged into the soft mud and two plank landing ramps were tossed ashore by the crew. A wheezing British truck, a legacy of World War II, rattled down onto the ramps and ashore. It stopped with a jerk of brakes directly in front of the ferry and a line of sweating, half-naked porters began tossing mud-smeared sides of bloody beef onto its flat bed. Hausa traders crowded onto the ferry for the return trip.

Big Boy vaulted out of the Land Rover. He rushed down the hill waving his arms. Craig lost sight of him as he plunged into the crowd of porters. Then he saw him climb onto the truck and reach into the truck's cab. A white-clothed figure, arms and legs spinning, arced out of the truck's cab and landed with a soft thump in the mud. The truck's motor revved painfully. The truck jerked forward and sideways, out of the rutted approach to the ferry. The vehicle tilted dangerously as its wheels sunk into the mud. A great din of angry shouting filled the air.

Big Boy jumped down from the truck's cab and walked back to the Land Rover. He grinned at Craig as he started the Land Rover down toward the ferry. A group of angry traders and porters blocked their way, shouting insults, waving their thin black arms. A rock bounced off the hood. Craig glanced anxiously at Big Boy. He was still smiling—but without humor. He gunned the engine and drove straight for the ramp, plowing through the crowd, scattering it to right and left, a tumbling mass of white teeth, shouts and curses.

They bumped roughly up the ramp onto the ferry. Passengers jumped from the flat ferry deck into the launch to get out of their way. Then Big Boy was gone again. Craig saw him run up to the launch captain, make a few arabesques under the captain's nose with the shining steel of a switchblade knife. "Move this damn boat," Craig heard him shout, "before I slice you like the butcher man!"

The impressed captain pulled hard on a lever, rang a battered bell and spun the small, spoked wheel. The ramps were pulled aboard. They fell away from the bank. A few more

§ **95**

rocks bounced harmlessly off the ferry as they drifted with the current, waiting for the engine to take hold.

Big Boy opened another beer and offered it to Craig. Craig took it and put it down on the floor boards. He wiped some perspiration from his face and neck.

"Sit down," Craig ordered.

Big Boy swung himself into the Land Rover. He looked at Craig innocently, expectantly.

Craig was furious. Already, before speaking, he knew words would be useless. This increased his anger. "Listen to me!" he said awkwardly, searching for the right approach. "No more of this rough stuff. You work for me and you'll take my orders, understand?"

Big Boy returned his glare. "Yes, Mastah," he said quietly.

For several seconds Craig played with the idea of reasoning sensibly with Big Boy. But he knew it would only be interpreted as a sign of weakness. "Next time you want to act tough you ask me first!" he almost shouted.

Big Boy ran his tongue over his lips and watched the great clumps of waterweed drift past. "Mastah," he ventured, speaking slowly, with great solemnity, "I am very sorry but I don't think Mastah knows the African man. Many fellahs are not Christian and they push, push. Bad tribes steal and fight and don't like Christ, so damnit—nice people, like Mastah and me, we got to push first. Amen, amen, and that is the truth."

He glanced at Craig to see the effect of his explanation. Craig was trying hard not to smile. Big Boy wasn't really funny. In the middle of the sun-lashed Bomasha River he was trying to discipline a dangerous brute who piously concluded his infantile reasoning with a heartfelt amen.

"There won't be any pushing from now on till I give the

word!" Craig said forcefully, trying to hold Big Boy's shifting glance. "Do you understand that?"

"Yes, Mastah," Big Boy replied with finality. "You are the boss man."

Chapter 8

.

Craig and Colonel Durand met for the first time in a small village not far from Ache. They climbed from their dusty vehicles, shook hands and entered a low mud building without windows by the side of the road. They sat at a wooden table on the pounded mud floor and were served warm beer and a plate of high-smelling roast goat.

The colonel sent the pock-marked proprietor outside and they were finally alone, facing each other in the flickering light of a badly primed kerosene lamp. The colonel lit a cigarette and Craig puffed on his pipe. It was cool and the night was full of the sound of crickets. There was a long, silent pause. Craig made up his mind not to speak first.

The colonel finally leaned forward over the table and spoke. "You speak French, don't you?"

"Yes, I do."

"Monsieur Craig, I believe it is important that we understand each other from the beginning." Craig nodded, listening, attempting to size up the man before him.

"You have just arrived, it is true. But we do not have much time. I shall be blunt. I feel a mistake has already been made by involving too many people in something that should be handled by a very few."

Craig put his pipe down on the table. He was exhausted from his trip but he knew that the first impression he made on Colonel Durand was important. He pushed his thoughts into line and spoke with as much assurance as he could manage.

"I agree we don't have much time. I've thought this over. I am sure the only tactic is to drive more of a wedge between the Bomasha and the river tribes—the Goka. I understand there is a strong doubt that the Bomasha will allow a Goka to become premier. I feel we can make sure they won't."

Craig paused, glancing at the colonel, who returned his gaze coldly, with no sign of approval or disapproval. He continued. "I believe we can begin with a campaign of rumor, or psychological 'intoxication.' A two-way campaign carried out simultaneously in Bomasha and Goka territory. The Goka have always feared the historical Bomasha drive to the sea. The Bomasha emirs have been talking about it for centuries. Properly handled this fear can be a powerful political weapon." Craig paused and took a sip of his beer.

"How do you suggest we carry out this campaign?" the colonel asked.

Craig resented this toneless questioning. It made him feel like a student reciting a lesson before his teacher.

"I have been told that you can help me. I know that the storytellers and holy men of the Bomasha tribes have for years been the political tools of the emirs. With their help, and that of the Bomasha in the army, the word can be spread. With the Goka it may be more difficult."

§ **99**

The colonel's fingers slid up and down his nose. He snuffed out his cigarette on the table, tossed it to the floor and stepped on it with his rubber-soled boot. He sighed.

"Your plan has some merit. You are correct in saying that the only procedure is to alienate the tribes. But I'm not sure we have time for rumors and campaigns of 'intoxication.' We may even now be too late. Our main hope is in action."

Craig frowned and the colonel smiled. "Ah yes," he said bitterly, "we don't have time for political theory. We have lost most of Africa with our lack of action and the worship of the word 'independence.' The communists are waiting like hungry vultures while the soft-headed liberals of the world prepare their next meal. I have seen it happen in Asia and in North Africa. I don't intend to see it happen in Bomasha. We want to split the tribes. Very well, we shall. But not with rumors and recitals of history. We must use facts and happenings that we, ourselves, bring about. I know the Bomasha. I've seen them at war. The news of a Goka at the head of the government will sweep through the north like a brush fire and bring them swooping down on the nearest Goka villages like avenging lions."

The colonel's eyes shone in the light of the lamp. "This country belongs to the Bomasha," he continued, "and not all the socialists and liberals in France or America or the United Nations can tell me that a Goka can serve as its first premier without handing it to the communists as a gift. This country is small but rich. It has a great potential. Under the guided rule of the Bomasha emirs it could become an arrow in the hide of a communist-dominated Africa and a bridgehead for the West."

"But your government is grooming a Goka, Mr. Tibaki, to be the first premier."

§ **100**

"My government? Don't make me laugh. The fatheads we have in Paris today match those you have in Washington. Once again they've chosen a man of straw hoping to control him after independence. But it won't work. Men of straw are outmoded. They have no staying power. They collapse at the first show of force or rebellion." The colonel sipped his beer and looked at Craig. Why, oh why, he asked himself, did they have to send an American?

"What is your plan, Colonel?" Craig asked.

"It's simple enough, as any military plan should be. I now have at my disposal a number of well-trained Bomasha tribesmen. Most of them are veterans of the army. In a few days I shall have some men to lead them . . ."

"Europeans?"

The colonel looked slightly surprised. He smiled. "Yes, Europeans. A Frenchman whom I know very well, having served with him before in some tight spots, and a South African who has been very highly recommended.

"Once they are here and have taken the group of Bomasha in hand we can start our operation. These Bomasha will wear army uniforms and pose as members of the defense forces. They will operate in Goka territory, demanding new taxes and putting restrictions on free movements between villages."

The colonel watched Craig expectantly as he spoke. He seemed pleased when Craig interrupted him.

"This, of course, will mean trouble," Craig said.

"Yes, it will." Colonel Durand sat forward, the muscles in his jaw flexing and his hands clasped around his beer bottle. "It will mean trouble—for we are seeking trouble. Africa has been called a sleeping giant. A very accurate description. The giant seldom stirs until it is forced to. The men who can make it move are those who understand this. The first Goka to

§ **101**

stand in our way will be shot down as will be the second and the third and the fiftieth. African history is built on blood and not all the bright young political scientists of the world can change this simple truth."

The colonel stopped talking and sat back. He rasped a match over the table top and lighted another cigarette. The soft sounds of insects battering against the lamp dominated the sudden silence. Craig studied the colonel. A lot of what he was saying was true but his manner was unsettling. His intensity worried Craig. It bordered on fanaticism.

He in turn bent forward over the table. He spoke slowly and evenly. "I don't need any history lessons, Colonel, and I'm not the type to faint when I see blood. I'm here to do a job. I've been hired and paid to do it. There are a lot of people watching what goes on here. Some of them are 'bright young political scientists' and you're making a mistake if you underestimate them. If we show our hand or call unnecessary attention to our work we'll have a U.N. investigation team breathing down our necks, or even more dangerous—we'll have Bomasha full of correspondents looking for a good story. This is exactly what we don't want. What happens here has to look like a natural clash of tribal interests—without outside interference."

The colonel nodded slowly. There was logic in Craig's reasoning. For a brief moment a shadow of respect crossed his face.

"Now," Craig continued, "you know Bomasha much better than I do. My instructions are to take my lead from you. What do you suggest as my first move?"

Craig knew this approach flattered the colonel. It would also expose a bit more of the colonel's character.

§ 102

"You are supposedly here to study the river tribes, the Goka?"

"That is correct."

"Good. There is a fishing village not too far from here that could be called the head village of the tribe. They don't really have any such organization but the headman of this village is a crafty little ape. Many of the other Goka headmen look up to him and go to him for advice. He hates the Bomasha and is not afraid to show it. It would be good to make contact with him from the beginning. You can feel him out. If he seems reticent you can stay behind your anthropological screen. If he seems willing to cooperate you might go a little further. As I say, he hates the Bomasha and other Gokas will listen to him. He could be invaluable for our purposes."

"What's his name?"

The colonel smiled. "He's called Pierre. That's all—just Pierre. I'll give you a map with the village marked. It's not hard to find. It's on a wide bend of the river."

"Does he know Tibaki?"

"Yes. And they are not friends."

"How are we fixed for money?" Craig asked.

"We have enough, for the time being," the colonel replied. "I don't think you'll need any for a while. First, see how Pierre reacts. I would like to avoid money transactions as long as possible. Things tend to get complicated the minute money changes hands."

"I understand," Craig said.

"Do you bring any word from Paris?"

"No, my contacts there were limited."

"It's just as well."

"There is something though. Before I left Paris I asked for

ten thousand small posters. Each one bears the portrait of Tibaki over a legend in the Bomasha dialect that identifies him as the first premier of the new Republic of Bomasha. These posters will arrive as communications equipment for the defense forces. The cases will be marked for delivery direct to you."

The colonel was listening carefully.

"Your men," Craig continued, "can see that they are posted at night in the larger villages of the emirates. This will confirm the distasteful rumors the Bomasha have heard that a Goka has been chosen to govern them. Once this thought has sunk in, you can order units of the defense force to move through the Bomasha villages ripping down the posters. This will add to their fears and create a good deal of confusion and suspicion."

Colonel Durand nodded. He didn't think much of posters or the other tools of a propagandist's trade but he had to admit that Craig's plan could work.

"I had one other idea," Craig continued. "I've checked over some maps and talked to some people who know Bomasha. If I am correct there are two central fishing grounds used by the Goka?"

"That's right," Durand murmured.

"In the dry season these fishing grounds, both wide spots along the river, turn into warm mud baths with just enough dampness left to keep the river fish alive. These fishing grounds are the only spots where the river Goka can find fish during the dry season." Craig drank the last of his beer. "If the Goka were to hear that the Bomasha planned to build dams upstream from their fishing grounds . . . I think the result could be as effective as any Bomasha raid on a Goka village."

Colonel Durand pursed his lips. "Possibly," he said. "You could mention it to Pierre if the opportunity presents itself. Incidentally," the colonel said, "some of my Bomasha veterans are nearby, if we need them."

"Armed with Belgian submachine guns?" Craig asked.

"Correct," the colonel replied sharply. "How did you know this?"

"Big Boy Eniki, my assistant."

"That fool talks too much," the colonel said with disgust.

"I didn't know you knew each other."

"He's worked for us for some time."

The colonel stood up. "I think I'll get some sleep. It's late and I've got to inspect my troops before the sun gets too high tomorrow."

They walked together to the low door of the building. There were still several roadside vendors squatting outside over the red coals of their fires. Strips of goat meat still sputtered and curled on the grills.

"Oh," the colonel said, reaching into his pocket, "here are two safe-conduct passes for you and Eniki. I have signed them myself. If you have any trouble show them to my men.

"I think your plan to use rumor, psychological intoxication and fear has its merits," the colonel said, settling his kepi low on his forehead. "I am used to working a bit more directly. I shall see that your rumors are based on fact."

He pushed his hand at Craig. They shook hands. "I will be curious to know how your meeting with Pierre works out," the colonel said seriously.

"I'll keep you informed," Craig replied.

Big Boy arrived a few seconds after Colonel Durand's jeep had driven off into the darkness. He brought straw mats and blankets. He tossed them on the floor and arranged makeshift beds.

"Now we go sleep like two pickin's," he said smiling.

He left and came back with the proprietor, both of them loaded down with luggage. They stacked the suitcases and haversacks in a corner. Big Boy took off his shirt. Spotting his shadow on the wall he shuffled and danced before it with the loose ease of a professional boxer.

Craig knocked his pipe out and sat down on his blanket. The solidity of the hard mud floor came as a surprise. He sighed and began to unlace his shoes. He glanced at Big Boy, who was punctuating his short jabs with guttural grunts.

"Why didn't you tell me you knew Colonel Durand?" Craig demanded.

Big Boy stopped his shadow boxing and came over to Craig. He crouched down and wiped the perspiration off his head and chest with his shirt.

"Oh, I know the colonel for some time. He get me my pass into Bomasha."

Craig started to ask another question but decided not to. He flopped down on the mat and pulled his blanket up to his chin.

"Good night, sahr," Big Boy said, as he too stretched out on the floor.

"Good night," Craig replied wearily.

He considered his first meeting with the colonel a success. At least there had been no open show of antagonism on the colonel's part. Coordination was going to be a problem. Durand still felt he could do the job himself but he seemed resigned to accepting Craig. With the colonel handling the Bomasha, who knew and respected him, and Craig handling the Goka it should work out. He corrected himself. It had to work out.

The proprietor still moved around behind the bar putting bottles away and filling cases with empties. Big Boy shouted something in a local dialect and the noise stopped. A few moments later the lamp went out with a pop.

Craig rolled on his side. He was suddenly hungry but he was too tired to budge. A sleep as heavy as death overtook him and he slid away with it, without dreams. Much later the noise of screaming awoke him and he conjured up a vision of a small black child tied to a post like a goat, dying slowly under a hail of heavy blows. Then, more awake, he identified the sound as animal. Reassured he fell asleep again wondering if it were a jackal or a hyena or maybe some bird.

Craig and Big Boy moved up along the Bomasha River. They stopped at several Goka villages. Craig took notes and Big Boy made valiant efforts to communicate with bits of the Goka dialect and elaborate sign language. This first trip was useful. It gave Craig an idea of the local geography that no map, no matter how recent and detailed, could explain. The innumerable jags and squiggles of the muddy river created strange divisions of land. Villages that were within hailing distance and ten minutes away from each other by canoe turned out to be two hours distant by road.

Their Land Rover slewed over the muddy trails, through the thick bush. Big Boy cursed continually under his breath. At first Craig's play acting as an anthropologist had amused him. But his amusement soon faded. He detested the Goka and Craig's insistence that he act as a translator infuriated him.

At sundown, with the help of Durand's map, they reached

§ **107**

their goal, the village of Pierre, the headman, one of the main Goka fishing grounds. There was a sudden break in the jungle and before them lay a broad bank of sand running down to the river. A rank of dugout canoes were pulled up on the sand. The canoes were piled high with fishing traps of reed and fiber. Dip nets hung from long curved poles anchored deep in the sand.

The harmattan winds had begun to blow south from the Sahara. A heaviness had settled over Craig and Big Boy like a penitent's hair shirt. Now, as they pulled to a stop near the river bank the orange sun retired behind a veil of red dust and the river seemed to reflect a far-off fire.

A number of naked Goka children appeared suddenly beside the Land Rover as if they had sprung from the warm sand. Craig climbed out and walked toward the river. The younger children scattered out of his path giggling and squealing. He stood at the water's edge with an unlit pipe in his mouth and examined the river. There were definite scum lines that marked the slow but certain fall of the general water level. The dry season was still three weeks off but there were already exposed rocks crowned with dry waterweed that disappeared in a puff of powder dust when he kicked at it.

Each day that passed now would see small groups of Goka leave their village and move toward this fishing ground loaded with their primitive fish traps. Throughout the dry season they would camp beside this broad elbow of the river with Goka from other villages, sloshing up to their knees through the warm mud in search of the whiskered suckerfish lying dormant, waiting for the rainy season and the return of the waters. The fish they caught would be wrapped in wet banana leaves and sent back to their villages on the backs of young porters to supplement the diet of salted stock fish that each Goka village kept in emergency reserve.

This fishing ground would be the first to be affected by the construction of any upriver dam. Craig walked back toward the Land Rover, the abrasive sand stinging his cheeks.

"Let's make contact in this village," Craig told Big Boy as he climbed in beside him. "We might as well stay here tonight."

He hadn't mentioned Pierre to Big Boy. Big Boy probably knew about his plans already. Big Boy grunted a reply and started the motor. They started over the sand but the wheels began to sink and lose traction.

"To the left," Craig shouted, "quick, down along the water."

The Goka children screamed with delight, bounding beside them as they wobbled forward.

Big Boy swung the steering wheel and they bucked out of the soft, dry sand and drove down to the water's edge, where the sand was wet and solid. The village was directly in front of them, a collection of palm-thatched huts, straggling out over the water on shaky stilts. Three skinny dogs with ridged backs came running toward them barking and snarling, their teeth bared. Craig slammed the Land Rover's door as a hound launched himself against the vehicle with a thump. They heard the distinct click of his fangs against the metal followed by a surprised yelp of pain.

Pierre was a short, wrinkled Goka with long arms, orange-palmed hands, and a dirty black beret. The whites of his eyes were the color of egg yolks. While Big Boy stumbled through the formalities of introducing Craig, the headman explored his own wide nostrils with a long finger, pausing occasionally to examine his findings with an air of scientific detachment.

A group of villagers formed around them, smiling and pushing each other closer as a sort of game. The odor of fish was overpowering. As Big Boy spoke and gesticulated, Craig examined the village. Behind the huts were brown woven mats covered with drying fish. There was a continual buzzing passage of slow-moving flies. Nets and fish traps were hanging between the stilted huts, and two petrol tins, their tops cut off raggedly to form crude cooking pots, were set over a fire of dry palm wood. The pots were tended by several young Goka girls who occasionally poked and stirred an odiferous fish stew.

Craig examined the Goka. They seemed almost amphibian, as if their living by the water had wrought physical changes in the race. He caught himself up short. My God, he thought, I'm beginning to think like an anthropologist!

"Phew," Big Boy shook his head. "That fish smell be mighty powerful. This fellah he wants us stay for chop. He invite us," he said sadly. "I don't think we say no."

Craig smiled at Pierre and nodded a pleased acceptance. He tried to breathe through his mouth to avoid the cloying odors.

"We follow this man," Big Boy said as the headman turned and walked off toward one of the huts followed by several men of the village. "I think this be good time to dash one bottle of Mastah's gin," Big Boy suggested.

Craig hadn't told Big Boy of the gin in his rucksack. He wondered if Big Boy had already gone through all his belongings.

"All right," Craig replied shortly. "You know where it is. Bring a bottle along. Lock the doors and tie down the rear flap."

§ **110**

Craig followed the headman to the hut and up the crude, notched pole that served as a ladder. He had to bend double to enter the dank interior. The odor here was more of damp thatch than of fish. The headman sat and motioned for Craig to join him. The other Goka sat beside them in a circle. Two of the men were stark naked. As they sat and crossed their legs they carefully lifted their sagging testicles with one hand. Once settled they released them gently. Their gesture had a certain dignity. Both of these men had bracelets of green reed tied around their upper arms. These were the reed wrappings used to close off one end of their fish traps. They had been working in the water when Craig and Big Boy drove up. The other Goka wore tattered shorts made from clipping the legs off light cotton trousers. For some obscure reason, one of the men periodically slapped his hands together. He wore a stained and stiff fedora, grease-blackened around the crown. He wore it with the entire brim turned down. When he wanted to glance at Craig he had to raise his head toward the ceiling.

Big Boy entered last and slipped the square bottle of gin to Craig. Grunting and wiggling his eyebrows Big Boy suggested that Craig present the gin bottle. Craig lifted the bottle with both hands in what he presumed was an impressive gesture and put it down in front of the headman. No sooner were his hands off the bottle than the headman lifted it up close to his face to inspect the label. He smiled and replaced it on the floor.

A young woman with huge, bare feet and the body of a young boy appeared from somewhere in the darkness behind the headman and put two drinking gourds before them. Outside the harmattan hummed and rustled through the tall palms.

§ 111

"Pierre!" the headman said suddenly, smiling at Craig. Craig smiled back, puzzled but game.

The headman opened the bottle after much unnecessary prying at the seal. At one point Craig was about to reach over and help but Big Boy stayed his hand. The others sat silently. The man in the fedora continued his periodic clapping but he now had eyes only for the gin bottle and the drinking gourds.

The headman splashed gin into the drinking gourds, filling them to the brim. He raised one to his mouth and tilted his head. Craig watched his Adam's apple bob up and down; one, two, three times. The headman stopped drinking and blinked his eyes, smiling. "Pierre!" he said, nodding, and passed the half-empty gourd to the man on his right. He then lifted the second gourd and repeated his performance. This time he made no comment when he had finished gulping the gin but passed the gourd to the man on his left.

By the time the first gourd reached Big Boy, who was seated on Craig's left, it was empty. Big Boy's wide mouth turned down at the corners and he glared at the Goka who had handed him the gourd. The gourd moving toward them from the headman's left arrived at Craig holding a quarter of an inch of alcoholic moisture. Craig made a broad gesture of drinking it down and was about to hand the gourd back to the headman when he noticed that Big Boy had passed his gourd back around the silent circle. Craig followed suit.

The headman poured more gin into the empty gourds. The girl returned with a large irregular earthenware bowl full of the fish stew they had seen cooking in the petrol tins outside. The steaming mass of boiled fish was the color of gray dishwater, shot through with the silver of fish belly. Reptilian fishheads lurked, half-sunken in the thick liquid. Craig hoped that next time the gourd would reach him with more gin in it.

The headman gulped again at the full gourds and passed them on. He reached behind him and picked up a rolled banana leaf. Unrolling it he shook the bright dust of pounded red peppers into his hand. He pulled the bowl closer and sifted the pepper powder over the scummy surface of the stew. Then he plunged his hand deep into the bowl and stirred the mixture around and around, impervious to the heat. The pepper changed the stew's color from gray to a gray-pink. With a gesture of finality the headman withdrew his dripping hand, licked at his fingers and pushed the bowl toward Craig.

"Pierre!" the headman said, his eyes now slightly glazed from the gin. The man in the fedora raised his head, almost crossing his eyes, in an effort to see.

Luckily one of the drinking gourds reached Craig with a surprising two inches of gin left. He didn't hesitate but drank it down quickly and while the liquor burned his tongue he dipped his hand into the bowl, sought out a solid sliver of fish flesh dripping with pink gravy and poked it into his mouth. The bright explosion of heat almost knocked him back against the flimsy wall of the hut. Flames of searing pain shot up through his throat, ripped past the tender roots of his tongue and the tissues of his nose to bring a gush of tears from his smarting eyes. He looked around in desperation for something to put out the fire, to douse the potent pepper. Big Boy, recognizing his plight, snatched a drinking gourd out of his neighbor's hands and pushed it toward Craig. Craig grasped it and gulped more gin, oblivious to the bite of the alcohol, aware only that the gin was liquid. He sat for a moment

§ **113**

gasping in gulps of air and looking around him through his tears. It was an underwater scene, blurred and shimmering. The Goka were eating unconcernedly, dipping their hands into the stew, munching great mouthfuls of fish and fish heads and spitting bones onto the floor. Big Boy was eating slowly, with a certain caution. Craig noticed that he was shaking each morsel of fish carefully, removing as much of the pepper-heavy gravy as possible.

The headman belched loudly, removed a long ladder of fish bones from his mouth and smiled. He patted his stomach, and emptied the gin bottle into the two drinking gourds. This time he ignored his own people, busy crunching and sucking at the fish stew. He handed a full gourd across to Craig with a gesture of magnanimity. At the same time Craig felt the ominous skittering of some tiny form of animal life high on his leg, moving toward his crotch. He took the gourd, smiling through his ebbing tears.

When they had finished eating the headman rattled off a few guttural phrases. His retainers wiped their mouths with the backs of their hands and left the room. He then stared directly at Big Boy. Big Boy took the hint. He was glad to get out into the fresh air.

Craig offered the headman some of his tobacco. He accepted it with a smile. He filled a short, chipped clay pipe and lit it. He sat watching Craig with tendrils of smoke leaking out of his nostrils and curling up over his black face.

"I speak French," he said suddenly, still watching Craig. "You English?"

"No, American."

"You mission man?"

"No," Craig replied. "I study tribes."

§ 114

"Why?" the headman asked, his bloodshot eyes studying the white man.

Craig was astonished that he had remained lucid after drinking so much gin.

"To learn their history," Craig said.

The headman looked blank.

"It is very interesting," Craig told him.

The headman grunted and looked bored. Craig decided to try a different approach.

"Much," he said seriously, "has been written about the Bomasha tribe but little about the Goka."

At the mention of the Bomasha the little man's lips curled with distaste. "Bomasha pigs!" he said vehemently.

"I have come to your country," Craig continued, "to study the ways of your tribe. Monsieur Tibaki is most interested in my research."

The mention of Tibaki brought a frown to the headman's face but he said nothing.

Craig explained his interest in the burial rites of the Goka and the place of the shark in the tribe's religion.

The headman listened, puffing on his pipe. He volunteered a grunt from time to time as a vague show of interest.

Craig spoke on until the headman seemed to be in a complete state of apathy. "I am afraid I may have come too late for my research," Craig stated, shaking his head.

"Oh, dry season not long," the headman replied, "Rains come again, river fill up."

"Yes," Craig said, "but I have heard the Bomasha were building dams upriver. I . . ."

"What you say!" The headman bent toward him, his eyes flashing, his pipe put aside.

§ 115

"It may not be true," Craig told him, watching him swallow the rumor like a baited hook. "A defense force sergeant told me about it," he elaborated. "The Bomasha want irrigation for their groundnuts." Craig caught himself. He had better be careful. He wasn't sure groundnuts needed irrigation.

"Impossible, impossible," the headman was mumbling.

"Bomasha no build dam," he said, but Craig could see that already his mind had moved to the fact that the Bomasha could build a dam if they wanted to.

"The government probably wouldn't let them," Craig said with the hint of a question in his voice.

Pierre shook his head. "French like Bomasha," he said bitterly. "Bomasha want dam—French don't argue."

"But surely, Monsieur Tibaki would intercede in such a situation."

The headman growled several words in Goka and sucked in his breath audibly. "Tibaki say yes, yes to French. Yes, yes, Tibaki always answer yes."

Craig was silent. He decided to stop guiding the conversation. The headman grimaced at the floor of the hut, still mumbling to himself. When he looked up again his face reflected a grim determination.

"Goka will not be pushed." He poked Craig in the chest with his forefinger as he spoke. "Bomasha think it is as before. Is not true. Our young men will fight. They are school-trained. Stupid Bomasha!" he exploded. "We rub their beards in the excretion of pigs!"

The headman recovered himself. He rubbed his chin and watched Craig. A smile crept over his face. "Thank you, American," he said, "for word of the dam."

"It may not be true," Craig replied.

§ **116**

The headman nodded. "It is well I know." He stopped smiling. "Goka need friends now," he said seriously. He reached out and shook Craig's hand. "Pierre," he said again, smiling broadly.

He directed Craig to the door of the hut. The interview was over. He followed the headman into the welcome fresh air.

Craig and Big Boy didn't sleep well during the night. Stretched out on the sand beside the Land Rover they were assaulted by mosquitoes, and disturbed by the slow scraping passage of land crabs. Big Boy covered his head with a blanket and snored intermittently. But the night held a great deal of interest for Craig and he was content to observe.

Since nightfall there had been a coming and going of Gokas. A hum of voices had continued from the headman's hut and canoes had pushed off into the river on mysterious voyages. Craig couldn't tell if the returning canoes were the same that had departed but each arrival brought an increase in the volume of the discussion.

He fell asleep with his head on his arms. When he awoke the morning sun burned white over the river and Goka fishermen were working the shallows.

The headman, accompanied by his retainers, came toward them, shuffling through the warm sand. Two women carried a fire-blackened pot of hot water slung between them on a pole. They shook hands and the headman offered them the hot water. Big Boy gave Craig a rough translation of the headman's rapid Goka. "He wants us to wash," Big Boy grumbled. "The water smells of fish," he added frowning.

Craig noted the headman's reluctance to speak French when in earshot of his own people. The headman gestured toward the tribesman in the battered fedora. The man had stopped clapping his hands and was examining their Land Rover with fascination.

"He say this fellah going to show you the river burial today," Big Boy translated. "There is a pickin' dead upriver. He's go take you there."

Craig nodded. He tried to look pleased.

"Pierre," the headman said smiling. He left them with his retainers following along behind. Craig's guide sank down into the sand beside the Land Rover, his face held high, watching them from under the shade of his fedora brim.

"We have an audience," Craig said as he dug for soap and a towel in his baggage.

"Stupid bushman," Big Boy grunted, staring at the Goka.

They didn't spend much time washing. The water was oily and it did smell of fish. They drank from their water bottles and ate some biscuits smeared with jam. Craig slung his water bottle over his shoulder. After a few commanding phrases of Goka from Big Boy their guide led them into the village.

Craig was anxious to learn what had caused the nightlong conference and the movement of the canoes. He first noted the increase in the number of canoes pulled up on the beach. Then he saw the young men gathered before the hut of the headman. Their guide tugged at Craig's arm, pulling him toward the river bank, away from the village. Big Boy had also seen the pile of assorted weapons that the young men were working on. Craig caught a glimpse of ancient rifles, braces of machetes and what looked like a few army Enfields.

"Oh ho!" Big Boy murmured, raising his eyebrows.

Craig allowed the guide to pull him down to a canoe at the water's edge. The skinny Goka spoke excitedly to Big Boy, waving his arms and pointing up the river. "He says he be the juju man of the village. He go show you burial ceremony."

Craig listened with half an ear. He was still looking toward the headman's hut. Then he turned to his guide. "Tell him he is very kind. I am honored."

The Goka smiled, bowing his head and motioning Craig and Big Boy into the dugout canoe.

Craig took Big Boy by the arm. "You stay here," he said. "Find out what's going on. Offer them any help they might need with that pile of rusty weapons. I'll be back as soon as I can. Now, push us off before our juju man has a heart attack."

Craig stepped into the narrow canoe and sat down. The Goka waited for Big Boy to climb in but Big Boy shook his head. He lifted the Goka bodily and placed him gently in the stern. He pushed the spear-shaped paddle into the Goka's hand and gave the canoe a mighty shove. It shot out from shore, riding lightly on the turbid water.

Craig ignored his guide's protests and waved goodby to Big Boy. Finally the old man ceased his chattering and began to paddle. Craig smiled, thinking of the young men in the village and the stack of arms. Pierre was obviously a man of action.

Craig fidgeted throughout the burial ceremony. The ceremony itself was a great disappointment. He didn't really give a damn but he wondered if anyone who knew the Goka would take him seriously if he continued to speak of his interest in their burial rites.

When they had landed on a shaky wharf in the center of a village of stilted huts the ceremony was already underway.

§ 119

The dead infant lay flat before the door of a hut. She had been coated with ashes and her skin was a ghostly gray. One of the child's eyes was open in a ghastly wink.

The village juju man shuffled in front of the child, and danced around her parents, chanting softly, shaking a gourd rattle. His head was covered with a raffia mourning mask. A crudely carved shark of water-bleached driftwood sat precariously on top of his head.

The family and the other members of the village gathered on the thatched porches of their huts or in floating canoes, watching the ceremony with no sign of emotion. A blank, transparent shade seemed to have been drawn over their eyes. Craig's arrival appeared to have gone unnoticed. He and his guide crowded in among the onlookers.

The unemotional ceremony seemed to drag on and on. There was only the murmur of the river, the cry of far-off fishing birds and the monotonous chant of the juju man.

Craig watched, wiping the perspiration from his forehead, and waited. Finally a jute sack was brought from the hut. Several villagers assisted the juju man in lifting the doll-like body and inserting it into its rough shroud. The juju man closed the sack by tying knots with raffia cord. He lifted the sack toward the parents and, with a quick motion of his shoulders, tossed it out into the mainstream of the river.

The sack sunk, bobbed to the surface and began its slow trip downstream. There was an audible sigh from the onlookers. The father of the dead child went into his hut and returned with three bottles of palm wine. The juju man removed his mask and mopped at the rivulets of perspiration coursing over his face and chest. He took a proffered bottle of palm wine and drank deeply. Craig was offered a bottle by the father. He drank some of the still-fermenting wine before passing the bottle to his guide.

They left when half the bottle was gone. Craig was in a hurry to return to the village and see what Big Boy had learned of Pierre's plans. He made a mental note not to insist on the importance of Goka burial rites in any future anthropological conversations.

Chapter 9

:

Big Boy was in his element. He squatted among the young Goka stripping down the most presentable weapons and laying their rusted parts on fly-covered straw mats. He shook his head and grumbled over the neglected rifles. He had wrapped a handkerchief around his forehead to keep the perspiration out of his eyes.

At first the Goka had been reluctant to admit him but he had bulled his way in, shouldering the youths aside, a look of disgust and anguish on his broad face, as if he were rushing to the rescue of a mistreated friend.

Pierre, the headman, had seen Big Boy's intrusion into the circle. He had watched with surprise and pleasure as Big Boy had taken an Enfield in his hands as if it were a toy and had begun to clean it. Before retiring into his hut, he had told the youths to assist Big Boy.

Big Boy brought a can of machine oil from the Land Rover and requisitioned a Goka woman's headcloth for cleaning rags. The Goka watched fascinated as his huge hands moved magically over the weapons and broke them into little pieces. The Goka had never realized that the rifles came apart. In his preoccupation with the weapons Big Boy forgot Craig's instructions to question the Goka on their plans.

He struck his thumbnail in the receiver of an Enfield and squinted down the barrel. The rifling was pocked and eaten with rust and filth. He called for hot water. He picked up an ancient Mauser with a cracked stock. The barrel was sealed with a plug of dried clay.

"You stupid bastard," he shouted at the nearest Goka. The man looked at him puzzled, ready to smile but unsure.

When Craig returned, there were two Enfields cleaned and oiled. The Mauser was almost finished. Several Goka were sorting out a pile of cartridges of various calibers, under Big Boy's supervision, and cleaning them in a tin of oil.

"Ah, Mastah," Big Boy greeted Craig as he approached. "These bushman don't know nothing. I never see such a mess ..."

Craig quickly took in what Big Boy had accomplished. He rubbed at the stubble on his own chin and pulled Big Boy away from the busy Goka.

"What are they up to?" he asked. "What are they planning?"

Big Boy shrugged. He realized he had forgotten to question the Goka. "Maybe they go hunt," he said without conviction.

Craig sighed with impatience. "Keep working," he ordered. "I'll be back."

He walked to the headman's hut and paused at the foot of the ladder. "Pierre!" he called, " 'Allo, Pierre!"

The headman's face appeared in the darkened entrance of the hut. He motioned for Craig to climb up and enter.

§ 123

Craig breathed a sigh of relief in the darkened interior. He couldn't go another day under the sun without a hat and he knew it. His eyes became accustomed to the darkness and he saw Pierre sitting alone in his usual place. The headman gestured for him to sit down. When Craig had settled himself the headman reached for a long bundle wrapped in dirty rags. It was heavy. The headman lifted it with a grunt and set it down between them.

"I want to thank you for the guide and the opportunity to see the burial ceremony," Craig said.

The headman raised a hand for silence and started to unwrap his bundle with great care. Craig watched the unveiling; the flash guard, the sight, the long barrel. When the last bit of cloth was removed the headman opened the bipod and the Bren gun was set up between them, dented and rust-spotted. The headman ran one hand over the weapon. He smiled with pride and nodded his head at Craig as if waiting for praise.

"Where did you find this?" Craig asked, surprised.

"Long time ago, long, long time," the headman answered, still smiling at Craig.

"Why all these weapons?" Craig asked innocently.

The old man's smile turned off. He tapped his skull with his forefinger. "In here I think. I think Goka be ready this time. Maybe Bomasha build dam, maybe not build dam, but Goka be ready. This gun be broken. I think your man," he motioned outside, "can fix it."

Craig looked doubtful. "I think this is a very dangerous thing. I am a man of peace and—"

"He can fix," the headman repeated, smiling at Craig.

"We must leave soon," Craig replied. "He can look at it before we go."

"Very good, very good," the headman said, satisfied. "You are a friend."

Colonel Durand felt he had put the 6th company more or less in order. Forty-eight hours of inspections, shouting and assigning punishments seemed to have had a healthy effect. The company commander had been caught flat-footed by the colonel's arrival. The young lieutenant was the son of a local emir and his taste for gazelle hunting from an open jeep had become a vice that kept him away from his command for days at a time.

Durand had found the men restless and ill-disciplined, the noncommissioned officers reluctant to act without authority. He had called for a parade and inspection under the searing midday sun. He had stood with them through it all, a lone, erect, leather-brown figure eyeing with disdain the occasional heat-struck collapse of a man in the ranks. The errant lieutenant had appeared halfway through the inspection, as the colonel was ordering punishment for three men who had filed teeth into their bayonet blades. Two magnificent dun and white gazelles were slung over the jeep's hood. The lieutenant had hurried over to the colonel, saluted and extended his hand.

Colonel Durand had measured him with a look of disdain. "Go to your quarters, *Corporal*," Durand had commanded. "I am occupied here with soldiers."

Before leaving the parade ground the young former officer had stood for a moment looking dumbly at his own empty, extended hand.

A veteran sergeant was now in charge of the company and the colonel was content. He knew he would have trouble

§ 125

with the former lieutenant's father but that, Durand felt, was a minor thing. He could handle it.

He was less content when he saw Craig's Land Rover pull up in front of the company headquarters.

"Hello," Craig said as he entered the open door.

"Come in," Durand responded with a thin smile of greeting. "Would you like some mineral water? I'm afraid that's all I have to offer you."

"I'll take anything liquid."

"My God," Durand said suddenly, "are you mad? To run around without a hat in this heat? Your head looks like a strawberry!"

Craig nodded in agreement. "I agree. I need a hat."

"Sergeant!" the colonel shouted. When the sergeant appeared he sent him off for a campaign hat for Craig. "Seriously," Durand said, "it is not very intelligent to go without a head covering."

Craig drank his mineral water. He could do without the colonel's lecturing. He had more important things to discuss. The colonel poured himself a glass of water. He glanced around at the headquarter's hut. "It is primitive here," he said, "but they do their best to make me comfortable."

The sergeant clumped in holding a broad-brimmed campaign hat. The colonel took it and dismissed the sergeant. "We are not to be disturbed, understand?"

"Yes, my Colonel."

He turned to Craig. "Here you are," he said, turning up one brim and snapping it. "Like the Australians."

"Thank you," Craig murmured, accepting the hat.

The colonel walked to the door. The parade ground was empty and quiet, "Well," he said, "how are our friends, the Goka?"

Craig sat down on one of the sand-filled animal skins that served as seats in the small room.

"They are not happy."

The colonel looked amused and raised his eyebrows.

"Pierre swallowed the story of the dam. At least he is very suspicious of the Bomasha and I could see it was the kind of thing he felt they might well be planning."

"Very good."

"They have collected a number of arms . . ."

"Arms?"

"Yes, they've brought arms in from other Goka villages and Pierre is having them cleaned and put into working order."

The colonel moved closer to Craig. He had stopped smiling. He looked very interested. "What do they have?" he asked.

"Not much. A dilapidated Bren, a few Enfields, some old Mausers and some firelocks or muzzle-loaders that would probably do more damage to the marksman than to the target. Big Boy helped them clean some of the rifles and he fixed the Bren but the clip is so badly dented it will only feed three shells at a time."

"They would actually fight the Bomasha?"

"Pierre would. He's called in a group of young Goka. They look tough. But I'm sure he wouldn't move first. He speaks of 'being ready' for the Bomasha. He sounds determined."

"Sacré Pierre!" the colonel said joyfully. He smiled at Craig. "Congratulations! You've only been here a few days and already the Goka are arming. It is almost unbelievable. Those scum actually think they can fight the Bomasha!" The colonel strode back and forth across the room. He was thinking and murmuring "Very well" under his breath.

§ 127

Craig lit his pipe. "What are your plans?" he asked.

"My plans?" Colonel Durand paused for a moment, thinking. "I will stay here a few more days with this company and then head south to make a report to the high commissioner and Tibaki. Oh," he said, striking his forehead, "I almost forgot. Your posters arrived. They're out there in that covered truck. Tonight the truck will be driven into the emirates and they should be posted within a day or two." Durand chuckled. "I took a look at that poster. Where did you get that portrait of Tibaki?"

"A friend on a Paris newspaper lifted it for me."

"It's perfect. Even a mother would turn away a son that looked like that. And your 'study' of the Goka?"

"I saw a burial ceremony. It wasn't much. I'll have to find other things of interest."

"You should see Tibaki. He's a fund of information on the Goka. What are your immediate plans?"

"I felt it would be best to return to Ikiri to help build the image of the busy anthropologist. Then I think it would be well for me to see Tibaki. You and I could meet again in the south."

"You're right. By then I should have the reaction of the Bomasha to your posters. I'll arrange a meeting with Tibaki for you when I return."

They walked together to the door. Big Boy was dozing behind the wheel of the Land Rover.

The colonel frowned. "Watch that fool," he said. "He'll try to take a case of brandy back across the border and it's not the kind of thing you should get mixed up in . . . right now."

Craig smiled. "I feel I could drink the whole case myself." He put on his new hat and tilted it at an angle.

§ **128**

"Very good," the colonel said. "I will contact you by telegram in a day or two. Where are you staying?"

"The Ikiri Rest House."

Durand made a wry face. "Eat well," he said sarcastically. "Goodby." He stood at the door until the Land Rover had disappeared from sight.

He turned back into the room. He smiled and rubbed his hands together. He rummaged through his baggage and opened a map case. He spread a map out on the shaky table that served as a desk and studied it carefully, running his thumb over his lip. Finally, he located the Goka village of Pierre, the headman. He took a short red pencil out of his blouse pocket and made a heavy circle around it.

So, he told himself, the Goka want to fight. This development was heaven-sent. Pierre was the only possible leader the Goka could ever call on. With him out of the way the Bomasha would have no worries. It was perfect. Even if there were trouble from outside it could be covered by the fact that the Goka were illegally hiding arms.

He made some measurements on the map and checked his kilometers. Satisfied he straightened up, his fists on his hips. He had a perfect first assignment for the two European mercenaries. It would be a good test of their ability. Smiling, and feeling once again the thrill of approaching action he strode out into the sunlight to see what had happened to the afternoon work bugle.

". . . Imam Habib, Sonny Agola, Mr. and Mrs. Holt of Kingsway," Alice Thompson read aloud the names of those to be invited to the Queen's birthday party. Her husband slumped in a chair under the ceiling fan, listening with his eyes closed.

§ **129**

"... L. S. Shetima, Mr. Magabian ..."

"That fool?"

"We can't leave him out, Robert," she said. "You know that."

"All right, all right."

"Michael Craig ..."

"He's out of town."

"I know, but we can send an invitation to the Rest House. He may be back soon."

Robert Thompson sighed. "If you insist."

"I think we had better set up the bar out in front and use the driveway for the party."

"Humph," Thompson replied.

"What is the matter, Robert? Are you ill?"

"No, blast it! I'm just thinking of all the liquor our noble guests are going to slop up. Means another cash outlay and a long wait for replenishment."

"Well, at least it's a change. It could be fun."

Thompson didn't reply. He hadn't had a drink that morning and when he half-opened his eyes he could see the hands of the wall clock creeping slowly, very slowly, toward eleven o'clock. Occasionally he did something like this to prove to himself that he wasn't an alcoholic. He also tried to think constructive thoughts and be sociable.

"Do you remember, Alice, the time I carried that secret dispatch for General Glanville in the Sudan?"

"Yes, dear," she replied, still busy with her list, tapping her lips with a pencil.

There was so little in Robert Thompson's life that he himself remembered. He liked to contemplate the high spots. "Right across the bloody desert," he said, his eyes still closed

§ 130

and a smile of pride on his face. "I didn't have any escort. A civilian doing a soldier's job."

The dispatch he spoke of had been a routine message. It had been marked confidential and the general couldn't, at the time, spare any of his staff officers. They had thought of the chubby foreign office type who had been assigned to their headquarters.

"Yes," the general had said at the suggestion of using Thompson, "get him out from under foot for a bit."

Through the years since the war Thompson's liquor-fed imagination had reconstructed the incident. It was one of his favorites. "Right across the desert with a Nubian guide. I think an Italian patrol almost caught up with us. But I made it." He chuckled. "Just like Lawrence—more or less, eh?"

"What, dear?"

"I said that . . ." He stopped speaking and his face clouded. The dark eyebrows dove into a frown. He felt the usual hurt. It kindled a burning anger. She never listened to him. Nobody listened. "Nothing," he said bitterly, hoping an argument would start. But she was oblivious to his mood, still bending over the writing desk, scribbling out her invitations.

He pulled himself up, tucked his shirttail in and walked over to the liquor cabinet. "I'm going to have a drink," he said defiantly. "You want one?"

"No, dear," she said, still writing.

"Well, I do." He poured himself a pink gin and went back to his chair. He shut his eyes and tried to go back, but he couldn't. He sipped his drink resentfully and glowered at the spinning blades of the fan.

She was almost finished with her invitation list. She wrote Craig's name on an envelope and hesitated. She reopened the envelope and removed the engraved invitation. "I look forward to seeing you again," she wrote boldly across the bottom of the card.

The act of putting her thoughts into writing confirmed her interest in Craig. She had thought of him frequently since his departure from Ikiri. She had told herself it was ridiculous. Pure curiosity had a lot to do with it, she knew, but there was more to it than that. A certain excitement was there too. She couldn't deny it.

She pushed her hair back nervously and put down her pen. "There," she said, sighing. "That's that! Can someone from your office help Ignatius distribute these invitations, Robert?"

"I suppose so."

She lighted a cigarette and walked out onto the veranda to examine the driveway and think of the placement of her buffet tables.

Alone in the room Thompson was able to slide back into his memories. Now the Italian patrol had caught up with him and he was fighting from behind his prone camel, a grim look on his determined face. He remembered it all as if it were only yesterday.

Chapter 10

:

The village of Pierre, the headman, awakened to a new day. The viscous mists clinging to the surface of the river dissipated into feathery vapors that rose slowly, fading into the higher heat haze clamped over the river and jungle by the morning sun.

The Goka had already begun work and their heads bobbed like black balls above the surface of the shallow, dun-colored river. They were working a net into shore, pushing slowly through the muck in a slow-motion ballet of straining muscles and shining teeth.

A scattered group of women and children waited on the beach. Some of the women were filling water tins and the children squealed and chased each other through the dry sand.

The two lorries with defense-force markings that pulled to a stop on the slight rise before the village went unnoticed for some time. Time enough for the uniformed, armed men to jump down onto the sand and divide themselves into two sections.

§ **133**

The children were the first to notice the visitors. They saw one of the sections starting off through the sand, skirting the beach, on its way to the other side of the village. Some of the bolder young boys approached the strangers, running, then slowing down, curious but cautious as they realized that the soldiers were of the Bomasha tribe.

They also saw the two Europeans. One was short and dark with black hair, long sideburns and a straggly black mustache drooping down at the corners of his mouth. He wore a parachutist's uniform. A red beret was pushed back on his head. A submachine gun hung across his chest and, as the children watched him, their eyes wide with wonder, he reached down and snapped the bolt of the weapon, feeding a shell into the receiver. The little man looked over the children's heads, ignoring them.

The second European was tall. He wore a broad-brimmed bush hat with a leopard-skin band. A shock of blond hair hung over his forehead and one of his eyes was a cornflower blue. The other eye was glass and of a different blue. It had been fitted into a socket with torn muscle tissue. It pointed up, staring toward the sky.

He wore a khaki hunting shirt and slacks. The shell pockets of his shirt glinted with brass cartridge cases. A well-cared-for automatic rifle hung, barrel down, in one of his hands and he held a long, lit cigar in the other.

The uniformed Bomasha tribesmen unloaded some ammunition boxes from one of the lorries. Their comrades in the other detachment reached the far end of the village. The tall blond officer put his cigar in his mouth, lifted his rifle and tapped the long clip extending from its underside.

More children came to look at the strangers. The younger

ones came forward, holding hands, their mouths open, expecting to be spoken to, to be noticed. The eldest were undergoing an intuitive change. Their simple minds were troubled by the silent Europeans, the weapons and the unsmiling Bomasha. They took a few steps backward and looked at each other, wondering.

The two Europeans exchanged words. The shortest turned to a Bomasha wearing sergeant's stripes and spoke a few words in French. He gestured with his arm, aiming it straight toward the village, raising it and lowering it as if he were cutting a pie.

The Bomasha nodded in agreement and shouted in Bomasha dialect to the other section, which was still moving forward. They halted, listened and began to pull back in reply to the shouted commands.

"Stupid Kaffir bastards," the blond mercenary said in English, shaking his head and smiling without humor. He turned to his companion and spoke in a halting French. "It's good it is not night. They were moving directly to our front."

Suddenly one of the older children, a long lanky boy with huge hands and feet, turned and started running back toward the village. A Goka woman, whom the Europeans hadn't noticed approaching, got close enough to see the Bomasha and the weapons. Her high, shrill scream of warning chilled the warm air, immobilized the Goka fishermen momentarily and spread panic among the children.

"*Merde!*" the Frenchman growled. He pushed one boot forward, bracing himself, and lifted his submachine gun. It was a new, light Belgian model and when he pressed the trigger it ripped the morning with a high metallic clatter, spewing an arc of empty, smoking shell cases onto the ground.

§ **135**

The tall boy leading the pack of screaming, frightened children cartwheeled into the sand with a thump and lay still, his limbs protruding like the legs of a crushed spider. The fleeing children broke and swept around him. The deeper sound of the South African's automatic rifle tempered the soprano of the submachine gun. Two small children fell together, arm in arm, as in a child's game.

The Goka men were moving toward the beach with frustrating slowness, trying to speed through the sucking mud and the pull of the sluggish current. The section of Bomasha now in place along the fringe of jungle facing the village and river opened fire with a cracking and sputtering of automatic weapons. The murderous flail of their bullets skipped across the water toward the struggling fishermen.

The tall South African signalled the Bomasha forward and he and his French comrade moved forward slowly, pausing occasionally to fire at scurrying targets as they presented themselves.

A group of Bomasha gave chase to the woman who had screamed, shouting and laughing as she ran back and forth before them like a cornered hare. The Frenchman's submachine gun rattled again. The woman came to a sudden stop and pitched forward slowly, face down into the sand. The Bomasha turned toward their officers, puzzled and resentful. The sergeant shouted angrily, shaking his carbine at his men and motioning them on to the village.

A few of the Goka fishermen reached the beach. They dodged the Bomasha fire, pushed the women and children behind canoes and fish traps under the stilted huts, picked up their weapons and came forward to fight.

A Goka Enfield thumped and one of the Bomasha sat down abruptly in the sand, clutching his bleeding thigh. A deadly cone of fire from the well-trained Bomasha silenced the Goka rifleman but his comrades came on.

The mercenaries stopped firing a moment to watch the Goka advance. There were eight men coming toward them at a run, their fish spears held in a throwing position, their machetes flashing at their sides. There was a moment of near silence as the other section found itself without targets in the village. The South African and the Frenchman stood quietly, waiting, their weapons held ready across their chests. The South African smiled, his eye cold, but interested. "We today have heroes," he said. When the Goka were close enough and they could hear them panting and gasping, he put his cigar back in his mouth, flipped the catch on his weapon to full automatic and opened fire. They stopped firing when four of the Goka had gone down, three silent and one kicking violently at the sand, moving himself in a threshing crablike circle, and the Frenchman swung his arm forward, loosing his section.

The Bomasha swept forward shouting their battle cry and went for the stunned, outnumbered Goka with fixed bayonets and spade-bladed throwing spears.

A fishing spear rose up out of the melee, wobbling slowly through the air toward the white men and fell flat on the sand at their feet. The Frenchman held his submachine gun under his arm and lighted a cigarette. "Let's go," he said without enthusiasm. "Let's get it over with." They walked down the slight slope toward the village as the last thunk of a Bomasha blade into flesh and bone ended the resistance of the village males. The other section moved toward the village eager to get their hands on the women and children.

The Goka women set up a chorus of screaming as the Bomasha approached. Some women tried to launch a dugout

§ **137**

but warning shots in the water beside them capsized the canoe, dumping them into the shallows. Another group of naked women, dragging a cluster of children with them, broke from cover and ran along the river bank, away from the village. The Bomasha shouted in triumph and took up the chase. The fastest Bomasha brought down the slowest Goka woman with a flying tackle. As they scuffled in the sand two of his comrades came to his aid. One wrenched the infant from his mother's arms, swung it around several times by its feet and sent the child flying, like a small, fat ebony bird out over the river. It hit with a light splash and promptly disappeared from sight.

The woman fought and struck out with her nails and teeth until a Bomasha raised his throwing spear and struck her on the side of the head with its butt. Her eyes glazed slightly and her arms fell limp to her sides. The Bomasha pried her legs apart and fell upon her, each in turn, shouting and laughing in triumph and pleasure as the woman's thin fingers clawed weakly at the damp sand. When they had finished, the laughter faded, frowns appeared on their scarred faces and one Bomasha raised his throwing spear and struck hard, blade down, at the quivering, violated belly.

The mercenaries moved cautiously among the huts. They knew the Goka had rifles and they meant to find them. They had managed to keep several disappointed Bomasha busy searching the huts while their fellow tribesmen enjoyed the fruits of victory. One of these Bomasha climbed up the notched-stick ladder to a large hut. He was about to enter the low doorway when a roar of firing sent him tumbling backwards into the mud of the riverbed, his face and chest shattered.

§ **138**

Pierre, the headman, came out of the hut hesitantly, blinking in the light, clasping in his hand the heavy Bren. At the tack-hammer rattle of the Frenchman's submachine gun he jerked, loose-limbed, in a sudden brief dance, fell back against the wall of his hut and slid to a sitting position.

The screams were fading now. Black clumps of slaughtered Goka dotted the sands. Already the vultures cast their gliding shadows over the village.

A group of Bomasha came toward the Europeans and their sergeant. They were dragging a young Goka girl along behind them. She had ceased to struggle. When they threw her before their officers she lay stomach down in the sand, her heaving shoulders the only sign of life. A Bomasha handed his rifle with its bloody bayonet to a comrade and knelt beside the girl. He reached down and gently cupped his hand over the girl's firm, round buttocks. He shouted to the sergeant.

The South African waited patiently for an explanation. The sergeant interpreted the Bomasha offer. "They have found this virgin and want you to have her." The Frenchman smiled. "Are you interested?" The South African took off his bush hat and smoothed his blond hair, now soaking wet with perspiration. "I don't like public love-making," the South African said abruptly, busying himself with a new clip for his rifle.

The short Frenchman shrugged and turned toward the sergeant. "Tell them we are proud of our Bomasha warriors. Tell them we give them this fine Goka virgin."

The Bomasha hesitated a moment. Then, grinning, they lifted the girl like a trussed pig and carried her toward a nearby clump of bush.

The group of men that had been searching the village came

§ 139

toward them dragging the Bren gun and an assortment of rifles and muskets. They threw them into one of the lorries.

"Is that all?" the South African asked.

"That is all," the sergeant said. "They were all in the headman's hut."

"Let's fire the village and get moving," the South African suggested, slinging his rifle. The Frenchman agreed and ordered the sergeant to send a team of men with jerry cans of petrol to ignite the huts.

The sergeant returned from the lorry with a bottle of whisky. "Ah, this is what we need!" the South African said in English. For the first time that morning there was warmth in his smile. "You may be black and stupid," he told the sergeant, "but you obviously have a heart." He explained what he had said to his French comrade and they both laughed, oblivious to the screams from the nearby bush. They drank in turn from the bottle and watched the smudge of black smoke rise over the crackling thatch of the Goka huts.

The next morning the inhabitants of three Bomasha villages woke up to find the flat, bespectacled visage of Jean Jaurès Tibaki peering at them from the walls of their huts and compounds.

The first dull shock gave way to noisy anger as the literate read the short text of the posters aloud to their fellow villagers. The very thought of a Goka as prime minister sent tall patriarchal Bomasha warriors into a rage and they vied with the children of the villages in ripping the posters from the walls and defiling them.

Two villages sent young boys sprinting to the seat of the regional emirate. The third village sent a messenger on a recalcitrant burro. The young boys had arrived long before the mounted messenger hurried through the gates of the emir's compound.

The compound was already humming and buzzing like an overturned beehive. The emir, a small, fat man, was swathed in blue robes. He wore a delicate white turban and a cheap pair of dark glasses with mirror-coated lenses. He was trembling with rage and his glasses reflected the angry faces of his counselors. He fingered his tufted prayer beads with such violence it seemed they would burst. He called on Allah to curse the Goka and he spit on the floor.

The young French lieutenant who served as the emir's military aide stifled a smile and wondered how soon he could discreetly inform Colonel Durand of the Bomasha reaction to Craig's posters.

Chapter 11

:

Some of the guests arrived early. The leader of the Muslim community and his suite crunched through the gravel and stood in a quiet, aloof group until Robert Thompson rushed down the steps to greet them, struggling with the tight collar of his uniform jacket.

Magabian strode in next, smiling and perspiring, shaking Thompson's hand with such enthusiasm that a cloud of disapproval settled on the district officer's face.

The British community sifted in, the men red-faced and uncomfortable in their baggy white suits, the women in flowered dresses and dated picture hats.

Alice Thompson met them with Ignatius at her elbow bearing a tray of ready-made drinks. The Rest House regulars, British construction experts and a few engineers arrived in the Rest House Land Rover and fell to work on the buffet with a minimum of sociability. Robert Thompson moved from group to isolated group, filling his role as host, secretly wishing he were alone, in shorts, under the ceiling fan.

Tobo Holman appeared with several young friends. They wore dark wool suits and high, stiff white collars. Tobo shook Thompson's hand with the limp grip he had learned in London and made excuses to Alice Thompson for his grandmother's absence.

Ignatius followed Thompson's explicit orders and supplied him with a steady run of double gins cut with a slight dollop of tonic. After several glasses Thompson began to feel better.

The driveway filled with guests and a conversational hum filled the still air. The Muslims sipped their lemon squash, exchanged rapid bursts of commentary in Hausa, shifted their voluminous robes on their shoulders and smiled at the other guests when they felt it was necessary. The British women settled into small clutches of four or five, gossiping and wiping away the bright beads of perspiration that seeped through their thickly applied layers of facial powder. Their husbands gathered near the buffet, chasing their gin and whisky with sandwiches, breaking off from their comrades occasionally to greet an African business acquaintance and chat the minimum of time required by social convention.

Some Yoruba merchants arrived with their families and the hum of conversation was livened by their wives' high-pitched, exuberant laughter. Their children's assault on the buffet brought summary parental punishment. But none of this seemed to disturb Robert Thompson, who by now was moving in a warm glow of gin. In this temporary happy state he failed to notice his wife's expression when Michael Craig arrived.

Alice Thompson sensed a great feeling of relief when she saw him. Several times she had glanced past the gate, casually inspecting the road leading toward the Rest House. She told herself she was being foolish, acting like a young girl. But now that he was there, walking toward her past the other guests and smiling a greeting, she felt pleased and grateful. The vacuum bell that had enclosed her party was suddenly broken for her and she sensed his presence and was excited by it. She veiled her feeling carefully with an undemonstrative welcome.

"Mr. Craig," she said, taking his hand, "how good of you to come."

"My pleasure," Craig replied, once again attracted by her voluptuous maturity, wondering how many other guests had received a penned note on their invitation card.

For Craig, the return trip to Ikiri had been a purgatory. The fiery sun had seemed to follow them and the air had been hot and dry. The colonel had been right. Big Boy had approached him before their departure from Ache with a case of French cognac and suggested that they hide it under their luggage. Craig's prompt refusal had plunged Big Boy into a sullen, uncommunicative mood that had lasted throughout the trip.

When they had pulled up at the Rest House the Land Rover had looked as if it had been chipped out of solid laterite and they had both been covered with the red dust. Craig had sent Big Boy off to the Ikiri Hotel with his pocket full of beer money. He had found the invitation to the Queen's birthday party waiting for him in his room.

His first impulse had been to ignore the invitation but then he had noticed the penned note. He told himself it would look best if he appeared. At one single appearance he could show the entire Ikiri community that he had returned from his first field trip.

§ **144**

She introduced Craig to an elderly British professor and his wife and left to attend to the other guests. Craig watched her go, noting the sheen of her chestnut hair, the roll of her hips and the solidity of her tanned calves as she walked toward the buffet.

Ignatius handed him a gin and tonic and he was engaged in a polite, exploratory conversation by the professor.

"Terribly hot today."

"Yes, it was."

"Understand you're in anthropology?"

"Yes, I'm here on a study grant."

"Lucky fellow. I'm stuck here on a teaching contract and can't move around much. Feel like a prisoner in my classroom."

Robert Thompson shuffled up, purple-faced and soaked with perspiration. "Well, Craig! Welcome!"

"Thank you. I almost missed your party. I pulled in this afternoon and just had time to wash off the laterite before coming over."

"Oh hell, should have left it on. Could have come as a bloody redskin—a real American!" Thompson roared with laughter at his own joke, oblivious to the lack of general mirth it produced. He glanced at his wrist watch. "Damn! Just about time for our toast." He rushed off toward the house, spilling some of his drink along the way.

The wincing scratch of a badly placed phonograph needle preceded the first blasting strains of "God Save the Queen." The chatter died in the driveway and all stood still, the British men attempting to pull their paunches in and their heels together in remembrance of their military service, the British women looking a little sad but deadly serious and straight

§ **145**

ahead. The Africans fell into a semi-silence. Some of the women giggled. They received dark looks of warning from their husbands. The children stopped their shouting, fascinated and pleased by the music.

The record ended and the silence was broken by the pop of champagne corks at the buffet. Thompson rushed unsteadily out of the house to grab one of the first glasses and propose the ritual toast to the Queen.

Following the toast there seemed to be a general relaxation. The volume of conversation rose and those who had held back with a forced show of decorum now attacked the bar and buffet with vigor.

"Do you like our party?" Alice Thompson asked. She had come up beside Craig quietly.

"Yes," he said, turning toward her, "very much."

She lifted her hand and pushed her hair away from her neck. She had had several drinks. She felt relaxed and adventurous. Drawing on her past experience she had decided to feel Craig out. For some reason it had suddenly become important to know if he was interested in her.

Craig sensed her mood. He noted the candid look in her eyes and the slight challenge of her smile. The solid contours of her figure under the light summer dress and the odor of her perfume sent a painful, pleasant lance of longing through him.

"Are you going to be in Ikiri long?" she asked, moving away from the main body of guests.

"Not too long," he replied, moving with her. "I expect to head back to Bomasha soon."

"We'd like to see more of you," she said, not meeting his eyes.

He watched her for a moment in silence, the opposition of

his physical longing and professional caution slowing his verbal reflexes.

"We?" he asked finally, a slight smile playing at the corners of his lips.

She raised her head. He saw her anger. "Damn!" she said, "don't toy with me."

"All right, all right," he said quietly. "Let me get you a drink." He took her by the arm and there it was. The spark that cheap song composers write about. The thrill of physical contact that travels like a flash fire, ignites the blood, cuts out the world and feeds on its own sensual promise.

As they walked toward the buffet Craig realized that he was now involved in a second conspiracy—one that could be just as hazardous as the first.

Colonel Durand returned to the south in good spirits. The raid on the Goka village had been successful and he had brought back the captured arms as evidence. If necessary that could be used as evidence of a Goka rebellion. He could also report to the high commissioner and Tibaki that the 6th company was once again a viable unit of the defense force.

Jean Jaurès Tibaki was not in his office. He was speaking at the commencement exercises of a Catholic school for girls on the outskirts of town. The colonel climbed back in his jeep and directed his driver through the dusty streets to the school.

The school was a low cement building isolated in the center of a dusty plain. The ceremonies were taking place outside under the brilliant canopy of a flame tree. The young African girls sat on rows of rough benches before a raised podium where the speakers and officials sat in a solemn cluster, the sun reflecting from their spectacles and the perspiration streaming down their faces. The uniformed girls looked like a field of black-faced daisies. The nuns were dark hummocks in the daisy field.

Colonel Durand saw that Tibaki was busy distributing scholastic prizes. He approached the ceremony and stood in the shade of the flame tree, biding his time.

He was eager to tell Tibaki of the outbreak of violence. He smiled as he remembered the report of his mercenaries. Pierre was out of the way for good. The Goka were stunned and almost helpless and the posters had done their work among the Bomasha. It was a simple thing but the American had been right. The Bomasha were furious. In one village they had poured petrol over two Goka travelers and burned them alive in the emir's compound. The sleeping giant was stretching. All the waiting and plotting would soon be replaced by action.

Tibaki finished the presentations and Kowo, his assistant, tapped him on the arm and indicated the colonel. An official from the Ministry of Education stood to address the students. Tibaki slid out of his chair and left the stand.

Colonel Durand saluted and they shook hands.

"Colonel, I am pleased to see you," Tibaki said, squinting against the leaf-filtered shafts of sun. "But I am surprised to see you here."

"It is something of great importance," Durand said gravely. "It could not wait."

"Ah?" Tibaki said, a frown wrinkling his forehead.

Durand walked several paces away from the nearest bench full of students. "There is trouble in the north."

"What?" Jean Jaurès Tibaki pulled his spectacles off and held his face close to the colonel's. "Impossible! Surely you are mistaken?"

"No. There has been a clash between the Goka and a group of Bomasha. We arrived too late to stop it but I have seized a number of arms that the Goka were hiding."

"My people hiding arms?" Tibaki seemed stunned. He walked a few steps, shaking his head. Then he swung back to the colonel.

"Was anyone hurt?"

"The whole Goka village was wiped out."

"And the Bomasha. You have captured them?"

"No, they must have taken away their dead and wounded."

Tibaki walked unsteadily to one of the nearest benches. The girls looked at him with curiosity and made room for him. The speaker droned on. Kowo stood by his side. The young man watched the colonel closely, suspiciously.

"Oh, my God, oh, my God," Tibaki murmured, staring at the dusty ground and fanning himself with a silk handkerchief.

"I must return to my office to see if there are any further reports," the colonel said.

Tibaki looked up as if in a daze. "Yes, yes, of course. I too must get to my office." He sighed and stood up. "Colonel, we must keep this quiet. We must have a full investigation. This violence must stop."

"Yes, certainly," the colonel agreed. "I shall keep you informed."

"Thank you. Kowo, call for my car."

The colonel's jeep sped back to his headquarters. The American would probably be upset with the speed of his action but he had had enough of waiting. Regardless of his experience, the *Amerlo* was still an amateur and the colonel's plans had no place for amateurs.

His sergeant handed him an envelope. It was a coded telegram from Paris. He shut and locked his office door and opened his safe. Removing a small notebook he took it to his desk and concentrated on the ciphers of the telegram, working slowly but precisely, marking down each word of the message with a blunt lead pencil.

He paused for a moment to wipe the perspiration off his forehead and went immediately back to work. When he had finished he held the sheet of paper before him and read the completed message. He grunted disapprovingly and read the message through again. His hand rose to his face and his fingers began a systematic massaging of his nose.

"No," he said softly, "I don't like it." He struck a match and held it to the corner of the decoded message, watching it absently as it caught and shriveled into ash. He let it drift to the floor and crushed it with his boot. He folded the telegram and placed it in the notebook. He returned the notebook to the safe and locked the safe's heavy door.

Deep in thought he strode to the window and stood with his hands clasped behind his back. He had always followed orders. Now he hesitated. He did not consider murder his business.

Chapter 12

.

Craig was shaving when a boy brought him the telegram. He tipped him, waited for him to leave, and opened the envelope still sticky with glue. "Developments warrant your immediate return. Durand." Craig put down his razor and sat on the edge of his bed. He was puzzled. Not a word about a meeting with Tibaki. He was surprised by the colonel's lack of caution. He expected any message to be couched in terms of his cover—a word about research or the promise of the interview with Tibaki. This telegram had a special tone of urgency. It made Craig uneasy.

"Developments." There was an ominous sound to the word. It couldn't have come at a worse time. He had spent a restless night weighing an important decision. Now that he had decided, the telegram prodded his conscience, a printed proof that his decision was a mistake.

He wiped the lather from his face and pulled on a shirt. His rendezvous with Alice Thompson was set. It was too late to back down. He ran a brush through his short-cropped hair and noted from the mirror that his expression was sober and worried. Maybe nothing would come from their meeting. It was something he had to get out of his system. But the fact remained that a few minutes after receiving an urgent telegram from his collaborator he was running off to meet a woman. It shook his self-confidence a bit, but not enough to change his plans.

When Big Boy arrived with the Land Rover, his previous curiosity over Craig's use of the vehicle was forgotten. He had news. He was excited.

"Trouble," he shouted as Craig met him on the Rest House steps. Craig walked with him back to the Land Rover, away from the Rest House.

"What is it?"

"I talk with one fellah who come in from Bomasha last night," Big Boy explained. "This fellah say Goka and Bomasha been fighting and the defense force running round like crazy shooting here, shooting there."

"Son of a bitch," Craig murmured, frowning.

Big Boy chuckled. "I think war be starting!"

Craig ignored this remark. "Listen," he told Big Boy. "Get ready to leave tomorrow morning. I'll bring the Land Rover back soon and you can check it over for the trip."

Big Boy raised his eyebrows and shrugged his shoulders. "We going back to Bomasha? Now?"

"That's right. Keep your mouth shut, understand? I want to pull out tomorrow before dawn."

"Okay, Mastah, okay with me."

"Good. You have the key?"

"Here."

"Thanks." Craig climbed in the Land Rover and started the engine. "I'll bring it down to the hotel when I get back."

§ 152

Big Boy's curiosity was piqued again. "You going for a ride alone?" Craig had covered this ground before. He didn't bother to answer.

They met by an abandoned shed that had been used to store hemp. It wasn't far from town but it was well hidden in thick bush. She was there when Craig arrived. He saw Thompson's Morris first, parked behind the shed. She was standing nearby, smoking a cigarette. She held a pale yellow lily in her hand. She had taken it from a plant that pushed its shiny leaves through the cracks in the dilapidated shed.

He shut off the ignition and got out. She turned toward him. She was nervously biting her lips. He was committed now and he knew it. He felt the thrill of anticipation mount as he walked toward her. She was wearing a white dress of light tropical material. Her chestnut hair was brushed back from her eyes. It looked damp as if she had just been swimming or had come from a shower. She wore a thin necklace of gold chain.

"Hello," he said, smiling.

She smiled back fleetingly and looked down at the ground. He stepped closer. "Look," she said with her head still down, "maybe this is a mistake."

He caught a scent of her perfume. His eyes traveled from the sheen of her hair down her shoulders to the swell of her breasts. He'd been without a woman for a long time and he had to clear his throat before responding.

"Maybe," he said tonelessly, watching her, waiting.

She sighed deeply, her breasts rising under the thin material of her dress, and looked up. Their eyes met. He moved to her, grasping her thick hair in one hand and taking her into his arms. Their kiss was hot and deep and desperate. She moved in against him and rolled her head back and forth, moaning

§ 153

slightly in his embrace. She broke away finally and put her lips to his neck.

"Come," she said huskily, "I've a blanket."

She led him under the sagging roof of the shed. A blanket was spread on the ground. He kissed her again and her teeth closed gently on his lip.

She pushed herself away, smiled, and turned her back. He unbuttoned her dress and she slipped out of it, neatly folding it and placing her underclothes on top of the pile.

Craig undressed and joined her on the blanket. His need and her eagerness brought them together in a frenzy of violent love-making. Her body was a supple, wild thing that he fought to master. He hammered at her sensuality, heeding the urgent pleas for force. Her nails drew blood, her moan rose in pitch and finally he dominated, feeling her capitulation and fulfillment and all was silence again except for the crackling of the sun-dried jungle leaves and their own heavy breathing.

They lay silent. She with her eyes closed and a smile on her face and he above her, resting on his elbows, holding up the weight of his body. She reached up and brought his head down and they kissed slowly, fully. The silent battle began again—more studied this time but with the same results.

Later she sat and lit a cigarette. He watched her. His experience told him: now comes trouble. He could sense the change in his own attitude. He found himself glancing at the jungle, wondering if anyone was around. He noticed how her eye make-up had smudged, how her breasts were not as full as he had expected. The usual dark moments and second thoughts now that the assault had been carried, the citadel won.

She blew smoke directly out before her without a word. Her eyes looked at nothing.

§ **154**

"That was good," he said, watching her.

She snuffed out her cigarette and lay down beside him. She put her face close to his and ran her hand over his cheek. "It was wonderful," she said softly but the words sounded hollow to both of them.

Their eyes met again and he read a truth in her tears. "Damn you, Michael Craig!" she said suddenly.

He didn't have a chance to reply.

"Sorry," she said quickly, looking away. "I don't mean it."

He sat up and shook his head. "We're pretty much alike, you and I. We'd like to blame others for our problems but we can't."

She smiled then and he put his fist to her chin and gave it a slight push.

"I must get back," she said, rising to dress.

They dressed silently and picked up the blanket. He put his arm around her as they left the hut.

"Are you going back to Bomasha soon?" she asked, recovering her usual voice, becoming once again Mrs. Robert Thompson.

"Yes, very soon."

She folded the blanket and placed it carefully on the back seat of her car. "I wish this hadn't happened," she said suddenly.

"I'm glad it did," he replied.

She came to him and they kissed. She smiled, brushing a wisp of hair from her face. "When will it happen again?" she asked.

"Soon."

She got into her car and started the engine. "Who are you, Mr. Craig?" she asked seriously.

"I am the man who has just made love to you," he said, smiling.

She shrugged. "Fair enough," she replied.

He watched her drive out onto the road before he walked back to the Land Rover. He felt good now. The expected complications had not developed. He had judged Alice Thompson pretty well. No need for love lies. There had been tears but they had been short-lived. He wasn't in love with her. That he knew. But she was his kind of woman.

Alice Thompson drove back toward Ikiri dry-eyed. Her tears were finished. She felt spent but physically at rest. Craig had been a good lover. She was glad that she had kept the rendezvous. Her only regret was the usual feeling of emptiness that settled on her. She felt her eyes moistening. She frowned, gripped the steering wheel tightly and set her mind to the future problems of bringing Craig to her bed. This blanket business was a bit awkward.

Commissioner Innes was surprised to hear that Harvey Klein was back in town. Klein, he thought, must have had just enough time to return to Paris, shower, shave and catch the next plane back to Africa. The commissioner was even more surprised that Klein had insisted on coming directly to his office without waiting for a meeting to be arranged at the American consulate.

The commissioner's curiosity vied with a certain irritation that Klein would pick a Saturday noon to come plunging back into his life, delaying his departure for the club and the period of easy relaxation he looked forward to each week.

He stood by the window looking down on the main street. It was fast emptying as the British sped home to drink their gin and bitters and eat their Saturday curry on the vine-covered terraces of their bungalows while the Africans parked their bicycles against the walls of a thousand small beer gardens to drink their beer and eat their palm-oil chop.

Two huge trailer trucks loaded with hardwood logs labored up the street, forcing the smaller vehicles off the road and leaving a scattering of angry, shouting taxi drivers behind them. There was a fifteen pound fine for driving such trucks through the main part of town. The commissioner shook his head slowly, a slight smile on his face, as the overloaded vehicles passed majestically by his headquarters apparently unseen by the constables on duty at the gate. A man had to master his blood pressure, the commissioner reflected, if he wanted to last in Africa.

A speeding taxi careened around a corner, narrowly missing the rear of one of the trailer trucks, and jerked to a stop before the police building.

The commissioner recognized Klein as he jumped from the cab, paid his bill and walked quickly toward the gate. He turned from the window and walked back to his desk. Something was up, that was a certainty. He sat on the edge of his desk and waited for the sound of footsteps in the corridor. His orderly knocked, entered and went through the formality of announcing Klein. The commissioner asked him to show the visitor in.

"Hello, Commissioner," Klein said, as he entered and they shook hands.

"Welcome back."

"Thanks."

The orderly shut the door. Klein wiped some perspiration from his brow. "Well," he said, "I could have saved myself a trip. It turns out I just missed a message that had been sent to me from Paris. They were quite surprised to see me when I walked in. Once they explained the situation it was a question of catching the next return plane. To make it short—Craig is a patsy."

"A what?"

"A patsy, a fall guy. He's just another part of the general plan to make Bomasha a complete international mess in the next few months."

Commissioner Innes frowned and sat down behind his desk. "I'm afraid you'll have to be a bit more explicit."

Klein sat down and yawned. "Excuse me, I'm bushed," he said rubbing his eyes. "French security picked up one of the big boys. He's a banker with a fine family, a chateau in the country and close government connections. He chose to talk and what he said was confirmed by the papers in his private safe. As an interesting sidelight to the over-all plan they decided to involve an American—an American with previous official status—and have him up to his ears in their Bomasha operation. Then, and this is what brings me back in such a hurry, the American is to be killed, murdered to be exact, in the most compromising situation possible, to indicate official American meddling in Bomasha."

"So!" the commissioner said, sitting straight in his chair.

"This whole thing," Klein continued, "didn't add up to me from the start. We know most of these people and I have never been able to convince myself that they would trust an American to work for them. Now, for the first time, the pieces fall together and it begins to make sense."

"Are you sure . . ."

"We're as positive as we can be."

"My God, this is serious." The commissioner got up and paced between his desk and the open window. All thought of the club had faded from his mind. "How much time do we have? Are there any dates?"

"No. Our source couldn't even give us an estimate."

"Is Colonel Durand involved?"

"I don't know. They seem to have kept the plan very quiet. Only a few of them know about it. One letter made a disparaging remark about the colonel's 'outdated sense of honor.' Maybe he's refused to go along with them."

"You don't sound very reassuring. I suppose a professional has been hired for the job?"

"Yes, but we don't know which one."

"Which one?"

"The two mercenaries. We're sure one of them has been chosen to kill Craig. But, damn it, we don't know which one."

The commissioner sat on the window sill, his arms folded. "Well," he asked, "what are your plans?"

Klein removed his glasses and shut his eyes. He rubbed his forehead slowly. "I've got carte blanche to handle this any way I see fit. The only answer is to get Craig out of Africa and the sooner the better."

"If he is on this side of the border it will be fairly simple. I'll have my people pick him up and deliver him to you all wrapped and ready for shipment."

"Yes, that would be ideal. Now that we've picked up one of theirs they'll realize we've also gotten our hands on some information. They'll be in a hurry to wind things up. I've got to reach Craig in time, the goddamn fool!"

"Does Hargrove know about all this?"

"I'm sure he does by now. The message they sent to me from Paris must have been received and decoded at the consulate but he has orders to keep hands off and take his lead from me."

§ **159**

"Poor old Tom, he must be in a real swivet about all this."

"Well," Klein said with a grim smile, "Hargrove is the least of my worries."

"Yes, quite." The commissioner rubbed his chin, thinking. "And the French?" he asked. "Are they going to help?"

Klein laughed abruptly. "It depends which French you're talking about. Their security people have helped us quite a bit already. Their intelligence boys are lukewarm. In fact, I detected a certain amusement among them that one of our black sheep had gone so far astray. As to their military intelligence, the less said the better. I have the feeling half of them would be pleased to do the job on Craig themselves."

"Yes, I dare say." The commissioner walked to a wall cabinet, opened it and took out his cap. He put it on slowly. He pulled out his black leather regulation belt and holster. He shook the belt before swinging it around his waist and several large flies buzzed lazily toward the ceiling. "Local leather— not cured properly," he stated flatly. He went back to his desk and took a key out of one of the drawers. With it he opened the metal arms locker near the office safe. He selected a regulation revolver and a clean white lanyard. He clipped the lanyard snap to the butt ring of the revolver, passed the loop over his shoulder, pushed the revolver into his holster and secured the leather safety flap.

The commissioner turned to Klein. "A few days ago I would have been most reluctant to go bashing about the country with you in search of Mr. Craig. Things being what they are, however, I think we'd best get a move on."

Chapter 13

.

Big Boy suffered from a beer hang-over but he climbed from his sagging bed and fought his way with difficulty out of its ragged mosquito net. He had finally bedded down with one of Magabian's house whores, a woman named Beatrice with an enormous, muscular bottom.

Now as he stood swaying by the side of the bed he admired her in the half light of dawn. She lay on her stomach. The smooth black mountain of her buttocks brought a tender smile of appreciation to Big Boy's hard face.

He threw some water over his head, gathered up his baggage and tiptoed out the door. He hadn't paid Beatrice. The way he looked at it she ought to pay him.

He fought Magabian's front-door lock, banging and cursing at it until it finally yielded. He breathed deeply, cleansing his lungs of the close air in the hotel. He had prepared the Land Rover for their trip. Oil, water, all was in order. Yawning, he climbed in and wound up the engine with no regard for Magabian's sleepy guests.

Magabian heard the engine of his Land Rover start and

his sleepy, fat face reflected the contradictions of his tumbling thoughts. He reached to his bedside table, took a bar of chocolate and unwrapped it. A fly lit on the discarded wrapper. Magabian smashed it with a swift, downward movement of his chubby fist.

Later in the morning, when an African constable came in to ask if he had seen Big Boy Eniki or the American, Magabian beamed with pleasure. Yes, he had seen them and he could tell the authorities quite a few things, including the story of a stolen Land Rover. But he must see a British police officer. He had no intention of being questioned by an African.

Big Boy told Craig about the Bomasha ferry. It had not appeared on the Ikiri bank for twenty-four hours. Rumors from Bomasha had it that the ferry had been confiscated by the defense force and that all traffic had been interrupted.

"What about the passes that Durand gave us?" Craig asked.

"Our passes be fine," Big Boy said, concentrating on his driving, "but we don't get this Rover across at ferry landing. But not to worry, Mastah. I know bridge upriver that go take us."

Craig examined the map he held open on his knees. "I don't see a bridge marked here."

Big Boy swung the Land Rover off the main road onto a small dirt track leading north along the river bank. "This bridge not on any map." He laughed and gunned the Land Rover forward along the road between the ocher spires of abandoned anthills.

Hours later they pulled to a stop beside the river. The Land Rover's engine steamed and clicked as they sat in the shade. Evening was close and a slight breeze blew from the north. Big Boy slumped behind the wheel, frowning and wiping the dust from his eyes. Craig's throat felt like a dried streambed. They had been traveling for some time over an overgrown track, thick with bush and pitted with potholes.

Big Boy lifted his hand and pointed a finger toward the river. "Here be old bridge. We go across easy."

Craig licked his dry lips and strained to see the bridge. He could see some thin trestles. Looking closer he noted that one of the trestle uprights had come loose from its foundation and was swaying with the force of the current.

"What bridge is this?" he asked Big Boy.

"This be old railroad bridge for banana plantation. They have one small puff engine bring bananas over from Bomasha. Now the engine be finish."

"How about border guards?"

Big Boy grinned through his thick coating of dust. "Not to worry," he said, "this good crossing for changing brandy and cigarettes. Police get plenty dash money. Beside, they tell all people bridge fall down long ago."

Big Boy knelt in his seat and dug into his rucksack. He sat down again and blew some dust off the blue steel of his Smith & Wesson. He put a small package of cartridges on his lap and proceeded to load the revolver. He sensed Craig watching him and shook his head.

"I don't worry about police but smuggler fellahs carry shotguns an' be nervous, too much."

Craig watched Big Boy's blunt fingers push the stubby cartridges into the chamber of the revolver. He in turn knelt on his seat and dug into his haversack until he had found his Colt and its cartridge supply. He laid both packages on the floor boards and unscrewed the top of their big, canvas-

§ **163**

covered water bottle. He drank, looking out at the flickering screen of leaves and the river that moved past them like a sluggish wash of diluted clay.

He didn't like the situation: the urgency of Colonel Durand's telegram and the reported outbreak of trouble in Bomasha confirmed by the closing down of the ferry. It looked to him as if someone had jumped the gun. The detour they had been forced to take put them another day away from contacting Durand. Craig rubbed the stubble on his chin and thought about the colonel. The possibility of a complete double cross hovered in his mind. He probably should have known better than to trust the colonel. But why, if Durand was at fault, had he sent the telegram? He thought of the twenty-five thousand dollars nestled in cool security in Switzerland. Linked with it was the memory of another rule he had learned in World War II. "When an operation begins to crumble, get out and get out fast! Don't try to put the pieces together again!" That was good advice—at the time— but it didn't quite apply now.

He got out of the Land Rover and stretched his legs. He pulled his binoculars from the luggage. Hunched over on the warm hood of the vehicle he scanned the trestles of the small railway bridge.

"You sure we can drive across? Won't our wheels get caught between the ties?"

Big Boy glanced over his shoulder at the bridge. "No, I cross many times."

Craig played his binoculars along the opposite bank. The trail leading away from the bridge on the Bomasha side was lined with row upon row of thick-stalked banana trees. Their wide yellow-green leaves formed a canopy over the empty trail. It looked like a cool, protected tunnel.

§ **164**

"I'm in charge here," the colonel said, fixing them both with angry eyes. "I don't want you to forget it."

The two mercenaries stood before him in the clearing, several yards from the road and the parked convoy of defense force vehicles. They listened quietly. The South African blew a chain of smoke rings into the still air and smiled. The short Frenchman shrugged his shoulders.

"We understand that, my Colonel," he said, "but you know yourself that these orders came from Paris."

"I don't care!" the colonel shouted. "We're not in the business of murder. Not while I'm in command."

Peter, the South African, cleared his throat and spoke in halting French. "Colonel, I fully recognize that you are in command. I only ask what difference the death of this American would make?"

The colonel glared for a moment at the South African. "I did not come here to argue," he said sharply. "You have your orders. Michel," the colonel addressed his countryman, "I wish to speak to you alone."

As the two walked a short distance away, the South African dropped his cigar and ground it into the dirt with his boot heel. "You have your orders," he murmured to himself, "and I, my dear pompous Colonel, have mine."

Alice Thompson was surprised to see her husband up so early. He sat over his tea, puffy-eyed and irritable, lighting cigarettes and absently snuffing them out. She sat down across from him and attempted a noncommittal "Good morning, Robert."

He glanced her way, nodded, as he would to one of his African clerks and replied, "Yes, quite."

She decided not to push the conversation and concentrated

on eating her pawpaw. He fidgeted with his cigarette, sipped some more tea and suddenly looked at her as if she had just come into his field of vision.

"Damn," he said resentfully, "haven't got enough problems around here. Now that bloody bore Innes is coming down."

"The commissioner?"

"Humph," he replied, affirming the question.

"Will he stay for lunch?"

"By God! That's a woman for you! Will he stay for lunch? Every time he shows up it means complications and trouble and all you can think of is 'will he stay for lunch'! How the bloody hell do I know? The stupid Highlander thinks he's a second Sherlock Holmes."

She watched her husband patiently, without interrupting. For a moment she visualized the rise of his blood pressure as the thin red line of a thermometer climbing up and up and she was secretly amused.

"It's that damn American. You know, Craig, the chap you invited to our reception."

"We both invited him."

"Well, all right. The point is that Innes is after him for some fool reason and when I mentioned that he'd been here Innes reacted as if I were the leader of a gunrunning gang."

"I don't see what Mr. Craig could have done."

"Don't be so stupid! I suppose you thought him handsome. That's all you need—a handsome American. As far as I'm concerned, the Yanks mean nothing but trouble. The more innocent they look, the more trouble you can expect."

Thompson pushed his teacup aside and buttoned his shirt over the large fold of stomach that hid his belt. "I daresay you imagined Craig as a fine between-the-sheets savory," Thompson said maliciously.

"Robert," Alice Thompson said slowly, white-lipped, "that was uncalled for."

"Don't 'Robert' me, Milady. I know what runs through that lily-white mind of yours. Expect to find you wrestling with one of the houseboys any day now."

"Robert!" Alice Thompson sat erect and stiff. She bit her lower lip but the tears couldn't be held back. They glided down her cheek rapidly and she wiped them from her chin with a napkin.

He glanced over at her, saw the tears and reddened. He rose awkwardly from the table, and shuffled about the terrace aimlessly. He broke the embarrassing silence by calling for his houseboy. "Ignatius," he shouted, "clear the table."

"Yes, Mastah," Ignatius replied, appearing on the terrace with a fixed, meaningless smile on his face and a toothpick held tightly in the middle of his mouth.

As Ignatius cleared the table Robert Thompson glanced again at his wife. She was still sitting stiffly erect but her head had fallen and she was holding one hand over her forehead in an effort to hide the tears.

"Well," Thompson said, clearing his throat, "I must be off. Work to do." He waited for Ignatius to leave the terrace and moved closer to his wife. "Sorry," he said, putting his hand on her shoulder. She recoiled from his touch so rapidly it made him jump. "Damn," he muttered under his breath. Without another word he turned and left for his office.

The commissioner and Harvey Klein landed on the Ikiri air strip an hour later. "Come on," the commissioner shouted to Klein, "I want to see if we can pick up Craig now."

"Fine," Klein replied, wiping his glasses. He was relieved to get out of the small police aircraft that had brought them to

Ikiri. The pilot seemed to have found his way to Ikiri by following the flow of innumerable rivers and as they constantly changed direction the sun had danced around the light plane like a golden ball.

Within half an hour of landing they knew that Craig had left and they were listening impatiently as Robert Thompson told them what he knew of the American. As he knew very little, he embellished his tale with rumor and shaky flights of imagination. As far as the commissioner was concerned, it was all beside the point. He wanted help from the district officer, not a rambling, disconnected recital of conjecture and speculation. He knew about Thompson's drinking but he was shocked to see how much it obviously affected his ability to tie thoughts and words together.

The commissioner cleared his throat and interrupted the drone of Thompson's self-satisfied voice. "Robert, I'm sorry if I seem to be continually in a rush but we have to be off shortly and I should like to tie up a few loose ends."

Thompson stopped speaking and looked at the commissioner, a vague smile on his face. "Certainly, Malcolm. I understand. You must find your American. Why, I can't imagine. Enough bloody Americans running around Africa today without searching them out." Thompson laughed and pushed his bulging shirt further into his walking shorts. "Oh," he said, glancing uneasily at Klein, "sorry."

"I'm sorry to be mysterious about Craig," the commissioner said, "but I must find him. I'm depending on you to help pass the word along the border. Mind you, I don't want a man hunt with every Goka fisherman out looking for a reward and Craig's head delivered in a sack. I just want some responsible men on the lookout and I want to be notified the minute they have a thread of information."

"Certainly, certainly," Thompson repeated, scratching his forearm.

"I suggest your forestry and game people might help. Seems to me there are some intelligent young chaps working close to the border. They've helped us out with some smuggling troubles in the past."

Robert Thompson suddenly looked belligerent. His bushy black eyebrows descended slowly and he pursed his lips. "I presume the police will be doing their bit?" he asked coldly.

Commissioner Innes was in no mood for Thompson's sarcasm. A sudden flame of Scot's temper brought him to his feet. He looked down at Thompson, his knuckles showing white where he grasped his swagger stick. "That was a bloody stupid remark, Robert!" he said slowly, glaring at the district officer.

Robert Thompson shrugged his shoulders. He got to his feet and glanced meekly at Klein. "I'm afraid no one seems to understand my little jokes," he said, sighing.

"I can do without such jokes," the commissioner replied, picking up his cap.

"Well, I shall get word to my forestry people. The game types will take a bit longer; I'm afraid our communications aren't very good."

"It's most important that I know the minute Craig comes back across the border."

"Yes, certainly, Malcolm. I say, how about a bash of brandy? I believe there's a bottle stashed away somewhere in the office."

"No thanks, we must be off. I'm taking a run over to the Bomasha ferry and up along the river border to check some of my posts."

"Very well, another time."

§ 169

"Yes, goodby."

"Cheerio, Malcolm. Goodby, Mr. Klein."

Robert Thompson stood for a moment looking out the door, watching the heat shimmer over the gravel walk. He waited till the police Land Rover carrying the commissioner had turned off onto the road and disappeared from sight. He walked back to his desk and sat down heavily in his chair, scratching violently at one forearm and then the other. The flabby undersides of each forearm were mottled with the heat and the sudden scratching was turning them scarlet.

Thompson grimaced as he scratched. He glanced overhead at the motionless ceiling fan. Must get that thing fixed, he thought, should do something about it today. He sighed and put his hand on the telephone. There it rested for a full minute, his fingers tapping out a tattoo of indecision. Finally they tightened around the receiver and he churned the bell crank with his other hand.

"Hello, hello, this is the D.O. Get me the forestry office—I want to speak with the foreman." Thompson waited, patient and inert, with his eyes closed. At the rasp of a voice, his tired eyes opened. "Hello, forestry? That you, Ajali?" He waited, listening, the thick eyebrows climbing up, up. "What? To his village? Damn! Who gave him permission? . . . Oh yes, I suppose I did. Well, yes. Very good. I'll speak to him when he gets back. Goodby."

Thompson replaced the telephone, slowly, frowning. "Balls!" he said aloud. He glanced at his watch. "Well," he said, brightening, "I do believe it's time for a little drinky."

Chapter 14

:

"Damn!" Commissioner Innes paced back and forth over the pounded-mud floor of the Ikiri police post, punching his fist into the open palm of his other hand. "Just missed the two of them! What rotten luck!"

Harvey Klein had changed from his suit into light khaki slacks and an open-neck shirt. He stood before the post's wall map of the territory, studying the roads.

"I didn't realize there were so many roads to the Bomasha River," he said, running his finger over the bug track of a red road line that ended at the thick green serpentine of the river.

"With the ferry out you can bet that Eniki is not using the main road," the commissioner said, putting his big, bony hand next to Klein's and tapping his fingers on the ganglion of several small road lines. "We might as well give up hope of catching them this side of the border. If London and Paris answer our telegrams soon, and they get that blasted ferry moving, we'll be able to nip across into Bomasha tonight."

Klein turned from the map and lit a cigarette. He took off

§ 171

his glasses and wiped them with a handkerchief. He glanced at the two leather-bound volumes on the nearby table. He had had one hell of a time getting through the binding but his hunch had been rewarding.

He picked up the pile of one-hundred-dollar greenbacks. "I think we better put these into a safe," he suggested.

"Yes, you're right," the commissioner agreed. "I'll see if we can get those bindings sewn up again. It won't be as good a job."

"As long as we get them back on the shelf in one piece."

The commissioner took the greenbacks and put them into a small metal strongbox. He locked the box into the police post safe.

"Craig's worked out his cover pretty well; books on anthropology, native carvings, a few old maps, but not one thing that really points to what he's really doing. Do you think we'll be able to get him out?"

"Well, when our people contact the French officially and Tibaki hears about this I'm sure we'll get some sort of help. What Colonel Durand will do, however, is another kettle of fish. With Craig playing the hunted fugitive it won't be easy."

"Well," Klein said, replacing his glasses, "shall we talk to the hotel owner?"

"My God, glad you brought that up. I'd almost forgotten him."

The commissioner called the constable standing outside the door and asked him to show Magabian into the office. Magabian had dressed for the occasion. He had on a porous white cotton shirt and cream-colored flannel trousers. A blue necktie stamped with the golden insignia of a British motor club held the curled collar of his shirt together. He wore a pair of magenta socks under his sandal straps. Magabian was subdued. He shook hands with both of them in a manner that suggested they were all involved in a very serious matter.

"Sit down, please, Mr. Magabian," the commissioner said, moving behind the desk. "Mr. Klein works for the American government. He and I are both most interested in hearing all you know in relation to Mr. Michael Craig and Big Boy Eniki."

"Yes sir, Mr. Commissioner," Magabian said in a dramatic undertone. He paused to roll his watery eyes toward the ceiling, obviously putting his thoughts in order. "Well," he continued, leaning forward over the creased melon of his stomach, "this Eniki chap is no good. I can tell you, he is a thief and a scoundrel. Many times I have known him to brag of the young Ikiri girls he has taken in the forest." Magabian licked his lips, searching for the words to describe the scene in his mind. "Yes, he has told me. He catches them cutting grass and he comes up from behind, throws their skirt over their head and—"

"Yes, quite," the commissioner interrupted dryly, "but we are interested now in when you first saw the American, Craig, with Eniki and what they did or what you heard them talking about."

"Eniki told me the American was a leader of mobsters!"

"A gangster?"

"Yes, Eniki told me he was from Chicago, where he had a yacht and the police were so afraid of him that they let him leave the country any time he pleased."

The commissioner glanced at Klein, who shrugged his shoulders and frowned at Magabian.

§ **173**

"I say!" Magabian said suddenly, snapping his plump fingers. "I almost forgot the most important thing. Mr. Craig no sooner arrived than they stole my Land Rover!"

"How did they manage that?" the commissioner asked.

"Eniki threatened me with death," Magabian said gravely, his brown eyes taking on a sad, spaniel cast.

"What did he say?"

"Commissioner," Magabian replied, straightening in his seat with indignation, "he said he would smash my head."

"Why didn't you report this?"

He slumped back to his original position, avoiding their eyes. "Well . . . I felt the police have many crimes to work on and I, as a good citizen, had no right to bother them with . . ."

The commissioner cleared his throat and flushed a red deeper than his normal sunburn.

"Look here, Magabian, save your little speeches for Empire Day. I know how much illegal brandy you bring over from Bomasha each month and I also know how you trade watered whisky in return. There are a few other things on your record that you may have forgotten. We haven't."

Magabian suddenly lost much of his color.

"Now," the commissioner said, "answer yes or no to the following questions. Did Craig ever speak to you or did you ever hear him speak of his business?"

"No, sir," Magabian replied, clasping his hands before him. "I only just met the gentleman at the Queen's birthday reception."

"Did Big Boy ever discuss his plans?"

"Yes. That is, he mentioned how happy he was to work with Mr. Craig. Early on he talked about showing people he was a big man. Oh, I knew that Big Boy was a bad black, a real bushman! And now they've taken my car."

§ **174**

"Did Big Boy say where they had gone? Did he mention the name of a town or a village in Bomasha?"

"No, no, I do not recall it. But he spoke of the Goka. Said they were animals and told me about their stinking villages."

"That will be all, Mr. Magabian, thank you."

Magabian looked from one of them to the other, his hands making futile circles in the air. "I want you to know I shall help all I can, Mr. Commissioner. It is not only because they took my car. I am a respecter of the law. I am a British citizen, a loyal subject of Her Majesty—"

"Yes," Commissioner Innes said, standing up, "we all know that, don't we?"

Magabian rose and turned to Harvey Klein. "I also have a cousin in America. He is a rich man."

Klein nodded, smiling, and shook the proffered hand. It was moist with perspiration.

"Oh, one other thing, Magabian," the commissioner said casually. "I suppose Big Boy is still armed?"

"Armed?" Magabian said, smiling through his feigned puzzlement.

The commissioner slapped his swagger stick against his shorts with a smart crack and his eyes fixed on Magabian, cold and hard. "Come off it!" he snapped. "We know you sold him a Smith & Wesson service revolver and ammunition to go with it."

Magabian looked crushed. He extended his short arms on both sides of his body in a gesture of despair and hurt pride. "But, Commissioner, I don't know . . ."

"All right, if that's the way you prefer it. But listen carefully, Magabian, not one word of all this to anyone—particularly to newspapermen. Not one word about Craig or Big Boy or our little meeting tonight. Understand?"

§ **175**

"Yes, yes, Commissioner, you can depend on me."

"Stick close to your hotel; we'll want to talk to you again. Goodby."

Innes waited for the door to close before exploding. "The bloody cheek of that bastard. Trying to put me off. He's been fairly harmless recently and we've left him alone. You ought to see his file. Tried to jump on the Jerry bandwagon during the war, jumped off that soon enough and tried the Vichy types and when their sun set he wrapped himself in the Union Jack. Lately he's been nosing around to see if it's time to change horses again. Can't quite picture him as a champion of African independence but I'm sure he'll manage."

The phone on the desk buzzed and the commissioner picked it up. "Yes, Innes here. Yes, all right." He listened without speaking for a minute or more, tapping his swagger stick against the desk lamp. At one point he winked at Klein and nodded his head. "Yes, very good. He's right here." The commissioner put his hand over the mouthpiece. "Well, we've got the go-ahead. We're authorized to go into Bomasha. The French weren't too pleased but there's not much they can do. They're putting Tom Hargrove on now. He wants to talk to you."

Klein took the receiver. Soon he heard the nervous, guarded voice of the American consul.

"Hello, Klein?"

"Yes, how are you?"

"Fine. Listen . . . uh, on this business. Ah . . . we must tell Tibaki what's going on."

"Yes, I see."

"Do you think . . . er, is there a chance you can find . . . the man you're looking for?"

"We hope there's a chance."

§ **176**

There was a sudden clicking and a snatch of local dialect, then the consul's shocked voice. "My God, this is supposed to be a secure police line! Hello, hello, Klein, are you still there?"

"Yes."

"Well, we'd better be careful. I'll say goodby. Oh, good luck."

"Thanks." Klein hung up, shaking his head. "What a circus!"

"Well, we're all ready," the commissioner suggested. "I'm taking a radio-equipped police wagon in addition to my own. According to headquarters they've put the ferry back into operation and Colonel Durand's defense force is to give us full cooperation."

"Very funny."

"Not really, old boy, not really. I suggest we have dinner on the road. What say you?"

"I agree, Commissioner . . . wholeheartedly."

Robert Thompson came into his house humming to himself. He shouted for a drink, pulled off his shirt and collapsed into a chair with a sigh, rubbing the sparse dark hair of his chest. Evening was the time he liked best. By then he had built his alcoholic cushion against the world and it carried him through what was left of the day. He heard his wife moving in her room and he decided to speak with her—as soon as he was served his drink. He stood up, swaying slightly, and accepted a glass of brandy and water from Ignatius.

She was sitting in a low chair, reading, when he entered. Her chestnut hair was pulled up into an unruly pile on top of her head. She was wearing white sharkskin shorts and a loose halter. Her husband stood for a moment without speaking, his eyes traveling over her body.

§ **177**

"So, got the bikini on again," he remarked, frowning.

She put her book aside and took off her reading glasses, folded them slowly and watched her husband. "It's not a bikini, Robert," she replied patiently.

"Well, who gives a damn," he said, smiling the liquor-etched, false grin she was so familiar with. "What are you reading?"

"A novel."

He walked over, lifted the book and glanced at its jacket. "Written by a Yank, eh? Should think you'd get tired of such trash. Always the same themes—their sad life as a child or their 'horrible' wartime experiences."

He threw the book onto the bed and sipped at his drink, eyeing the firm white circle of her breast showing along the edge of the halter. He sat on the arm of the chair and cautiously ran his arm over its top till his fingers were close to her bare shoulder.

"Well, I guess our friend, Innes, the Guinness drinker, is being led a merry chase. Stupid bloody Scot! Thinks he can come dashing down here into my district and start giving me orders. I'm not one of his black constables!"

He inched his fingers forward and rested them lightly on his wife's tanned shoulder. She tensed automatically but he preferred to ignore it. He slipped his hand further onto her shoulder and she moved forward in her chair, temporarily out of his reach.

He flushed, gripping his glass and reached out for her but she stood up quickly and he lunged forward, off balance, and fell into the vacant chair, spilling his drink over himself and the floor.

He looked up at her, breathing hard, his lips working, and

§ **178**

saw the disgust on her face. Two of the buttons on his shirt had popped off with the strain of his sudden move. The flabby pink bag of his paunch protruded over his wrinkled trousers.

"You bloody bitch," he panted through clenched teeth. "You're fair asking for it. Been visiting any hemp sheds lately?"

She couldn't hide a quick look of fear.

"That's it," he went on, noting her reaction with the sure instinct of a chronic alcoholic. "I may be your drunken Robert but I know a thing or two."

He recovered himself, cleared his throat and sat up straight. The smile reappeared. He reached out toward her. "Come here, Alice," he said softly, putting his glass aside, avoiding her eyes. "You and I can discuss this like adults."

There was no movement. His wife was staring at him in disbelief. He saw the tears filling her eyes but they didn't dim the look of pure hate. He winced, searching for appropriate words. She left the room. He heard the bathroom door slam behind her.

He shook his head slowly and reached for his drink. He drank down all that remained in the glass and walked unsteadily to the bathroom door. He thought he could hear her crying. He tapped on the door gently.

"Alice," he said contritely, "I'm sorry. I didn't mean what I said." There was no answer and he pounded on the door with his fist and shouted. "Alice, don't you hear me? Stop crying!"

There were more choking sounds. Then her voice came through the door with the keeness of a rapier. "I'm not crying, Robert! I'm being sick!"

He stood away from the door, his mouth working, beads of

§ **179**

perspiration on his forehead. He turned and walked into the living room. He opened the liquor cabinet and poured himself a fresh glass of brandy, this time without water.

"They don't understand. None of them understand," he said to himself in a puzzled tone. He gulped down three quarters of his brandy. "Well, then," he stated as if reason had returned to the world, "bugger them all."

Chapter 15

．

Jean Jaurès Tibaki walked back and forth behind his desk as he spoke. The Goka notables who crowded his small office nodded in agreement with his words or murmured darkly in support of his negative remarks. "Anarchy will not be tolerated here," he stated firmly, pausing to remove his spectacles. "There are forces that wish to destroy our nation before it is born. We will not allow it!" He sat down hard behind his desk. "We will not allow it," he restated with less certainty.

He busied himself with his glasses, wiping them with his handkerchief. Taking his silence as a signal, most of the notables rose, bowed once toward Tibaki and backed toward the door and out of the office.

Finally there was only one man left. A young man with light brown skin and curly hair the color of gray dust. The doors were closed and the two were left alone. Tibaki replaced his glasses and glanced over his desk lamp at the young man. "My dear Kowo," the future prime minister said quietly, speaking in French, "they are all fools. You are the only one I can talk to truthfully."

Kowo lighted a cigarette and listened.

"Freedom," Tibaki continued, "is ever harder to find. The fools who just left heard what I said but did not understand. Their freedom is the right to go after the Bomasha with machetes."

The young man smiled and nodded. "It is sad," he said.

"There is not much we can do," Tibaki continued. "I cannot trust the defense force and thus there is little we can do openly. The police report on the fishing village raid points to defense force participation." He was silent for a moment, thinking. He turned to his record player and soon the soft cool notes of Brubeck spread through the dark room. Tibaki smiled, tilting his head and tapping on the top of his desk. Still tapping, he spoke over the sound of the mellow, calculated discords.

"Kowo, I want you and your people to seize Colonel Durand." Tibaki glanced up at his friend. "The Colonel despises me. I am, to him, a symbol of what he hates in Africa. So be it. But I am well aware that he is playing a double role here. I could not prove it in court but that does not bother me. Without him the defense force loses its brain—an extremely desirable condition under the present circumstances."

The young man smiled and blew a quivering smoke ring into the still air of the stuffy office. "Agreed," he stated flatly.

"This," Tibaki continued, "is a job for you and a few of your most dependable companions. Avoid violence. Avoid bloodshed. I want the colonel to disappear for a time. I shall leave the technical planning to you. In the meantime I shall scream to the world of our situation—to the U.N., to the Russians, to the Americans, to the British . . ." The little man

§ 182

paused and smiled, slowly shooting the cuffs of his white silk shirt. ". . . and even to our friends in Paris.

"You know, Kowo, it has already begun. The British police commissioner from across the border and an American agent will be here shortly to search for the American who came to Bomasha as an anthropologist. I do not have the details but Paris has requested us to cooperate with them. Our territory has become an international hunting ground."

"Our territory has become a land of warring anthills," the young man said bitterly. "There is smoke rising over the villages in the north and our own people no longer heed our commands."

Jean Jaurès Tibaki shook his head sadly. "For years I have been working and hoping. I have watched people, white and black, laugh at me openly and behind my back but this was only a further goad to remain, to hold tight. Someone once said that freedom must be fought for and won. This is both true and false. I feel like a fisherman who has sacrificed both his arms to a hungry shark and is waiting in fear and pain for the shark to digest his offering and return for more. Maybe," Tibaki said doubtfully, "freedom is not worth our trouble." Resolve returned to his voice. "We must try, Kowo, we must try."

The young man stood up, stepped over to the desk and clasped Tibaki by the hand. For the first time he noticed that tears glistened behind the gold-rimmed spectacles. The record player clicked and Brubeck gave way to Gillespie.

Craig and Big Boy drove south along the Bomasha bank of the river. Big Boy had been the first to point out the red glow of fire along the horizon. Both of them had heard the sound of shouting and far-off rifle fire.

§ **183**

Big Boy spun the wheel suddenly and pulled the Land Rover off the road behind a clump of oil palms. Two defense force trucks came careening toward them, headlights blazing, their occupants loosing random shots into the night. They both climbed out of the Land Rover and fell flat in the dust. One of the trucks skidded to a stop a few hundred feet away. Big Boy silently thumbed back the hammer of his revolver. Craig crawled a few feet away from Big Boy for a better view of the road. He brought his Colt up, his arm free and ready before him.

They heard the shouting, laughing men relieving themselves, the crash of a breaking bottle and a few shouts of angry commands. The truck ground into motion again and rolled on down the road, a fast-disappearing pinpoint of light.

Big Boy pushed himself up on one elbow, shaking his head. "They go bush, those soldiers!" he said puzzled.

"Come on," Craig said, "let's get moving. The sooner we find Durand, the better."

They continued south, hearing the ominous sound of far-off firing throughout the night and the early dawn. The sun hopped into place against the clear sky as if a puppeteer had pushed it up on a stick from behind the garishly painted backdrop of the jungle.

Craig took the wheel and let Big Boy sleep. As he drove he reflected on Colonel Durand's comment of "the sleeping giant." From what he had seen in the last twenty-four hours, Durand's sleeping giant awoke too easily. He glanced at himself in the rearview mirror. His hair and beard had grown in the last few days, gray hairs dominating the black. His skin was tan under its primary coat of sunburn. He reached down with one hand and loosened the laces of his rubber-soled, canvas-top boots without taking his eyes off the road. He had put his Colt .38 into one of the broad pockets of his bush jacket. He reached down and unbuttoned the pocket flap as he applied the brakes.

The defense force radio jeep was parked at a crossroads. He could see the soldiers sitting around a smoldering fire, heating their rations. As he slowed and rolled to a stop they scrambled to their feet and leveled the blunt muzzles of their automatic weapons at the strangers.

Big Boy awoke and rubbed his eyes. "Sweet Jesus," he murmured, watching the tense trigger fingers. A tall sergeant detached himself from the group and came forward. He stopped at a safe distance and motioned for them to get out of the Land Rover.

Craig forced a smile and held his safe conduct pass out to the sergeant. The sergeant saluted Craig hesitantly, in deference to his white skin and accepted the safe conduct pass. He examined it closely. Finally he smiled and nodded his head. The submachine guns lowered.

"Have food with us," the sergeant offered, indicating the tins being heated by the fire.

"Thank you," Craig replied, breathing a secret sigh of relief.

Squatting on their haunches they shared the soldiers' rations. The Bomasha watched them with curiosity. The sergeant told them there was much trouble in the country.

"I must contact Colonel Durand," Craig told the sergeant. He pointed at the jeep's aerial. "Can I use your radio?"

The sergeant pondered the question for a moment. He seemed puzzled, unable to make up his mind.

"Damn fool don't know how to use that radio," Big Boy muttered.

The sergeant put aside his half-finished tin of rations, wiped

§ **185**

his mouth and walked to the jeep. Craig followed. The sergeant switched on the radio, put on the earphones, and picked up the mouthpiece. The radio hummed and whined. The sergeant turned some dials, reduced the whining and began calling in Bomasha. He repeated his call signal several times, waiting for a response. Finally a gravel voice rasped in reply and conversation went on, back and forth, interrupted by static. Craig lit his pipe and Big Boy fidgeted.

They heard the name Durand mentioned several times in the flow of incomprehensible Bomasha. Craig waited patiently with his back against the canvas covering of the jeep. The sergeant reached out and tapped him on the arm without turning from the radio or halting his conversation. Craig moved closer. The sergeant smiled and handed him the earphones and the mouthpiece. There was a humming void. He heard someone cough.

"Zebra here, Zebra here," a voice erupted in slightly accented English. "Do you read me?"

Surprised, Craig fumbled for the transfer switch, found it and spoke. "Craig here, Craig here," he shouted into the mouthpiece. "Who is Zebra? Who is Zebra?"

There was more silence and a steady clicking. Then the voice came on again speaking slowly, spacing the words. "A . . . fellow worker, Craig. Fellow worker—and friend of the colonel."

Craig listened, frowning. He knew now that he was speaking with one of the mercenaries. "Urgent I see Durand," Craig replied. "Urgent I see Durand."

"Roger, can do. Put the sergeant on. Put on the sergeant."

Craig passed the earphones and the mouthpiece back to the sergeant, who resumed rattling off long sentences in Bomasha.

Craig relit his dead pipe and wondered about the mercenaries. He must have spoken with the South African. The slight accent was not that of an English-speaking Frenchman. Thank God he had made some contact. There was nothing worse than operating in the dark.

The sergeant finished and switched off the radio. He shouted something to his men and indicated that Craig and Big Boy should follow his jeep. Big Boy asked him a question in shaky Bomasha.

He translated the sergeant's reply to Craig. "He go take us to his officers. They be not far from here."

"All right," Craig said impatiently, waiting for Big Boy to start the engine. "Let's get moving."

Colonel Durand received Commissioner Innes and Harvey Klein in his office. He sat behind his desk bracketed by two flagstaffs, one bearing the tri-color fanion of his old regiment and the other the yellow and brown flag of the Bomasha defense force. He studied the two men before him, wondering how much they knew.

"We are pleased with your cooperation, Colonel," the commissioner said in faltering French.

"I speak English," the colonel replied shortly, irritated at the commissioner's linguistic ineptness.

"Mr. Klein and I are going to need all the help we can get."

The colonel glanced at Klein. "Is that so," he said, rubbing his nose, mad at himself because his mind was wandering and he wanted to get rid of his two visitors as soon as possible. He addressed himself to Klein. "Well, we have no word of your compatriot returning to Bomasha," he said, shrugging his shoulders. "He hasn't crossed at the ferry and my men have

§ **187**

not seen the Land Rover you describe." He paused, looking down at his desk, frowning. "What is this nonsense about his life being in danger?"

"I don't think it's nonsense," Klein replied seriously. "Our information comes directly from your intelligence people in Paris."

"Oh," the colonel said negligently, "our people often make mistakes. Put a man in civilian clothes, give him a shoulder holster and tell him to gather information and you soon find he makes it up—or exaggerates, depending on the case."

Klein and the commissioner exchanged a significant glance. The colonel saw it and realized he was sounding too negative.

"Nevertheless, I shall see that all my men are on the alert. I understand you have some men with you. Do you need further help?"

"No," the commissioner replied. "I've brought my own radio car. I plan to leave early tomorrow and nip up around the river areas. I understand there is trouble between the Goka and the Bomasha."

"Yes, I am afraid this territory is not pacified like your own. A Goka village has been attacked and wiped out by the Bomasha. Now we hear that tribal warfare has broken out in the north and along the river."

"Damn!" Innes murmured under his breath.

"Yes, it is a mess," the colonel said and he fixed Klein with a hard look. "We are experiencing the new Africa, Commissioner," he said bitterly, still looking at Klein, "the emancipation of the black. Unfortunately, Mr. Klein, we haven't reached the point of development here that your country has in Georgia and Mississippi. We lack airborne troops and national guardsmen."

§ 188

The commissioner broke in before Harvey Klein could reply. "But surely your defense force can keep things under control?"

"My defense force, Commissioner, is ninety percent Bomasha and their interest in the survival of the Goka is slight."

It had grown dark while they had been talking. A single drum thumped somewhere out in the bush and an off-key bugle sounded scratchily in the defense force compound.

"Well," Commissioner Innes said, getting to his feet, "we appreciate your offer to help and we'll be in touch. Goodby, Colonel."

"Goodby, Commissioner. Goodby, Mr. Klein."

They shook hands and left the colonel standing behind his desk, erect, chin in the air.

"Hard man, the colonel," the commissioner said as they walked down the cement stairs of the defense force headquarters. "I was afraid for a minute there that he'd put you on about the Georgia business. Expected a dustup, right there in the office."

"You'll find, Commissioner," Harvey Klein said quietly, "that I have a mighty thick skin."

"I'm beginning to find that out."

"He's a great psychological study, our friend the colonel," Klein said as they climbed into their station wagon. "A real Gallic stew of conflicting drives."

"Looks like a dangerous type to me."

"You're so right, Commissioner."

"I say," Innes said grumpily as he started the engine, "suppose we drop the commissioner business. My first name is Malcolm."

§ **189**

Colonel Durand sat down slowly after his visitors had left. He sat back in his chair and watched the ceiling fan slice the air slowly. He wondered who had been chosen to kill Craig. It must be the South African. Michel wouldn't stoop to such work. He'd been a good *para*, one of the best. His memory went back to the Suez operation and Michel sprinting across the hot dust of an Egyptian street, loaded down with full canteens for the wounded. The image faded and a darker picture replaced it. That of Michel in an Algiers bar, drinking with O.A.S. gunmen. He sat up, sighing, and pulled on his kepi. Things were getting out of hand. To succeed, the Bomasha subversion had to be carefully controlled. He couldn't allow things to disintegrate.

He picked up his brief case and left his office. The defense force sentry at the door made a clumsy attempt to present arms with his carbine and almost dropped it on the tile floor.

His Peugeot sedan was waiting for him and the chauffeur rolled out of the rutted compound and turned into the paved road leading toward the colonel's quarters. He sat back and relaxed. Well, he thought, it's easy enough to send telegrams from Paris where there is nothing more to do than curse de Gaulle over a big lunch. Here in Bomasha he was still in command.

His driver slowed for a turn and suddenly jammed on the brakes, throwing the colonel forward against the front seat. "Name of a whore!" the colonel shouted. His driver pointed frantically toward a native cart full of bananas that had come into their path.

The colonel opened the door and leaped from the back seat. He strode toward the complacent African cart owner, who seemed to be enjoying his predicament.

"You stupid ape! Can't you—"

§ **190**

The colonel was borne down by several husky young Africans who had come silently from behind his sedan. Muscular arms pinioned him to the ground. A dirty cloth soaked in ether blotted out the need to struggle. The thump of a wooden club silenced his driver.

They worked swiftly, dumping the colonel into the back seat and piling in beside him. Kowo slid behind the wheel and swung the Peugeot out and around the banana cart. They sped down the empty street, headed for the native section of town.

A young Goka in the back seat ran his finger over a welt on his cheek raised by the colonel's brief case. "Dirty bastard," he shouted, inches from the colonel's face. "You filthy white scum!" And he spit into the colonel's face.

"Enough, Bola!" Kowo ordered from the front seat. "Cowards are brave in the face of the sleeping."

The night that fell over Bomasha was spotted with yellow flame. International air flights over the territory livened their passengers' voyage by banking as they passed over the river area so that the bored businessmen, government officials and serious-faced educators could gaze down on the points of fire. Clutching their after-dinner drinks they clucked and shook their heads over the state of things in Bomasha.

Thousands of miles away, over the ocean, the halls of the U.N. echoed with the name of Bomasha. The French delegate was exhausted after a full day of debate. When he spoke, his disdain for his Soviet colleague was painfully obvious.

"Mr. Chairman, I believe the delegation of France has already fully explained its position and its knowledge of the events in Bomasha. It is obvious that certain delegations prefer to make this a propaganda platform. The Soviet delegation

§ **191**

has engaged in accusations that would be extemely shocking if we were not inclined to weigh their seriousness against their source. The delegation of France has nothing further to add to the debate at this time."

The Soviet delegate once more took the floor. The French delegate shrugged his shoulders and poured himself some water.

"We have just had a very good example of the contempt with which the colonialist powers approach the shameful and bloody situation in Bomasha. We are not asleep in the socialist world. We know of the devious, cut-throat operation of the infamous Colonel Durand.

"This same mercenary has learned his trade crushing peoples who seek their freedom and independence." There was a moment's pause as a young, tousle-haired aide handed the speaker several papers. "This man's record," he continued, "is there for all to see. Indo-China, Algeria, Suez, and now the tiny, defenseless Territory of Bomasha."

The litany of past colonial wars brought a murmur of disapproval from the Afro-Asian delegations. Encouraged, the Soviet delegate waved a thin sheet of paper over his head.

"The Soviet delegation has received a plea for assistance from Bomasha. In times of persecution and colonial piracy," the Soviet delegate intoned dramatically, "our African friends know where to turn for help."

A scattering of applause followed the Soviet statement. The chairman granted the floor to the British delegation. The British delegate, a thin man, looked surprisingly like a praying mantis as he hunched over his microphone. He cleared his throat and spoke.

"Her Majesty's delegation, while retaining the floor, asks

§ **192**

that the full text of the telegram referred to by the Soviet delegation be read to this assembly and entered in the record of this debate."

While the chairman gave the necessary parliamentary instructions and clerks collected the telegram from the Soviet delegation the British delegate blew his nose. He then sent a member of his delegation on a quick round of whispered consultations with the French and American delegations.

The chairman called for order and the text of the telegram was read.

"Brothers across the seas. Bomasha needs your help in its time of birth. Democracy in Africa is dying. We count on you and your great nation. Jean Jaurès Tibaki."

The Soviet delegate smiled, for the first time in many months, and settled back, satisfied.

"Mr. Chairman, fellow delegates," the British delegate intoned dryly, "it seems that Her Majesty's delegation, the delegation of France and that of the United States share with their Soviet colleagues the honor of receiving individual telegrams with the identical text from Mr. Tibaki."

He paused, craning his neck toward the Soviet delegation and allowing a quick shadow of a smile to pass over his long face. "We request that all of these telegrams and the manner of their receipt be entered in the record of this debate."

There was a brief huddle around the chairman. Then the chairman's rapid Portuguese set most delegations grasping for their translation headphones. To the telegrams already mentioned, explained the chairman, must be added another with the same text, just received by the chair.

Chapter 16

•
•

The South African called Peter puffed on his long cigar and poured more whisky into Craig's glass. He smiled, his glass eye tilted up, scanning the roof of the tent. It had been a relief for Craig to find someone he could talk to. He was relaxing. The tension of the past twenty-four hours was dissolving before the amber glasses of whisky and the jovial conversation with the two strangers that the Bomasha sergeant had conjured up from the depths of the jungle.

Even Big Boy had rediscovered his smile. He sat across the table from Craig, laughing heartily at everything that was said, gulping large mouthfuls of whisky and water and trying hard to look like a man of the world.

A soldier brought them a plate of soggy meat patties and they wolfed them down, laughing and talking as dusk fell and mosquitoes clustered around their heads.

Peter and Michel told Craig they were waiting further orders from Colonel Durand. They knew that the posters had been Craig's idea. They told him of the results in the north. Peter told of the fury of the Bomasha at seeing the posters.

Slapping Craig and Big Boy on the back, they promised them a guide for the morning. "The colonel will be glad to see you," the French mercenary said, pouring more drinks. "He thinks you are a sympathetic American. Not like the others."

They all drank to the sympathetic Americans, not like the others. Big Boy rose, nodded to his drinking partners and staggered outside.

Craig watched the two Europeans. He wasn't as drunk as they thought and some of their remarks had put him on his guard. Their comments had an acid quality. He slowed down on his drinking, lifting his glass to his mouth several times but only sipping the whisky.

After a time he reproached himself for being thin-skinned and accepted another brimming glass from the hands of the South African, who was telling them of buffalo hunting and the importance of well-placed shots. Halfway through his narrative, as they discussed cartridges and powder and the weight and feel of specific hunting rifles, the bottle went dry. There was a moment of mournful silence as all eyes fell on the drained bottle.

Craig brightened. He remembered the bottle of gin remaining in his rucksack. He winked at Peter and Michel. He stood up and made a grand gesture. "Gentlemen, we shall now change our drinking habits. I shall return with some gin." The two mercenaries shouted approval as Craig passed through the tent flaps and disappeared into the night.

The defense force tent that had been allotted to Craig and Big Boy was about two hundred yards away. Craig could mark it easily by its bright kerosene lantern.

He paused for a moment, looking up at the night sky, admiring the incandescent sparkling of the faraway stars. He decided to relieve himself. He walked into the bush, still watching the sky and enjoying the night. Big Boy had gone to the tent for some reason. Craig could see the bulk of his form outlined darkly against the gold shroud of the lighted canvas. He noticed the red glow of Peter's cigar nearby and was about to welcome him to the African night when he saw the glint of moonlight on the dull steel of a rifle barrel. He caught his breath, fascinated by the red beacon of the cigar and the upward swing of the rifle. The crash of the report and the flash of fire seemed to rip away the cover of night. He felt exposed and vulnerable. A surprised groan linked itself with the blast of the weapon. Big Boy's dark silhouette grew suddenly larger and then was gone with a thump as if some hidden genie had pulled it into the earth by its feet.

"Good shooting." Michel's words carried to Craig through the stillness.

He sunk slowly to his knees, listening, alert.

"This Mauser pulls to the left slightly," he heard Peter say in his halting French. "I think it's the trigger."

"Where could his black be?"

"He looked very drunk when he left. He is sleeping somewhere or he took to the bush when you fired."

Craig felt his legs shaking. He breathed deeply, straining to hold every limb still and silent. The South African moved back toward the tent.

"Aren't you going to make sure of the American?" the Frenchman asked.

The South African answered with a grunt of disdain. "Go look yourself if you're worried. I assure you it was a clean head shot." He re-entered the tent.

Craig was momentarily alone. Perspiration covered his

§ 196

brow. He knew he had to move but to strike out into the jungle without food, water or a weapon seemed pure suicide. He glanced at his lighted tent, gnawing on his lower lip. He hated uncertainty. He had his share of it now in the seconds that thumped past in an eternity of time.

He reached around him, keeping his eye on the other tent. He could hear them talking and the metallic sound of shells being ejected from the chamber of a rifle. His hand found a piece of wood that seemed solid and longer than the others. He lifted it, felt its weight and grasped it tightly in his right hand. It wasn't worth much as a weapon but it made him feel better.

He pushed himself up into a crouch, glanced at the inviting silence of the jungle and back at the golden canvas of his tent. He felt as if he were standing on the edge of a pool of mountain water, building his physical courage before the shock of diving into its burning coolness.

He started across the clearing, moving quickly but cautiously, every sinew and nerve aware of the movements within the other tent. His ears followed each rise and fall in the mercenaries' conversation. It seemed strange to him that the Bomasha troopers hadn't come rushing from their bivouac following the shot. He imagined they had had their orders.

He reached the tent. His hands touched the canvas and he moved around to the tent flap, quietly cursing the triangle of bright yellow light from the lantern that he would have to cross. He scuttled across the few feet of light, and stopped, panting, on his hands and knees within the tent. He saw his haversack and crawled toward it to avoid showing a silhouette. He pulled it open, perspiration pouring freely from him and dripping off his chin. He pushed the .38 into his belt and the two small square cartons of cartridges into his trouser pockets. He reached up and pulled his bush jacket down from the bed and stuffed it with a tin of bully beef, two bars of concentrated chocolate and his compass.

He looked up from his frantic packing and came face to face with Big Boy. The shock of confrontation knocked the wind from his lungs. He had completely forgotten Big Boy in his rush to escape. A feeling of guilt took hold of him. It passed quickly. There was nothing he could have done. Big Boy lay dead. He was flat on the ground, stomach down. His huge head was settled chin forward, serpentlike. He already seemed part of the earth. The top of his skull had been shattered and pushed forward over his eyes in a gelatinous scramble of brain and blood, like a misplaced black beret. One of his arms was bent under him but the other was stretched out to one side. Clamped in his bloody fist was the opened top of a smashed gin bottle. Craig gathered up his bush jacket. His glance at Big Boy had taken only a few seconds and he felt resentment that the crushed effigy had taken so much of his time.

"Don't forget the gin!"

He recognized the South African's voice. He pushed himself under the loose canvas in the rear of the tent and paused for a moment, listening. He heard the crunch of approaching footsteps. He reached for the .38 in his belt and simultaneously cursed himself for not having loaded his revolver. Fear released its hold and he struck out into the jungle at a trot, guided by the bright moonlight, avoiding clumps of brush and scatterings of branches and twigs, leaping over stumps, listening over the thump of his own pounding blood for the sounds of pursuit.

§ **198**

The future prime minister of Bomasha received Klein and the commissioner on the veranda of his spacious home. Before they could sip the cool drinks a house boy served them, Jean Jaurès Tibaki announced with appropriate gravity the disappearance of Colonel Durand. Commissioner Innes looked up quickly from his glass into Tibaki's placid, serious face, searching in vain for an indication of what Durand's disappearance meant. Harvey Klein shook his head slowly. The Bomasha situation was a new and totally unpredictable addition to his experience.

"I am afraid his kidnaping has political implications," Tibaki said, chasing a beautiful white moth off the arm of his wicker chair. "His chauffeur witnessed his abduction by young toughs." The small African sighed and gestured toward the darkness out beyond the lights of the veranda. "Tonight there is violence in Bomasha. Killing and the filth that goes with it; robbery and rape. It is very sad, very sad."

Klein was about to speak but Tibaki, roused from his moment of sadness spoke again. "You are here to find the American?" Tibaki asked. "The anthropologist?"

"Yes," Klein replied. "We're here to find Michael Craig. He is not an anthropologist."

"I know," Tibaki said in a tired voice. "I know. I have been informed by the French." He pushed himself forward and spoke in a confidential tone. "Mr. Klein, I am not anti-American. But what am I to believe? Why does this fool Craig come to our country. Why must he add to our troubles?" His voice was bitter. "I have traveled. I know the world and I take things with a grain of salt. The communists have told me you are all rotten exploiters and colonialists and you people tell me the same about the communists. And I say

§ 199

damn both your houses! Find this Craig and take him away. Get him out of my country!" Tibaki was almost shouting.

The commissioner cleared his throat in irritation.

"I have worked with white men all my life," Tibaki continued, "but maybe my young hotheads are right. Maybe we should chase all the white men from Bomasha."

"Monsieur Tibaki!" The commissioner's voice was calm but heavy with reproof. There was a moment of uneasy silence. Tibaki sighed and made a helpless gesture with his hands.

"I apologize," he said sadly, shaking his head, the light dancing on the rims of his spectacles.

"We are here to help," Klein said, feeling sorry for the confused little man.

Tibaki nodded. "I know, I know," he said quietly. "And I shall try to help you find this Craig."

"We would like to find him and get him out of Bomasha before the journalists find out about him," the commissioner said.

"And before he is killed?" Tibaki asked with a weak smile.

"You know of this?" Klein asked.

"Yes, I have heard of the plan to kill your American. It is very difficult. Bomasha may look small on a map but—I don't have to tell you, Commissioner, it is a very big country when you are trying to find one man." He paused a moment, thinking. "Of course," he continued, "he is white and that is to your advantage. But you do not have much time."

Tibaki stood up, ending the audience. "I am sorry," he said regretfully as they shook hands. "I am very nervous. I am unable to trust people."

He didn't say "white people" but both Klein and the commissioner knew that was what he meant.

§ **200**

Craig moved all through the night. There was an ominous lack of audible pursuit. He thought of them—no longer drinking companions—caressing their weapons and talking the cold technicalities of man hunting. Thank God for the clear sky. With the help of his compass and the stars, he knew he was moving north, bearing away from the main road. But the narrow trails seemed to lead back toward the main road. He had to watch carefully and thrash around through the bush in search of new trails that were oriented toward the northwest. He knew he had not gone far but he continued, walking as fast as the trail would allow, slipping and tripping over vines and rotting wood. Once he had to pause silently, fearfully, as a large animal, an ape or leopard, crossed the trail ahead of him. He crouched on the damp ground and slipped six shells into his .38, with the realization that it was a small, ineffectual weapon.

As he pulled himself panting to the top of a small rise, he saw the flicker of village cooking fires. Again he turned toward the west, knowing his main salvation would be the village of Pierre. It would not be easy to locate but the compass helped. The bridge he had crossed with Big Boy was too far to the north but if he could get a canoe from Pierre and cross into Ikiri he might be able to pick up his money and get out. There was no doubt in his mind. He was a blown agent. The sooner he pulled out, the better.

Dawn came suddenly, a rose wash on the skirts of the night sky. He turned off the trail and climbed over the bone-white trunks of several fallen trees before collapsing under a jutting branch. He felt no hunger, only thirst. It was all he could do to roll his bush jacket as a pillow before he fell into the muscle-jerking sleep of complete exhaustion, the .38 lying in his lap and his back against the hard carcass of the dead tree.

He shifted and groaned in his sleep. Big Boy lectured him, shaking a long black finger in his face but he couldn't hear what Big Boy said. It was just a repetitive ra-ra-ra-ra of sound and Big Boy would disappear in a great, silent, slow-moving explosion of color only to return again, his finger shaking and his thick lips undulating, threatening, around the steady emissions of ra-ra-ra-ra. Then Big Boy faded upward, out of his dream. Alice Thompson came toward him, walking backward, completely nude, walking toward him across the market place and he felt sorry and embarrassed for her and tried to reach her to cover her up, but then he noticed that the Hausa merchants had all turned their backs. And she stood before him, her desirable back and buttocks shining in the sun of the market square. He reached for her shoulders and swung her around and it was Big Boy and the finger shook under his nose and the ra-ra-ra-ra sent the Hausas scurrying out of sight like frightened, white-robed crows.

He rolled, groaning, and woke up with a start, his lips parched and his neck stiff. He felt a strange, full feeling around his ankles. He loosened his laces and gingerly pulled his shoes off. The red dust was crusted moistly over the burst blisters on his ankle. With a shock he saw the purple, grape-like leeches clustered on his ankle and lower leg. They were taut, solid with blood. He sat for a moment looking out at the jungle. The sun was high in a sky of dull, heat-washed blue. The jungle was quiet, crackling with dryness and apparently empty. He flexed his arms and rubbed his stiff neck. He pushed his revolver into the pocket of his bush jacket and brought forth a packet of matches. He carefully lit the match and tried to burn off the leeches without burning his own flesh. It wasn't easy. The leeches were tough and the

§ 202

winnowing flame of a match didn't have the direct searing power of a glowing cigarette end. Cigarette smokers, he thought, are lucky when it comes to leeches.

He had used half of the matches in his box before the last leech changed color, pulled in on itself and fell onto the dry leaves. He put his socks back on carefully, laced his boots and ran his dry tongue over his cracked lips.

His need for water fought with the common-sense caution of traveling only at night. He stood up, leaning on the white tree trunk, feeling the bite of his blisters and rubbing the stubble of his coarse beard. He oriented his small hand compass, hitched up his trousers and started again along the obscure animal trail he had been following during the night.

The gray, vine-cluttered boles of ageless trees surrounded him in the hot silence. Strange bushes with lush green and yellow leaves lined the trail. They often joined overhead in an undisciplined arbor. A foot-catching net of berry vines was hidden a few inches under the acrid mulch of the jungle floor. Craig moved slowly, lifting his sore feet high and kicking himself free of their persistent grasp.

From time to time he thought he heard the rush of a spring or small stream but it was only the rare passage of an errant wind through the topmost branches of the trees, too high and too brief to cool the natural oven of the enclosed jungle.

Later, as the shadows lengthened, he munched one of his chocolate bars and felt it stick to the roof of his mouth like dry mud. He had to work hard to raise enough saliva to swallow. When he did, the chocolate sat heavily on his stomach.

§ **203**

Chapter 17

●
●

Kowo and his group worked quickly and efficiently among the ruins of the village. They took photos and made notes reconstructing the raid and gathering evidence. The dead had been ripped by vultures, disfigured by hyenas and dried by the sun. A subtle odor had replaced the stench of putrefaction. The village smelled like a tannery.

The young Goka wore bush shorts and sport shirts. They were armed with revolvers. Kowo had placed one of his men as a lookout. The rest were busy digging a long narrow grave for the mutilated corpses.

A low whistle from the lookout sent them all sprawling behind the cover of a charred hut. Kowo alone remained in the open, on one knee, the camera put aside and his revolver ready. He bit his lips and watched the jungle waiting for a sign from his sentry. He could hear someone coming. He rolled slowly to one side and slid into the freshly dug grave.

Craig came forward cautiously, his Colt in his hand. Kowo watched him. He noted the surprise on Craig's face as he saw the ruins of the village. The sentry stepped out of the bush and leveled his weapon at Craig's back. Kowo pushed his own revolver into his belt and stood up. Craig started and swung toward him.

"Put down your gun," Kowo ordered. "You are our prisoner."

The others came out from behind the hut. Craig heard a movement behind him. He was temporarily paralyzed by an empty feeling of indecision. He could break and run; he could fire and hope for the best. He lowered his Colt and dropped it onto the sand. The sentry behind him moved forward and picked it up.

Kowo motioned them forward. Craig was puzzled. He knew these men were Goka but he wasn't sure where they had come from or what they were doing. He glanced at the ruined village, taking in the collapsed hut of the headman, the shallow grave and the fly-covered bundles of dried flesh and white bone.

Kowo searched him. He took Craig's ammunition and handed it to the sentry. "Sit down," he said, when he had finished.

Craig sat on the hot sand and Kowo stared at him, frowning. "Aggh," he suddenly grunted in distaste. He swept his arm toward the dead. "White man's work," he growled, nodding his head up and down. "I hope you are proud."

Craig remained silent.

"We know about you, Craig. Monsieur Tibaki will be pleased that we have found you. I shall take you back with us and put you on exhibit. I shall be anxious to see what your government has to say! We have already put away your friend, the Colonel Durand."

Craig's heart stood still. His last bridge was down. He had to think and think fast.

"The colonel is in a cell within walking distance of his former office but he is a changed man. We took away his clothes. It is surprising how quickly a proud peacock can become a sorry sparrow."

Kowo turned and walked down to the river followed by four of his men. The sentry remained a short distance from Craig, watching him. Kowo and his men waded toward a fish weir. Craig presumed they were looking for their lunch.

"Can I have some water?" Craig asked his guard in French. The Goka shook his head and shrugged his shoulders. Craig made signs of drinking. The young man understood. He moved a few steps and cautiously handed Craig a dented army canteen that the gravediggers had put to one side. Craig drank the warm water slowly. He was surprised at his own self-control. He put the canteen aside and sighed. He felt slightly rejuvenated.

Kowo and his companions returned with several fish. They built a small fire and roasted the fish on the coals. Craig watched them eat. They ignored him, squatting on their haunches and licking their fingers. They glanced up briefly when they heard Craig rip open the wrapping of his last chocolate bar. He felt the strength of the sun and wished he had not left his hat behind.

The jeep came out of the jungle and braked to an abrupt stop. There was a frozen moment of mutual shock and surprise. The Frenchman fired first, one leg out of the jeep, bracing his firing position. A young Goka said, "Oh," and slumped face forward into the sand. The others fired back, their revolvers jerking in their hands. Instinctively Craig rolled over and sprawled flat. He saw the stocky French mercenary jump into the air as if he were trying to avoid the hail of bullets. He fell soundlessly, hanging from the jeep by one leg. The South African gunned the jeep's engine and swung the wheel, throwing a fountain of sand into the air. The jeep leapt toward the jungle, the dead Frenchman dragging and bouncing beside it like a mail sack.

Craig gathered all his strength and launched himself at the sentry. His head drove into the man's stomach. They went down together and Craig struck hard with the heel of his palm, smashing at his guard's Adam's apple. He jumped clear, snatched up his pistol and rifled the Goka's pockets for the ammunition they had taken from him.

He scuttled along on all fours, keeping a screen of ruined huts and debris between himself and the Goka. He reached the river and the line of beached canoes. Several were badly holed but he finally found one that looked undamaged. He pushed it into the water, and flopped face down as the current caught its bow. Ashore the shooting continued as the South African returned fire from the cover of the jungle.

The small convoy was parked in the shade at the side of the road. Harvey Klein sat beside Jean Jaurès Tibaki in the back seat of Tibaki's sedan. They were waiting for Commissioner Innes. The commissioner's Land Rover and radio car were in front of them. Three of Tibaki's police jeeps, loaded with heavily armed policemen, completed the convoy. They were parked beside an ice house. It was a squat, square building owned by a Lebanese who supplied dirt-peppered, milky ice to the surrounding district at outrageous prices.

The heat crept into the sedan despite the shade and Klein could feel his damp shirt sticking to the upholstery. Tibaki seemed perfectly comfortable in his dark wool suit. The chauffeur had gone to sleep as he did at each stop.

Klein had lost his detached American gloss. His usual com-

§ **207**

posure had vanished and he fidgeted, crossing and recrossing his legs. The pressure was on. At first Washington had wanted little or nothing done in the Craig case: "Just watch him and keep us informed." Now it was "Get Craig out of Bomasha SOONEST!" Klein found himself chewing on a hangnail. He sighed in exasperation, silently cursing the desk specialists at home to whom things always looked so simple. Why was Innes taking so long?

Monsieur Tibaki was preoccupied, worried. He tried to make conversation with the American. "They will be here in two days," Tibaki said, as if speaking to himself.

Klein turned toward him. The little man got on his nerves. "Who will be here in two days?" Klein asked with an attempt at cordiality.

"The U.N. investigation team. They will be flying to Ache. I must meet them."

"Yes, certainly," Klein didn't like to be reminded of their arrival.

"As you know, I have ordered the defense force to remain in their barracks. Some of the units have disobeyed this order and the killing continues between Bomasha and Goka. I have doubled my police force but I must have help from outside." The future prime minister turned toward Klein. "Do you think the American has left Bomasha?"

Klein winced. This was the third time in the course of the morning that Tibaki had asked the same question. He was spared the ordeal of replying. The commissioner came out of the ice house and walked toward them. He was holding a handkerchief over his nose and after a few strides he stopped and spit on the ground.

He put both of his freckled hands on the door of the sedan

and poked his head in the window. He was pale under his normal ruddy crust of sunburn. "It's Big Boy, all right. No bloody doubt about it."

"But are you sure, Commissioner?" Tibaki asked.

The commissioner paused to spit again into the dust. "Normally, I wouldn't go before a court and swear it. He hasn't exactly undergone the gentle care of a trained undertaker. But he did have a tattoo and it still shows, right where it should. Regardless, with your permission, Monsieur Tibaki, we'd like to run a dental check against whatever old army record he might have. But, frankly, that will take time. I believe we can rest assured that the mess in there was Big Boy."

"God rest his soul," Tibaki said quietly.

"Yes, quite." The commissioner had regained some of his color. There was a moment's silence. A dust swirl, spinning toward them down the empty road held their attention for a moment, swept past and was gone.

"Well," Klein said, "we know you must get on to Ache, Monsieur Tibaki. Thank you for your help. We may need more shortly."

The small African sighed and spread his hands in a gesture of helplessness. "Gentlemen, I'm doing what I can under the circumstances. I had hoped our independence would be a joyful event. Now even the possibility of achieving it is in doubt. Mr. Klein, I am sorry about your American and I hope you find him. I must tell you, however, that one life and even the possible embarrassment of your great nation puts very little weight on the great scale of sorrow before us."

Klein climbed from the sedan and joined Commissioner Innes. They shook hands with Tibaki. Tibaki poked his sleep-

§ **209**

ing chauffeur in the ribs and soon the sedan and the escort jeeps pulled away.

The commissioner and Klein watched the departure in a haze of slow-settling dust. "What do you think?" Klein asked.

"I'm not sure. Is the little monkey sincere?"

"I think he is. Goddamn it, don't call him a monkey!"

"My, my, slightly edgy, Harvey. No reason for it, you know."

Klein sighed, inwardly ashamed of his outburst, yet ready to defend it even if his own words somehow rang false. "The poor little bastard has been handed an impossible situation and he's doing his best and risking his neck at the same time. I don't call that being a monkey."

"Oh, that was just a figure of speech."

"You're damn right it's a figure of speech! The kind of talk you people and the French have been using out here too long."

Innes changed abruptly. The light smile that had been playing on his lips was swept away. He drew himself to his full height, poked his swagger stick under his arm and frowned at Klein.

"Just a minute there, old chap. I know you're tired and you're not used to this heat. I apologize for the lack of air conditioners and Coca-Cola—but let's not get onto that. Look, Harvey, I've been running my bloody ass off for the last few weeks, and so have my men, because one of your benighted countrymen has decided to stick his nose into other people's business. Now you and I are working together to send this idiot back where he came from—even if that means feet first. Let's not get sidetracked over my respect for African independence and Monsieur Tibaki's racial pedigree."

§ **210**

Klein wiped his brow with an already sweat-stained handkerchief.

"OK, Malcolm, OK," he said sighing, fervently wishing he'd kept his mouth shut.

"Well," Innes said, dropping the matter, "they may have gotten to Craig in the same way. If so we'll probably never know. On the other hand, the fact that he wasn't lying about when Big Boy's body was found may mean he's given them the slip. They won't give up the chase. I know the type. They have a certain professional standard to maintain, to say nothing of the pay for a job well done."

Innes wiped his forehead with a handkerchief. "I think we'd better get back to Ikiri. It's the only chance left to him."

"If he still thinks his cache of dollars is waiting."

"No reason he shouldn't."

The moon was orange, tinged with the redness of the northern dust. It was almost too beautiful. Ikiri had changed. It was noisy and not just with the shouts of mammy wagon drivers or traders. The bright lights of the Rest House flickered through the trees. The night echoed with laughter. The still air received the raucous shouts and the clink of glasses and threw them back into the valley with an increase in volume.

Alice Thompson drew deeply on her cigarette and let the tendrils of smoke curl slowly from her lips. She sat back in her chair and tried to relax but her nerves wouldn't allow it. There was a certain electricity in the air, a strange, nervous feeling of excitement. Perhaps it was the unaccustomed noise.

The journalists had arrived like a detachment of airborne shock troops. They had come roaring into Ikiri from the air strip laden with baggage, portable typewriters and cameras.

After a brief skirmish at the Rest House bar they had descended on the district officer with a hundred technical requests, questions and outright demands. Robert Thompson had been taken completely by surprise. Surprised, then shocked, then angry, he had telephoned his superiors in the capital, expecting sympathy and solid support in the face of the undisciplined ruffians who called themselves journalists. Instead, he was treated to a blistering lecture that removed several strips from his backside.

He had been ordered to put himself and his office at the disposal of the representatives of the press. They did not yet have permission to cross into Bomasha. For the time being, their press headquarters would have to be Ikiri. Thompson was told to make the best of it. Still shocked and upset at his superiors' lack of understanding, he allowed himself to be led out of the office and up to the Rest House bar by the newsmen. After several gin and tonics, the governing of Ikiri seemed much less important than his new-found comradeship with the hard-drinking correspondents.

Mr. Magabian, resenting the monopoly of the Rest House bar, installed two tired prostitutes in his upstairs rooms. He then sent one of his houseboys to the Rest House with orders to pass the word that young women with solid, pointed breasts and skin like freshly ground cocoa were available at the Ikiri Hotel.

Alice Thompson stood up and walked to the edge of the veranda. It was late. The lights of a Land Rover swung through the darkness and the vehicle crunched to a stop on the gravel in front of the guardhouse. It was time for the midnight guard relief. She could hear the guards talking in low voices and the high-pitched laughter of the African policemen. Fruit bats were flying overhead, conversing in metallic chirps as they dipped among the tall trees.

She watched the moon. It seemed to glow with a strange promise. She stretched, yawning, feeling the pull of her breasts against her dress, aware of the arch of her back and the tightness of her hips. There was an unsought but strangely welcome warmth playing over her body. She thought of Michael Craig and the warmth left her.

Her husband knew what had happened. He'd hinted at it ever since Craig had left. She didn't know how he'd found out but he knew. It gave him something to taunt her with. Day in and day out she had lived with his smirking innuendos and sudden fits of self-pity. He had hinted that her meeting with Craig was common knowledge in Ikiri.

The door to the boys' compound banged shut. She jumped at the sound. She stood nervously for a moment, feeling drained and alone. Ignatius came out of the boys' compound, paused to look at the moon, and went behind the bushes to relieve himself.

She backed away from the edge of the veranda and walked carefully and silently into the house. She shut the door and threw the bolt. She could neither laugh nor cry. The lamplight accentuated the lines of her face. She frowned fiercely at herself in the pitted wall mirror. Where, she wondered, was the nearest psychiatrist? She glanced blankly toward the sideboard and the half-full bottle of brandy sitting like an upright sentinel among the tray of empty glasses. She poured the brandy into a glass, still frowning, her shoulders sagging. "Good evening, Doctor," she said, staring at the amber liquor. "I'm so glad you could come."

Chapter 18

.
.

The canoe nosed into a soft sandbank and swung around broadside to the Ikiri bank. Craig remained flat, hoping that the current would catch him again and move him farther downstream. The moon was rising over the trees, throwing long shadows onto the sand and laying an amber sheen over the river's surface. He heard only the subdued gurgling of slow-moving water.

Craig moved quickly. Rising out of the canoe, he pushed it off into the current. In four strides he was lost in the shadows and bush. He breathed a deep sigh of relief and listened to the night, attempting to interpret the different degrees of silence surrounding him.

He had to plan ahead. He would have to get a plane out of Ikiri. It was a simple race against time. If he could get back to the Rest House and pick up his money without running into trouble, it would be fairly simple. He knew the South African would still be after him—if Tibaki's men hadn't killed him at the village. He doubted if Tibaki's people would chase him across the border. He frowned, trying to think of every dangerous angle.

It was his best survival insurance. The possibility that Tibaki might have warned the authorities in Ikiri crossed his mind. He thought of Alice Thompson. Would she warn him? Could he trust her? He had trusted a woman once before, a long time ago, in a similar situation. It had almost cost him his life and he had sworn never again to work with women, even professional agents. He smiled grimly and shook his head. Alice Thompson was far from being a professional agent but she was the only contact left to him in Ikiri. He had no other choice.

He moved on all fours, climbing cautiously up the slight rise of the riverbank until he found a fairly comfortable, well-hidden spot. The moon, the river, and the nearby trees seemed unreal, from another age. He settled down, his Colt within reach, his jacket bunched as a pillow. At dawn he would strike out for the main road to Ikiri. According to his calculations, it ran parallel to the river and it shouldn't be too hard to reach.

He examined the situation objectively and felt a surge of pessimism. He countered this sudden depression with a mental review of the day's happenings, judging them and classifying them in a coldly clinical fashion. Wondering if the French mercenary was dead or merely wounded, he reflected that his chances were considerably improved if the man had been killed. He thought of Colonel Durand and puzzled over the Goka he had run into at the village. Tibaki was obviously more politically intelligent and active than he had been led to believe.

He closed his eyes and suddenly realized how nerve-tired

§ **215**

and exhausted he was. As he slid into sleep, a succession of far-away scenes ran through the slowing machinery of his mind, soothing his senses with their appeal. San Francisco in the winter sunshine; his father teaching him to fly-cast in the cold Sierra morning; his wife laughing as she cooked his breakfast; the dark brown depth of her eyes as she came to him in the warmth of love. This last vignette lingered and he felt it tarnish before him. Tenderly he pushed it away, closing off his mind to its own vulnerability.

Colonel Durand raised his head groggily as the door opened. He couldn't see well in the sudden light and he put his hands up automatically to ward off any blows.

"So, Colonel, we meet again." Tibaki's voice held a certain sadness. "I did not want this," he continued, "you brought it upon yourself."

The colonel could make out Tibaki's small figure among the group of men before him. The cell-like room was fetid and close and Tibaki shook out his handkerchief and held it over his nose. He shook his head sadly, still looking at the colonel.

Durand wore a dirty pair of undershorts. His face was bruised from the beatings he had suffered and one eye was swollen shut. A beard darkened his chin and his hair had grown out. He sat watching Tibaki, still stunned by the situation and his own misfortune. He shook all over, suddenly unable to control the fever that burned in his body and made the men before him sway like seaborne weeds.

Tibaki stepped closer. "I want a doctor to see the colonel," he ordered. "Then I want the colonel shaved and you must give him back his uniform." He turned and walked toward the door. He paused on the threshold and folded his handkerchief. "We are planning a press conference for you, my Colonel. It is time to speak of your mistakes. You can help us. Don't plan on any assistance. Your fellow workers are either dead or on the run," Jean Jaurès Tibaki left and the door was bolted and locked.

Colonel Durand sat silently in the darkness. He sensed a burning coldness in all his joints.

Harvey Klein felt better after washing off the dust of their trip. Ikiri did appear as an oasis of civilization after Bomasha. He tucked in his clean shirt and buckled his belt. He was beginning to resent Craig. Craig had first appeared as an abstract—a name on official documents. Now Klein thought of him as a thorough scoundrel, an irresponsible crackpot and the cause of all his problems. Washington was still waiting for him to deliver the goods. A plane was standing by at Wheelus Field to take off for Ikiri the minute they got the word and whisk Craig away from the Bomasha hot spot and into the shadows.

He glanced at the mirror and ran his comb through his hair. He had suddenly developed thick sideburns. He was beginning to look like a heavy in a television western. He slipped his glasses back on and the world lost its soft edges. He pulled his suitcase out from under the bed, reached in his pocket, shook out a cluster of keys and opened it. He reached into the jumble of socks and extra shirts and pulled out a snub-nosed police revolver in a small, new waist holster of unstained leather that unaccountably smelled of vanilla. He held it in his hand for a moment, frowning before pushing it back among the shirts and locking the suitcase. "The hell with it," he said quietly.

He walked out of his room and onto the veranda of the

§ **217**

Rest House. He passed a table of British and American newspapermen. They were drinking and laughing but they stopped when he walked past, eyeing him with curiosity. Oh God, that's all I need, he thought, avoiding their eyes. He walked down the stairs and over to the police Land Rover that was waiting for him. He climbed in and the driver headed for the Ikiri police post. The moon was up. It had lost its orange coating.

Commissioner Innes was trying to decide what to about Alice Thompson. A woodcutter had seen Thompson's Morris parked out by the hemp shed. He had mentioned it to a clerk in one of Ikiri's shops. The clerk had mentioned it to his friend Ignatius and Ignatius had innocently asked his master about the hemp shed as he had some relatives that needed shelter over their heads during the rainy season. Robert Thompson had questioned him in detail and Ignatius had grown nervous, noting the unnatural glaze in Thompson's eye and the bitter pleasure with which he carried out his inquiry.

Ignatius passed the word to the cook and the story spread like a flash fire, distorting itself as it went until Major Bedwell picked it up. The major put the pieces together and reported it to Commissioner Innes clean-cut and corroborated by the woodcutter and several Hausa merchants who had seen both Alice Thompson and Craig leave and enter Ikiri by the north road on the same day, at approximately the same hours.

It was messy. Something would have to be done. The commissioner was not sure just what. He was sipping a mug of hot tea and pondering the problem when Klein arrived. "Hello, have some tea?" Innes asked.

"Thanks," Klein replied and the commissioner filled another cup from his thermos.

§ **218**

An African constable was hunched over a radio, one hand on the earphones, the other fiddling with the dial. The ear-splitting squeaks and wails of static filled the small building.

"You should have stayed up at the Rest House, Harvey," Innes said, handing him his cup. "There's not a bloody thing new. I'm going to catch a bit of sleep later myself."

Klein sat on the edge of the wooden table near the radio. He sipped the strong tea, frowning. His headache had come back. "Does he have to make such a goddamn racket?" he asked.

"He's trying to raise one of our border posts," Innes replied coldly and turned his back to look out the window. "We're putting out a fifty-pound reward for information leading to Craig's capture. I don't have an authorization yet but even if they don't agree I can cover it out of my budget."

Klein had been dozing, his head resting on his arms. He awoke with a start when Magabian erupted into the police post all mumbles and wild gestures. Commissioner Innes put aside the magazine he had been reading.

"Well, what's up with you?" he asked.

"Commissioner, I have come to make a report," the Armenian said nervously, glancing over his shoulder as if expecting someone to appear behind him.

"At three in the morning?"

"Commissioner, I—oh, good morning," he said, noticing Klein for the first time.

Klein nodded. His eyes felt as if they were coated with sandpaper and the steady hum of the radio seemed to bore into his brain.

"Commissioner," Magabian continued, "I have one roomer

§ **219**

who is most suspicious. He is a European. He is without papers and he has a large rifle that I don't think is for hunting."

The commissioner showed sudden interest. He swung his long legs down from the table and put his cap on his head. "What does this type look like?"

"He's tall and blond. Speaks with a foreign accent. There is something about him that reminds me of a German I once knew."

"Anything else? Anything different about him?" the commissioner asked.

"Ah, yes," Magabian said, smiling. He was enjoying himself. He was the undisputed center of attraction. "He has an eye that goes like this." And Magabian pointed one pudgy finger toward the ceiling.

Commissioner Innes jumped up. "That's the chap," he said, speaking over Magabian's head to Klein.

"The South African?"

"Yes, fits him perfectly. Sergeant!" the commissioner shouted as he strapped on his holster.

Magabian looked from one to the other, already beginning to feel left out. "I shall show you his room," he offered.

"Do you have the key?"

"No, but I have the hotel pass key," the Armenian replied, fumbling in his pocket. "Here."

The commissioner took it. "Thanks." A sleepy sergeant appeared at the door. "All right, Sergeant, let's get a move on. I want three men to go with us and I want them awake; now hop to it."

"Sahr!" the sergeant replied, grinning as he saluted.

The commissioner turned to Klein. "You ready?"

§ **220**

"Sahr," Klein replied.

The commissioner smiled. "Very amusing," he said as they walked toward the door.

Magabian started after them but the commissioner stopped him at the door. "You stay here, Mr. Magabian, if you will."

The pained expression of one who is often misunderstood returned to Magabian's cherubic face. "But, I—"

"Corporal." The radio operator stood up expectantly. "Get Mr. Magabian some writing paper and a pen." The commissioner took Magabian by the arm and guided him to the table. "I'd like you to write down all you know and can remember about this chap's arrival. It will be very important to us."

Magabian brightened. "Yes, Commissioner, I shall make a first-rate report."

"Good, now . . . what room is he in?"

"He's in room eight on the second floor."

"Very good."

Magabian was left behind with the silent corporal and the humming radio.

The sergeant and three sleepy constables were waiting outside. They walked up the road to the Ikiri Hotel, the commissioner leading the way. "The wolves are closing in," he muttered.

"Yes, Craig's reception committee seems to be growing."

They halted in the shadows near the hotel. The commissioner placed two men outside to cover the windows of the second floor. The sergeant and another constable accompanied them up the stairs and into the fetid interior. Sleep was heavy in the halls. Moving quietly toward the sagging stairway, they heard the snores and uneasy moaning of Magabian's roomers.

A sudden rush of water and the rattle of plumbing echoed in the corridor. A tall Hausa, clutching a towel around his waist backed out of a hall toilet. His eyes widened and he stopped with his mouth open at the sight of the commissioner's drawn pistol and the determined constables.

"Quiet!" the commissioner whispered, his finger to his lips.

The Hausa put a shaking finger to his lips and nodded his head.

The commissioner came closer. "You—stay right here. Don't move, understand?"

"I am an honest trader. I go for toilet . . ."

"Quiet," the commissioner repeated and the sergeant emphasized the order with a poke of his riot stick.

They climbed up the stairs. Each creak of the dry wood seemed like an alarm bell. The commissioner located the room with a small pocket flashlight. "You'd better stand back," he whispered to Klein. "He may come out shooting."

Klein agreed. He was content to observe. The commissioner motioned the sergeant forward, placing him on the other side of the door. Klein heard the faint scratching sound of the key entering the keyhole. The door swung open. Light flooded the room.

"Lie still," he heard the commissioner's command, loud and calm.

Klein moved quickly to the door. The man lay belly down on the bed, completely nude under the mosquito net.

The commissioner was standing by the light switch, his revolver ready. The sergeant had already snatched up the South African's rifle. He lifted the mosquito net and secured it over the bed.

The man's fingers wiggled upward under his pillow. Innes

sprang forward and pressed his pistol to the base of the mercenary's skull. "None of that—or I'll blow your head off."

Klein felt suddenly cold. The defenselessness of the nude body under the threat of the cold pistol sent a chill up his spine and he found himself repeating a personal prayer. Don't let him do it. Don't let him do it.

"Goddamn you Scottish Glasgow bastard!" the enraged South African grumbled, face down in his pillow. "I'm trying to get my eye!"

Innes removed the muzzle of his pistol from the man's neck. He picked up the pillow and tossed it to the floor, revealing the lifeless blue stare of the lone glass eye.

"Sorry," the commissioner said apologetically.

The South African lifted his tousled blond head and rose onto his elbows. The glass eye rolled down the dirty sheet toward him. He picked it up, licked it thoroughly and popped it in his eye socket with a deft twist.

"All right," the commissioner said. "Hands behind now."

The sergeant snapped on a set of handcuffs.

"You, get up," Innes said. "Help him dress, Sergeant."

The South African turned over and swung himself into a sitting position. He looked at Klein and then saw the sergeant hand his rifle to the other constable. "Careful with that rifle, you stupid bushman," he snarled.

The sergeant upended him and roughly began to pull his trousers on. The commissioner went through his suitcase. The South African stared at Klein for a while. Klein returned his stare even though the orientation of the glass eye made it difficult.

The mercenary spit onto the floor. "Who's your Jewish

friend?" he asked the commissioner. "Not a very talkative kike."

Klein felt as if someone had slapped him in the face. He hadn't expected it. He hadn't heard anything like it for years and he wasn't prepared to hear it now, deep in Africa.

"That's enough of that," Innes replied sharply, a sudden flush around his ears.

My God, Klein thought. He's embarrassed for me.

"Caught by a stupid Jock inspector, a dirty Jew and a bushman. I hope they don't hear of this in Jo'berg."

"All right, Sergeant," the commissioner said. "Get him out of here."

The sergeant dragged the mercenary to his feet and pushed him toward the door. "I'll get you, you goddamn ape!" the white man growled at the sergeant as they went out the door. Once out of the commissioner's sight the sergeant gave the handcuffs a strong twist and the South African cried out in pain.

"That's enough of that," the Commissioner called after them as he continued to rummage through the mercenary's baggage.

Klein sat down on the bed. "A real Nazi!" he said, still shaken by the man's bitterness.

"Yes, a bad apple, that one. We know a bit about him. Irony is he won the V.C. fighting the Jerries at Tobruk. That's where he lost his eye."

"*Plus ça change*," Klein murmured.

"What's that?"

"Oh nothing. Are you going to be able to hold him?"

"Bloody well right I am! Illegal entry, unregistered arms— I'll bash him on Big Boy's death if I can."

§ **224**

The commissioner straightened up and sighed. "Well, not much here. I—hold on, what's this?" He lifted a pipe out of the suitcase and inspected it closely. "Craig smokes a pipe, if I remember correctly?"

"That's right."

"Well, it could be a coincidence but this pipe is of American make. I happen to know our South African friend is a cheroot man." He pointed to a box of long cigars on the bedside table. He sniffed at the pipe, shrugged, and stuffed it into his pocket. "Let's get some fresh air. Magabian's hotel smells like a grease trap."

They walked down the stairs and the commissioner paused to speak with the constables he had left outside. He ordered a thorough search of the room and questioning of all the hotel's guests. Then they walked back toward the police post.

"Well, we'll see how Magabian is coming on his masterpiece," he remarked cheerfully. Klein was lost in his own thoughts and he only mumbled a reply.

Chapter 19

•
•

The mammy wagon was parked by the side of the road. It sagged in the middle. One of the tires was almost flat and strips of rubber were wound around it like black bandages. The cab was painted royal blue and the body red. A dirty brush had snaked a broad yellow stripe under the open windows. A white sign above the cab bore a crude drawing of a crescent over English lettering spelling out "Allah Wills It?" A pot of stockfish bubbled over a small fire, sending a sharp odor into the morning mist.

The fat Yoruba owner sat on the dented running board. His agbada was pulled up over his knees and tucked in at his crotch. He was a Muslim and his three wives were seeing to his needs. One crouched over the fire poking at the stiff stockfish with a stick while the other two prepared bowls and listened to their husband's jokes. He was a jolly man and his round face was constantly creased by a toothy smile. His wives showed their appreciation of his wit with shrieks of throaty laughter.

There were no passengers in the mammy wagon. When Craig rose out of the bush at the edge of the road, no one noticed his approach. The happy Yoruba was the first to hear the approaching footsteps. He stood up slowly.

Craig moved toward them. "Do you have some water?" he rasped.

"Water, water, give this gentleman some water," the Yoruba commanded, trying an experimental smile in the white man's direction.

Craig slumped against the mammy wagon. His lips were swollen. He took a gourd of lukewarm water and downed it in a few gulps. It tasted of petrol.

The fat Yoruba shifted nervously. Craig accepted another gourd full of water. He sipped it slowly and poured the dregs over his head. "Do you have any bread?" he asked.

"Yes, yes," the Yoruba assured him. "Get Mastah bread!" he shouted to his wives without turning toward them, keeping an uneasy watch on Craig.

Craig took the chalky white loaf. He chewed the bread for a long time before swallowing it. When he had finished half the loaf he felt better.

"How far is it to Ikiri?"

"Ikiri be six miles down this road," the Yoruba replied. "I take you, Mastah."

"No," Craig said, sighing. "I'll take your truck."

"Take my truck? Oh, no, Mastah." The Yoruba started a slow dance of pain and incredulity. "Mastah no go take my lorry? She be all I got. Oh, Mastah no do that?"

"I'm afraid so," Craig said with finality. "I won't hurt it. You'll find it later."

"Oh, no, Mastah not do that?"

Craig drew his pistol and swung it toward the cab. "You get in and start it. And no funny business."

The women started to wail in unison. The pot of forgotten stockfish boiled over onto the road.

The Yoruba climbed up into the cab, great tears rolling down his jiggling cheeks. "Ohhh, ohhh," he repeated, striking his head with a closed fist. The engine turned over, caught hold and the whole mammy wagon vibrated with its steady growl.

"All right," Craig said, feeling slightly dizzy and wanting to leave the wailing women far behind. "Climb down and stand clear."

"Oh, Mastah! Mastah no do this to Hafik?"

Craig swung up into the cab, located the handbrake and released it. He found the clutch, identified the footbrake, jammed the gearshift into low and started forward slowly in a series of abrupt jerks. Cursing, he pushed down on the gas pedal and the truck sprang forward, leaving behind the wailing women and the owner, who was now stamping on his skull cap and shaking his fist toward his one and only beloved mammy wagon.

The mammy wagon yawed as it sped downhill. Craig held his breath, nursing the loose wheel as he aimed the awkward vehicle at narrow bridges and guided it around abrupt curves. He passed a truck park. A group of mammy wagon drivers gathered for breakfast gaped at the passing white man.

On a long, misty stretch of road traversing a gray swamp he saw a small vehicle coming toward him. His fingers tightened around the wheel. A dryness clutched his throat as it approached and he recognized the muddy blue paint of an official police Land Rover. They rattled closer. He looked desperately for a turn-off but there was none. He kept his foot heavy on the accelerator, hoping to cut the seconds of possible recognition to a minimum.

There was a quick roar of sound, a passage of air. He forced himself to look at the car as it sped by. The two African constables kept their eyes to the front, oblivious of the speed of the passing mammy wagon.

The mammy wagon labored up a grade, steam sifting back over its hood. He watched the hill crest and listened to his heart beat, waiting for the appearance of more police vehicles or another lorry. The road ahead was empty. He lifted his feet from the accelerator, letting the weight of the truck loose.

Public works department laborers appeared along the wide shoulder of the road. They were bent double, backs to the asphalt, swinging long machetes at the encroaching bush. Craig felt he was running a silent gantlet as he sped by.

Another rise in the pot-holed road and Ikiri jumped up before him. Not wanting to get too close, he eased the wobbly brake down until it caught. The truck snaked a protesting trail of hot rubber across the road and clanked to a stop against a tall oil palm.

He jumped down from the cab, his hands shaking, fingers curled from their tight grip on the wheel. He moved quickly into the jungle, away from the road. He stopped, eyes closed, and tried to think out his orientation. His exhausted mind made a valiant attempt to respond but Ikiri appeared as a badly done sketch in a child's smudged exercise book.

He rested for a moment. Then he began a wide circling movement that he hoped would take him close to the Rest House without touching the village. It was hot work and by the time he could see the Rest House roof he had developed another aching thirst. He crawled forward on his stomach and peered out of the jungle. He decided it must be close to noon. A number of sedans, jeeps and Land Rovers were parked in front of the Rest House and the noise from the bar carried up to him.

He rested his head on his fists and thought. There were too many unanswered questions in his mind to risk walking into the Rest House openly. He weighed the possibility of entering his room through a window but rejected it. He looked up again and for the first time noticed an African constable walking back and forth in the Rest House parking area. He watched him until it became obvious that the man was a stakeout.

He rolled slightly to the left and parted some leaves to get a better view of the district officer's home. He would have to wait until dark and make his approach from the rear, out of earshot of the sentry box. He crawled back into the jungle and shut his eyes, trying hard not to think of water.

The guinea hen was cold and tasted like flaccid leather. Alice Thompson picked at it and finally pushed it away. It had been a dull, hot day and Robert had not returned for dinner. Ignatius came and silently gathered up her dish.

"Madam like dessert?" he asked.

"No. That will be all." Her words were slightly slurred and she smiled vacantly. Too much brandy before dinner had taken away her appetite. She sat alone and silent, listening to the far-off sounds from the Rest House. The crack of a breaking dish came from her kitchen.

"Damn," she muttered nervously, reaching for her cigarettes and a match. She lighted her cigarette and sat back to enjoy it. Her hair needed combing and she ran her fingers through its brown thickness, feeling too lazy to look for a comb.

Finally she left the table and went to her room. She shut the door and turned the key. She didn't want to talk to Robert. It would only mean unpleasantness. She had made up her mind that she would spend a weekend or maybe a week in the capital. She felt a pressing need to get out of Ikiri.

A cluster of mosquitoes left the tightness of the net over her bed and circled around her head. She sat down and combed her hair, watching herself in the mirror. She pushed a handful of hair onto the top of her head but dropped it quickly when she saw how it uncovered a few new wrinkles at the base of her neck.

On a sudden impulse she got up, went back into the living room and returned with a bottle of brandy and a water glass. She twisted the cork and broke a fingernail. She poured herself a good three fingers and sipped from the glass. She continued to look in the mirror. Suddenly she felt a cold, heavy fear. She saw it in her own eyes. The word "breakdown" slid unwanted into her thoughts. To drive it away she shut her eyes and took two deep swallows of brandy.

She filed her broken nail and finished her brandy. She took off her gold earrings and undressed before the mirror, examining her body critically, holding in reserve a certain prejudice that told her the tanned solidity and curves would still interest any man.

She shook her hair out, raised her arms above her head, watching her breasts lift. She flattened her stomach, tightened the muscles of her buttocks and peered into the mirror with

§ **231**

half-closed eyes. She thus pushed the slight sags and wrinkles back, regaining a few years.

She swung around quickly to see if Ignatius had shut the wooden louvers of her bedroom windows. They were shut. She smiled with relief, feeling slightly ridiculous and wondering what difference it would have made if they had been open.

Later, Robert Thompson thumped and banged his way into the house, rousing his wife from a deep sleep. She soon drifted off again despite his grumblings and eventual snoring.

Ikiri quieted down. The last drinkers in the Rest House bar reluctantly watched the barman stop the fans and begin turning out the lights. A late customer in Magabian's hotel was fleeced out of an extra three pounds by a husky, broad-bottomed prostitute and the radio continued its crackling and humming down at the police post. The moon traveled across the sky, occasionally covered by powder puff clouds that threw small, fast-moving shadows over the jungle and the tin roofs of the town.

At first she thought it was a bush rat scraping at the window. Then, half awakened, she realized that the scratching was too high. She held her breath, lying perfectly still, and thought of Robert's service revolver. But it was in a bureau drawer in the other room. A rush of images—snakes, leopards, a drunken houseboy—sped through her mind as she blinked in the darkness.

The scraping changed to a distinct slow knock, muffled but sure. She slid through the mosquito net and looked around in desperation for a weapon. She snatched up a dressing gown and, pulling it around her, tipped over the empty water glass on her bedside table. It rang against the floor in the quiet like the bells of a hundred burning churches. She seized the bottle by its neck and moved closer to the window. She forced herself to speak and heard a voice she could not identify as her own.

"Who is it?"

"Michael Craig." The reply was whispered close to the louvers. "For God's sake let me in."

Trembling she opened the latch and swung the louvers wide. Craig dragged himself through the window and slid to the floor. "Get me some water," he said slowly. "I need a drink."

She stood over him, her mouth slightly open, the moonlight softening her face. If Craig had raised his eyes he might even have looked beautiful.

"Please," Craig said, wiping at his dry lips. "Water."

She left the room, walking quietly, aware of the snoring from Robert's room. When she returned Craig was still sitting on the floor with his back propped against the wall, his head back and his eyes closed. He opened his eyes when she handed him the water. He drank down the whole pitcher, spilling it over his jacket and chest. She saw the revolver in his jacket pocket.

He finished drinking and put the pitcher down. For a moment they stared at each other without a word. She hadn't spoken since his arrival. She searched the floor for the fallen water glass, found it and poured it half full of brandy. She handed this to Craig. He took it and drank. He pushed it back in her hand and shook his head.

"I didn't think I could make it."

She swallowed with a great effort and sipped at the brandy before she could find her voice. "Why did you come here? You can't stay."

§ **233**

"I know, I know. I've got to get out of Ikiri. Out of Africa. Where's your husband?"

"He's asleep in his bedroom." She glanced over her shoulder. "I don't think he'll bother us. I normally keep my door locked."

Slipping out to the bathroom she brought him a basin of warm water and soap. While he was washing she went to the kitchen and hurriedly sliced some bread and cheese. With this under her arm she tiptoed back into her room and locked the door after her. He sat on her bed and wolfed down the sandwiches.

Her mind was confused. It jumped from one hypothesis to another without settling on a solution. She sat beside him. "They're after you, you know," she said, tapping at her glass with one fingernail.

"Who?"

"The police."

Craig frowned. "Where are they?"

"They're all over town. The commissioner has been using the police post as his headquarters and he has constables stationed about . . ." She looked at him and there was a certain tenderness in her glance. ". . . presumably waiting for you."

"Son of a bitch!" he said bitterly.

They sat in silence for a moment. She reached over and put her hand on his. "You shouldn't have come here," she said sadly. "I can't help you."

"You have already," he said, trying to think. "I didn't know they were after me on this side of the border."

"Why don't you give yourself up?" she asked.

"No," he said without hesitation. "That's impossible."

She sighed and shrugged.

§ 234

"I have enough money to get out of here if I could get to it. It's in my room at the Rest House. Two leather-bound volumes in a rack by the bed. If someone could get those books I'd have a chance."

"They're watching the Rest House, expecting you to come back."

He stopped speaking and listened for a moment to Thompson's snoring. "Do you have a houseboy or someone you trust who could get those books out of the Rest House?"

She shook her head and reached for the brandy bottle. She poured more into her glass. She drank and bent forward slightly as the warmth seared her throat. A wisp of a smile brightened her face.

"I could probably get them for you," she said in a faraway voice. "No constable would bother me. I could tell anyone who might be curious that I had loaned you those books before you left town."

"It might work," he said hopefully. "It just might work."

"I won't be able to do anything before tomorrow morning," she said. "They would think it strange if I walked into the Rest House at night or too early in the morning."

Craig nodded, yawning. "I can wait . . ." He gestured toward the window. ". . . out behind the house—in the jungle."

She raised her head and looked directly at Craig. "You might as well stay here until dawn. The mosquitoes would eat you alive outside. Robert won't bother us."

She stopped talking and ran her tongue over her lips. She stood up, a bit unsteadily. The day's drinking was taking effect. She slipped out of her dressing gown. She paused for a moment, turned toward him in silence. She bent forward and

§ **235**

found his mouth, grinding her lips against his, her body warm and responsive to his hands as they closed around her waist.

They moved under the net, seeking each other hungrily, her hand slowly exploring his body. In the slash of moonlight from the open window he could see that her eyes were closed. She was on her side, her brown hair mussed, her lips slightly parted. Her perfume only partly hid the odor of cognac that came and went with her heavy breathing. Her nudity was emphasized by the two white bands of untanned flesh left by her shorts and halter.

Her hand moved slowly down his chest, over his stomach and found him. He touched her chin gently, expecting her to open her eyes. Her eyes still closed, she lifted herself up even with him, the warmth of her breasts touching his chest.

"Be quiet," she whispered, her fingernails digging into his arm. "I don't want to talk. Oh God, come on . . . come on."

Her sudden need was infectious and he responded, clumsily taking her, forgetting the odor of cognac in the soft clash of their lips. The world was temporarily frozen, set aside. They writhed on the warm bed, he with one foot caught awkwardly in the sheets and she, demanding, receiving, absorbing. Theirs was a roaring cloudburst of physical desperation and need, a strange contest in which the gladiators sought salvation in the blows of their opponents.

She broke from his grasp, and knelt on the bed, holding her breasts slightly raised in her hands, her teeth bared. She was breathing heavily and seemed to be searching for fresh air. He paused for a moment, puzzled. "Leave me," she moaned, "Oh God, leave me."

Even as she said it she moved slowly toward him. He took her without gentleness and had her again brutally and finally.

§ **236**

Chapter 20

.
.

Ignatius waited patiently, his head cocked to one side. He decided to knock again. After knocking he glanced at his new Swiss wrist watch. He couldn't understand it. At six-thirty Madam was always awake, waiting for her morning tea.

He had been noticing the drop in the level of the brandy bottles. Madam go get soft head, he thought to himself, drink that brandy like Mastah. He put the tray down on the floor. He walked through the hall and out the back door. He paused on the back steps. Maybe Madam go be sick? Maybe she be hurt from Mastah full of brandy. He turned toward her bedroom window and was surprised to see it open. He approached the window hesitantly, his bare feet silent on the gravel. He shot a quick look over his shoulder at the servant's quarters. It not be good for his wife go see him at Madam's window.

The sound of breathing from within reassured him. He rose on tiptoe, grasping the sill to peer through the open window.

For a moment he paused, transfixed, his eyes wide. Then he let go of the window sill. "Haaa," he muttered, frowning and walking fast toward the boys' quarters. He rounded the corner of the low cement building. His wife was working outside, preparing food. She was pounding cassava root, swinging a long double-ended pestle with both hands. The children were sitting in a circle playing.

His wife smiled at him and paused to wipe her glistening face with her headcloth. "What you do here, man?" she asked.

He walked into their quarters, kicked off his working shorts and pulled on a patched pair of dark trousers. His wife followed him, curious.

"Where you go? Mastah tell you go for market?"

"Catch my shoe, woman, and stop the talk-talk," he replied, frowning.

She handed him his black leather shoes and he laced them tightly. Standing up, he tucked his collarless blouse into his pants, pulled on a wide-lapelled wool suit jacket, jammed a small bowler onto his head and picked up his black umbrella.

He smiled. "Woman, I got work with the constable. I go come back with plenty shillin'." He held a finger to his lips and winked before he crunched over the gravel on his way into Ikiri.

Craig had awakened at the sound of someone walking over the gravel. He had seen the momentary outline of Ignatius' head in the open window and heard the retreating footsteps. He saw the sunlight and cursed himself for oversleeping. He swung out of bed and inched his way to the window in time to see Ignatius disappear from sight in the servants' quarters. He waited by the window quietly until he saw Ignatius come rushing out again, dressed for his trip into the village. This may be it, he told himself, you may have blown the whole thing.

He had planned to leave in the darkness of early dawn. His exhaustion had betrayed him. There was still a chance and he had to take it. He pulled on his clothes and shoes. He placed the Colt in his belt and went back to the window. It seemed quiet outside. He could hear sounds of movement from the servants' quarters but the open space between the house and the jungle seemed clear.

He glanced back over his shoulder at Alice Thompson. She was sleeping soundly. He was surprised at the tightness in his chest, the sudden, unexpected feeling of regret. He swung himself over the window sill and dropped to the ground.

The noise of the Land Rover skidding to a stop in front of the house awakened Alice Thompson. Her eyes blinked open and she stared for several seconds at the empty bed.

She slipped on her dressing gown and sat on the edge of the bed with her head in her hands. Heavy footsteps sounded in the hall and a thunder of urgent knocking filled her ears.

"Open up, Alice!"

She recognized the voice of Commissioner Innes. She kept her eyes on the door. There were a few muffled words, a ripping crash. The door buckled and lifted sideways, hanging on its hinges.

Commissioner Innes appeared, his face strangely white around the eyes. He was holding a revolver, muzzle up in his hand, tense fingers curled outside the trigger guard.

"Sorry, Alice," he said softly. Then loudly, with obvious anger, "Where is he?"

§ 239

She shrugged her shoulders and looked away. The commissioner strode to the window. He swung himself over the sill and onto the ground. Three embarrassed African constables followed him through her room and out the window.

She raised her head and saw her husband standing in the doorway. He looked like a fat little boy and there were tears on his cheeks.

"You've ruined my career," he sobbed, his lips quivering. "You've ruined my career and . . ." He glanced around the room. ". . . I can't find my brandy."

"Come here, Robert," she said, "come over here."

When his head was lying on her breast she stroked his unbrushed hair gently. "There now," she said, staring once again at the floor, "don't cry. Ignatius will fetch us another bottle soon."

Craig was soaked with his own perspiration. He slumped heavily against the thick bole of a palm and tried to recover his wind. He gasped at the air as if it were a cool liquid. His pants were torn and his face bloody from fighting through a maze of sharp vines. He was tired and his knees shook with the strain of his escape. He had made a wide swing through the jungle, hoping to reach the road to the river but he had found no road and he knew that the river was a long way off.

He tried to listen for the sound of passing mammy wagons but he heard only the distracting boom of his own heart. The survival process of his mind focused on the river and Port Akodu. A freighter. He could hide aboard until they were clear of the coast. He could guarantee the captain a good sum when they reached Europe. Or he could give himself up.

He raised his head slowly, wiping the sweat from his eyes.

§ **240**

He was alone in a green kingdom. The leaves around him shimmered in a soft, warm breeze. A small white-faced monkey watched him from its perch high above on some rubbery vines. It scratched its head and chewed absently on a leaf. A chain of busy, heavy-headed black ants threaded its way over the ground, making a slight detour around the toe of his shoe.

A branch snapped in the jungle and he tensed, turning his head slightly, listening. The monkey imitated his movements. It suddenly moved off through the trees, agile and frightened. He heard another noise, light and indefinable. It sent a chill through him and he moved behind the tree.

There was no doubt about it, the noise was something and that something was coming in his direction. His fingers tightened around his revolver. His eyes searched for movement in the living screen before him. The sounds were close now. He could define them as footsteps.

Harvey Klein pushed through the bush, tripped over a vine, cursed and regained his balance. Craig watched him as he wiped the perspiration from his forehead and looked apprehensively at the surrounding jungle.

Craig was puzzled. He'd never seen the man before. He obviously wasn't a policeman. But there was no doubt that he had been following him.

Klein moved forward again. Craig pushed himself against the trunk of a tree, trying to keep out of sight. Klein came on, directly for him. Suddenly they were looking at each other, both puzzled and slightly embarrassed, like men caught in a children's game of hide and seek.

Craig's Colt was aimed directly at Klein's belt buckle. Klein removed his glasses and wiped his eyes with a handkerchief.

He suddenly felt more angry than frightened. "All right, Craig," he said, surprised at the steadiness of his own voice. "It's all over."

"Who the hell are you?" Craig demanded. Klein noticed that he had thumbed back the hammer of the revolver. Klein swallowed and tried to maintain his composure.

"My name's Klein, Harvey Klein. If you'd put that gun away I'll show you my credentials."

Craig shook his head and took a step backward. "I'm getting out of here, Klein," he said with determination. His mind raced, trying to find the way out.

"Don't be a goddamn fool," Klein said, losing his patience but keeping his eye on Craig's trigger finger. "You haven't got a chance of getting out of here and you know it."

"Shut up," Craig ordered. He felt dizzy. The thought that he might black out crossed his mind.

"Look," Klein said, trying to sound reasonable. "I'm not enjoying this any more than you are. I've come to get you. I'm not armed because I felt you would listen to reason."

Craig smiled. "Listen to reason?" he asked sarcastically. "What the hell are you, a vice-consul playing cops and robbers?"

"Washington sent me to get you, Craig, and I intend to do my job." Klein shook his head. "Listen, what I tell you is the truth. I'm not the only one looking for you. The British police, French Security and a team of U.N. investigators are all on your trail. The people who hired you in Paris are eager to shut your mouth, permanently. You're lucky I found you first."

"Turn around," Craig shouted, his voice bitter with frustration. Klein obeyed slowly, half paralyzed with fright. "Kneel down."

§ **242**

He heard Craig's orders and he fell to his knees. The words of a long-forgotten prayer returned as he waited, dry-mouthed and shaking slightly. Why hadn't he waited for the commissioner? Why hadn't he brought his revolver? These questions were academic now but they kept him from thinking of the pistol in Craig's hand.

Craig stared at the back of Klein's neck. Waves of dizziness swept over him. His body felt as if it were being crushed in a vise. I wish I were in Paris now with Anne, he thought, or in Switzerland with my fifty thousand dollars. He felt like vomiting and his hand shook.

Klein heard Craig sigh. "Give it up," Klein said softly. "Give me the gun."

"No," Craig replied, as if he were speaking to someone far away. "You see, Mr. Klein, I just don't give a damn."

There was a moment of complete silence. Klein thought of his family. The shot thudded, muffled. Klein's blood froze, his whole body tense. He swung around in time to see Craig fall. He jumped to his feet and ran toward him. Craig had placed the muzzle of the Colt in his ear and pulled the trigger. It was all over. Klein stood over him, helpless, nauseated, watching the unspeakable oozing.

"Jesus," Klein said under his breath. "Oh, my God."

The Ikiri air strip was almost deserted. Three Hausa traders were laying out their wares behind the administrative building and the barman had driven into Ikiri for some ice. The C–47 parked at one end of the tarmac caught the crisp warmth of the early morning sun, its silver fuselage sparkling against the green of the surrounding jungle.

Harvey Klein and Commissioner Innes stood alone at the rattan bar and sipped their lukewarm beer. They looked tired

§ **243**

and slightly gray around the eyes. The commissioner yawned and rubbed his chin. He glanced at his wrist watch.

"Well," he said, "the first of the U.N. troops should be arriving in Bomasha about now. The Swedes were supposed to be first in but according to the latest it's the Nigerian battalion." He smiled at Klein. "Something to do with skin pigmentation, I imagine."

"Their timing couldn't have been better," Klein said, "for us, that is."

"Yes, I must admit they drew our press colony off. Don't think there's one left in Ikiri. At least, I hope not."

Klein walked to the open door, shielded his eyes against the sun and looked toward the C–47. "I'd better get moving." He put out his hand. "Well, Malcolm," he said, "If you ever get to Paris look me up."

"Not bloody likely," the commissioner replied, smiling. "Good luck."

Klein turned and walked toward the plane. He was suddenly filled with a great lassitude. He swung himself up and into the fuselage.

The coffin was secured near the cargo door. It was of fresh-cut light wood. A native carpenter had carved a crude cross in the center of its lid. There were no hinges. The lid was nailed down. It had been circled with steel packing bands.

Klein stood for a moment staring at the coffin, smelling the sweet fresh wood. He lifted a paper baggage tag that was fastened to one of the metal bands. "Craig, Michael" someone had written on it with a shipper's grease pencil. Klein moved on past the coffin and settled himself in a bucket seat.

He had fastened his seat belt and settled back to sleep when a sergeant from the crew sat down next to him. He smiled and shouted to him above the sound of the engines. "I understand this is all a big hush-hush deal."

"That's right," Klein replied, hoping he would shut up.

"You with Intelligence?"

"That's right," he said, trying to be as rude as possible. He succeeded. The sergeant moved several seats away.

They bounced along the strip, stopped for a moment while the engines revved again and jerked forward, rushing over the tufts of grass, vibrating like a tin torpedo. They lifted off the ground and Klein strained around for a last look at Ikiri. He saw only some palms and a patch of corrugated tin roofing, then the wing lifted, blotting out his view. They climbed high. Bright shafts of sunlight reflected off the wings and cleaved through the shadows within the cabin. A green velvet carpet of jungle spread out as far as the eye could see below them.

Klein suddenly remembered he had come away without one souvenir of his African assignment. The hell with it, he thought. He settled back against the hard, cold metal of the fuselage and went to sleep.